SILVER MOON

OVER 100
GREAT NOVELS
OF
EROTIC DOMINATION

If you like one you will probably like the rest

NEW TITLES EVERY MONTH

All titles in print are now available from:
www.onlinebookshop.com

Electronic editions of all titles can be found at:
www.adultbookshops.com

If you want to be on our confidential mailing list for our Readers' Club Magazine (with extracts from past and forthcoming titles) write to:

SILVER MOON READER SERVICES

The Shadowline Building
6 Wembley Street
Gainsborough
DN21 2AJ
United Kingdom
or
sales@babash.com

or telephone
01427 816710
(UK office hours only)

NEW AUTHORS WELCOME

Please send submissions to
Silver Moon Books Ltd.
PO Box 5663
Nottingham
NG3 6PJ
or
editor@babash.com

First published 2005 Silver Moon Books
ISBN 1-903687-57-8
© 2004 Tessa Valmur

TANYA'S TORMENT

BY

TESSA VALMUR

ALSO BY TESSA VALMUR
THE ART OF SUBMISSION
BOUGHT AND SOLD
DARKER DREAMS
DARKEST DREAMS

All characters in this book are fictitious, and any resemblance to real persons, living or dead, is purely coincidental.

THIS IS FICTION - IN REAL LIFE ALWAYS PRACTISE SAFE SEX!

CHAPTER ONE

'Welcome to Scawder Lodge, Miss Raglan,' extending his hand, the man smiled warmly. Tanya shook hands with him. He was thin, tall, in his early sixties and dressed in a flannel suit and cravat. He gestured to her to take a seat and he settled himself on the edge of his large, mahogany desk, one leg balanced over the other.

'Now Miss Raglan,' said the man, 'firstly let me say how pleased I am that your Godfather put you forward to work with us here. Film work attracts so many young people but so few have anything to offer. I can see why your Godfather felt you 'd be the exception.'

Tanya kept silent, all too aware of how the man was feasting his eyes on her but also she was well aware that her physical appearance was at the moment her best, indeed her only, asset. She had no parents, no money, had just been expelled from university and frankly she would rather make a living posing in front of a camera than doing some physically or mentally demanding job.

'I've read your previous university reports,' said the man, 'I know why you were expelled and I've a clear idea of the sort of young girl you are. You're obviously very bright and have been given every opportunity, but sadly you're also a rather irresponsible young lady who seems to think she's above having to conform to some of society's rules. Now let me make it clear that...'

'That's not fair, I only...'

The man coughed heavily, glaring at Tanya until she fell silent and he was able to continue.

'As I was saying, let me make it clear that none of that counts against you as far as I'm concerned. I'm in the film business and if you're willing to work hard and you can act the part I have in mind for you, then I see no reason why you cannot be usefully employed working for me for a while. I don't suppose that your Godfather told you much about the sort of films that I make?'

'No, only from what he hinted at, I kind of guess I may have to do some nude scenes?' Tanya suggested, glancing up coyly at the man who had been introduced to her as Mr Campbell. Tanya decided it was best not to admit to what her Godfather had really said. He had told her in no uncertain terms that he knew someone who made porn films and was on the scout for some fresh young girl to be in a new film he was making. Her Godfather had then bluntly suggested that given Tanya's penchant for numerous sexual liaisons that she might enjoy such an opportunity.

'And you don't mind that?' the man asked.

'No, I'm game for pretty much anything… I have done a bit of nude modelling…'

The man smiled and nodded, glanced at the younger man stood in the room, then he ran his hand through his silver grey hair and standing up he slowly circled Tanya, regarding her as critically as if he was judging the value of a new purchase he was considering.

'Yes, your Godfather brought that to my attention… good photos I have to say.'

Tanya blushed as she guessed that her Godfather must have gone through her flat on one of his occasional visits. She had done the modelling shoot one summer when she was strapped for cash for a holiday and he'd refused to give her any more of an allowance until the next term. The men's magazine had paid well enough and she had actually enjoyed flaunting her naked body for the cameraman. Of course she'd kept a set of the photos in an album in a chest of drawers buried below her underwear. Just what the hell had her Godfather been doing rummaging through her clothes whilst her back was turned, she asked herself.

Since she was fifteen when her parents had been killed in a car crash, Tanya had been looked after by her Godfather; a distant cousin who lived in the Scottish Highlands. He had kept her at a boarding school before university and made occasional trips down to the south of England to check up on her and until a week ago he thankfully paid little attention to the nineteen year old girl in his charge. Tanya had nearly completed her first year at university when after a drunken night's revelry she had been caught in the boys' dormitory engaging in sex with several of the male students. The incident might have passed off without more than a mild rebuke had Tanya not then asked the male tutor who had discovered her, if he fancied caning her first then fucking her afterwards. Despite pleading that she was acting out of character because someone had spiked her drinks, Tanya was summarily dismissed. If this episode taught her anything it was that she'd have to learn to lie more convincingly.

When she phoned her Godfather and explained what had happened he told her to pack her bags and get on the next train to Inverness. Since he had provided her with generous living expenses and had paid for the rent for her flat, Tanya decided that she'd best do as she was told. She had only been at her Godfather's house, a large but neglected mansion house perched on a hillside overlooking Loch Marrich, for a couple of days when he announced that he had arranged an interview for her with a friend who was a film maker and who was looking for a young girl for a new project.

The silver haired man now standing before her gestured to the young man who'd greeted her at the door of the hunting lodge, to pour them each a Scotch from the crystal decanter that was on the rosewood sideboard. Tanya sat wide eyed with surprise as three crystal tumblers were given generous measures of whisky and the young man handed first one to her and then another to Campbell before taking the third for himself.

'Tanya, both your Godfather Donald and I feel confident that you'll settle into your new job here well,' Campbell smiled reassuringly and gestured for Tanya to start her drink. Needing no more encouraging, Tanya allowed a generous mouthful of the heady, amber liquid to fill her mouth and slip down her throat.

'A pretty girl like you, with your willingness to please, shouldn't have to struggle too much for work in our line of business. Wouldn't you say so Miles?'

'Absolutely sir; I'm sure she won't have too much of a struggle.'

'All you have to do to get on well here is to perform to your best,' Campbell smiled, took a large gulp from his glass and placing it down on his desk walked across to where Tanya was sitting, a sheaf of papers in hand. 'This is your contract, it's all pretty standard, but we do need your signature before we can get started. You should find our payment terms quite generous.'

Glancing at the document, Tanya saw what she was to be paid per day and needed no more encouragement, she eagerly scrawled her signature on the document.

'Excellent, now I think that we should get you settled in. Stand up Tanya and let me have a proper look at you.'

Tanya did as she was asked. As Campbell circled her she forced herself to relax and, all too aware that he was physically appraising her and desperate to get the job, she drew in her stomach and pulled back her shoulders to emphasise her cleavage.

Five and half feet tall, Tanya knew that she had the sort of looks that would give most men an instant hard-on and from as soon as she'd fancied it, she had enjoyed no shortage of boyfriends and casual lovers. Keen on racket sports and jogging she kept slim and her muscles were pleasingly firm and toned. She had a slender waist, pert buttocks, high generous breasts and a thick mane of honey coloured hair. She'd quickly learnt that with her looks she could ensure she'd be well spoilt by any man she fancied as long as she gave him a good time in return. She made sure that even if she only slept with a guy once he'd have to buy her dinner in the best of restaurants at the very least and if he wanted a second night with her it would cost him more dearly still. At just nineteen, her mercenary strategy had paid dividends; she had jewellery and expensive clothes in abundance.

Whilst the man circled her, Tanya forced herself to relax. A naked photo shoot and now some nude film scenes, what difference was there?

'Well Tanya, I have high hopes for you. I think it's time for Miles to show you around.'

'What part exactly will I be playing? I don't know anything about the film.'

'Oh, the outline is in your contract, didn't you read it? I shouldn't worry too much: basically all you have to do is to be yourself. The plot of the film is that you have been brought to a private school to be properly disciplined.'

'What do you mean, disciplined?'

'The plot is really secondary; the action is what will carry the film. You'll get the hang of it as you go along,' Campbell smiled and gestured for the young man to show Tanya from his study.

'Hang on a minute, what do you mean disciplined?' Repeated Tanya, suddenly a little concerned at the prospect of what might lie ahead.

'What I mean Tanya, is that you're playing a naughty teenager who has been brought to a strict private college where troublesome young ladies get taught to behave properly.'

'You mean caning and stuff?' Tanya asked, raising her eyebrows at the thought of being filmed supposedly getting such punishment. There was something rather erotic about imagining this, she realised, but she wasn't going to let on to this man what she thought.

'Precisely. I trust you don't have a problem with that? You have now signed your contract agreeing to such conditions.'

'No, I don't mind... after all, it's only acting isn't it?' Tanya said.

The man smiled but didn't answer.

Tanya followed the young man from the office. That sod Donald, her Godfather must have known what sort of a set up this film company was, she thought. What was now running through her mind also was whether Donald had not only looked at the compromising photos she'd kept hidden in her underwear drawer but if he'd read some of the diary she also kept there.

The diary she had started after her first sexual encounter and she had wanted to put down her feelings and the excitement she had felt at waiting for the next time she would have sex. Over the years she'd kept it the diary not only charted all her sexual adventures but she recorded in it her fantasies and desires as well. If Donald had read it and told these people about it then they'd know that she had engineered getting herself gang banged by four male students at the university and that she had relished the relentless shafting by the lads and although she'd begged them to let her go, she'd secretly been delighted when they ignored her, held her down and each in turn had fucked her, despite her breathless pleading for them stop.

* * *

Dear Diary Sunday June 5th.

Quite a day yesterday! After staying the Friday night with Mr Wilmot, I apologised to him for not being able to stay longer but had to meet my sister who was coming to visit and I was obliged to spend the weekend with her. I can't bring myself to write about him in first name terms as he's so much older and I feel absolutely nothing for him. Worse still, I suppose, he is a friend's father. At least he's divorced; well separated and soon to be divorced. Anyway, Emma has absolutely no idea I've been shagging her father and why shouldn't I? He's fit enough and has loads of money, which he's more than willing to spend on me.

Anyway on Friday he took me out to a smart country

house hotel far enough from Oxford for no one to recognise either of us. Of course there was still a chance we'd be spotted but I guess that just added to the excitement of it all. The dining room was all candles and long white table cloths and silver cutlery and whilst we ate, I can't really remember what we had other than I ordered fresh asparagus in butter to start so that I could delicately lick and suck the ends whilst keeping eye contact with him and thanks to the long table cloth I was able to stroke his groin with my toes without anyone knowing. Needless to say by the time we had finished the meal he was gagging for it and we took our coffee and Cognacs up in our bedroom. A bit too Laura Ashley for me but the bathroom was to die for. Well, since he did give me a lovely necklace and had been so nice I gave him one of my best blowjobs and woke him up early enough in the morning for us to have a shag before breakfast. He certainly can't say I didn't spoil him too and he should be very grateful, as he's older than I'd normally choose.

Anyway, he drove me back to my digs on the Saturday morning even though I had originally promised to spend two nights with him and he'd booked the hotel bedroom for two nights. Still, he swallowed the story about my sister, (men are so gullible!) and drove me home after I promised I'd see him again next weekend. Of course I've no intention assuming something (someone) better comes along, so I'll just send him a text message on his mobile and keep him in reserve for another weekend. I had to cut short our hotel episode because whilst we were shagging and I was thinking about how varied men's dicks are, I suddenly remembered that I'd promised to meet Julian on the Saturday evening. He is not my type at all but Susannah has, when pissed, confessed to me that he's not altogether her type either but he does have an enormous cock and he is seriously fit. Well, as I told you dear diary, a few weeks ago I did get Susannah separated from Julian long enough for me to persuade him to give me a quickie and since then we've both been trying to find time for a proper fuck without darling Susannah finding out what we're up to.

So this Saturday was our night together and the plan was simple, I would accidentally bump into Julian when he was out with some mates at a bistro and we'd slip off together. So as planned I ran into him and he invited me to join him and his three friends for dinner, which I did. I have to confess that they were all really rather tasty and I got this crazy idea in my head that maybe I could get a shag from all four of them. Well, after a few too many glasses of Chardonnay I guess I'd made it pretty clear what I fancied and we finished our meal and headed back across town to their college. They all shared a four bedroom dormitory apartment and it was easy enough for them to smuggle me in through a window since it was on the ground floor in one of the quadrangles.

Well, the guys must have half imagined that I was teasing or joking but when after some beers in their little sitting room I asked who wanted to be first, two of them nearly choked on their mouthfuls of lager. I was too drunk to remember who actually suggested it but it was decided that we'd use the sitting room floor and they didn't need much encouragement to help me out of my clothes.

Of course what I really fancied was experiencing having all four of them involved at once and to feel as if I was actually being gang banged. I had this fantasy going around in my head of being held down by a group of men whilst each took it in turns to fuck me. The boys were, I quickly realised, going to be far too nice and gentle with me unless I engineered it otherwise so after giving them a chance to get an eyeful of the full Tanya package, I spent some time playing around with each of them, getting them all well and truly worked up. I then told them that I felt too tired and drunk to carry on and wanted to go to sleep. Thankfully they weren't willing to let me slip off to bed and when I tried someone caught me and dragged me to the floor.

I made a show of trying to get away but what chance did I have, one slender little girl against four young guys? It was quite intoxicating, I have to confess and the guys worked admirably as a team. Whle Julian held my arms pinned down above my head two of the others each took a hold of one of my ankles and this way three of them were easily able to keep me held down flat on my back whilst the fourth guy fucked me. All I could do was struggle and make a show of protesting. Initially I just begged and pleaded with them to let me go but after the first one had had his turn I thought I'd up the stakes a bit and when the second guy tried to get his cock into my pussy I began to beg them to stop. To my delight, Julian abandoned his hold on my arms with his hands and instead pinned my arms down by sitting over them. This left him his hands free and after forcing my panties into my mouth he clapped one hand across my mouth to keep me quiet. The sensation of being silenced this way whilst one of his mates fucked me and the other two guys held my legs spread was quite enough to make me come. But of course they were by no means finished with me and by the time all four had helped themselves to what was on offer I'd come again and was feeling deliciously exhausted.

It was, I have to confess, a deeply satisfying experience and as I write this I keep thinking about the feel of having my legs forcibly held spread and the sensation of being gagged. I felt tempted to ask the guys if we could arrange for another session but something more imaginative but I decided against it. On reflection they're really too nice and now my appetite has been whetted I'd like to taste something a little bit more demanding. Time to stop writing, so until the next entry, that's all for the moment.

* * *

Her Godfather had driven her to the film company's base and left her saying he'd call back for her at the end of the day. Now, stuck miles from anywhere, she felt more than a trifle anxious at the thought that she had not only signed herself up for a day's work with the makers of porn films but that her Godfather might have read her diary and told these people that she actually fantasised about the sort of sexual activities that would make her an ideal subject for some hard core sex. Of course, everything would be all right but in case it wasn't he should have at least waited for her. The bastard had left her stranded! There was nothing she could do, the house, a former hunting lodge was set miles from anywhere. The last houses that they had passed on the way had been a cluster of cottages beside a bridge that crossed a broad boulder strewn river where they had turned off the main road. Tanya reckoned that they must have then driven up the private estate road leading to the old hunting lodge for maybe ten or fifteen minutes, so that would mean a walk of perhaps eight or ten miles back to the road. In her high heels and wearing no more than her short skirt and T-shirt such a walk was hardly an option, she told herself.

The young man led Tanya back down the main corridor to the entrance hall where another man stood waiting, a film camera balanced on his shoulder; its fake fur-covered microphone looking like some fox's brush. The man, he was young, shaven headed, dressed in black jeans and a black T-shirt, grinned at Tanya then drew some headphones over his ears and nodded to the young man accompanying her.

'We just want to shoot some demo pieces of you; ignore him and act as if he's not even there.'

'So what do I have to do?' Tanya asked.

'Pretend that you've just arrived at this college and that I am showing you around. Just talk, relax, be yourself.'

The man started to climb the broad flight of stairs and Tanya followed, her mind racing with the prospect that she was already being filmed and more exciting still she guessed that she was being dragged into starring in some seedy sex film. There was something deeply exciting about what she'd let herself in for and the possibility that these people actually knew about the sort of sexual fantasies she harboured gave a deliciously dangerous edge to the prospect of what might lay in store. If she could find out whether they had been given access to her secret diary and they wanted to film something headier than just a naughty schoolgirl getting caned then, Tanya mused, she might have the chance to actually act out some of her fantasies and the bonus would be she'd be getting handsomely paid for it!

'So how old are Tanya?'

'Nineteen,' Tanya answered as they climbed the stairs. The man with the video camera was following behind them.

'And what subjects interest you the most?'

'Sports really; I like to keep active,' Tanya exchanged glances with Miles, who smiled approvingly at her impromptu reply. Warming to her task, she then asked,

'So how many students are there here?'

The young man paused upon reaching the top landing.

'Not very many…' he smiled enigmatically and gestured for Tanya to follow him.

'And what subjects do you teach?' Tanya asked.

'Well, the Rutherford specialises in schooling girls who need, what shall we say? A firm hand? Yes, like you, our pupils are all in need of a bit of extra discipline.'

They had reached a broad door; painted gloss white with a brass door handle and a matching name plate. Tanya glanced at the brass plate, which read "Games Room". Turning the handle, the man gestured for Tanya to enter.

The room was large, with tall windows, through which the late morning light flooded the mahogany floored room. There was an array of gym equipment, horseboxes, heavy ropes, exercise mats and benches. Standing at the far end of the room on a raised platform was a man in a tracksuit, a whistle dangling from a red cord around his neck. Four young girls, barefoot and wearing only pants and bras were darting around the room. It took Tanya a moment, as she stood transfixed by the spectacle, to realise that three of the girls were in fact trying to catch the fourth. For a few more moments the girl being chased evaded capture but then she became cornered and when she tried to dart away one of the girls lunged, caught her streaming hair and with a cruel jerk brought her to heel.

Tanya watched, mesmerised as the pack of three girls fell upon the fourth. Struggling every inch of the way, the unfortunate girl was dragged by the ankles across to where two ropes dangled from the ceiling. Unlike the ropes Tanya had first noticed hanging in the centre of the room, these were slender and ended about six or eight feet above the floor and from their ends dangled what looked at first glance to Tanya like dog collars. The man with the camera had advanced past where Tanya stood transfixed and he was now obviously filming the struggle between the four girls.

A shiver of excitement ran down Tanya's back and her pulse quickened as she watched the three girls wrap and buckle fast one leather collar around their victim's left wrist and then the second around her right. The victim was then held still by two of the girls whilst the third took a thin roll of black electrical tape and pressing the victim's thumb against her palm she taped it in place wrapping the tape several times over the thumb and around the hand across the knuckles. Cutting the tape with a small pair of scissors she then applied more tape around the girl's fingers so they were bound together. A moment later and the same procedure had been applied to the victim's other hand.

The tethered girl shook herself free from the grip of her assailants and backed nervously away. She saw Tanya and the man stood in the doorway but she didn't call out, though her pretty eyes were wide with fear. She was a pretty convincing little actress, Tanya thought to herself.

One of the three girls clapped her hands in amused

satisfaction as their victim tested herself against the cuffs around her wrists and the ropes. She could move a few yards in any direction but that was all. The ropes also had sufficient play in them to enable her to reach one hand with the other. Try as she might though with her fingers and thumbs bound with the sticky tape there was no way she could unbuckle the wrist cuffs.

While she was allowed to come to terms with her predicament the tallest of the other three girls jogged across to a bench on the far wall and picked up a long whip. Glancing at the man supervising for approval, she waited upon his nod before eagerly returning, the evil looking whip in hand, its snake-like length of black, plaited leather trailing behind her.

Tanya glanced at the man next to her. She felt her cheeks crimson. The girl with the whip placed herself about five yards behind the tethered girl's back. Tanya could see the tethered girl's bare legs trembling, her slender arms pulling ineffectually against the ropes. She guessed that the girl was of a similar age to herself and that the other three girls were perhaps a couple of years older at most. The girl with the whip flicked her hand back then her wrist forward a second later, the coil of leather trailing about her feet leapt upwards, blurring, then came a soft 'crack' followed instantly by a winded grunt of pain as the tethered girl fell stumbling forwards under the impact of the hard leather across her bare back. Tanya felt a cry of alarm rise in her throat but she quelled it. The blow from the whip had been for real!

One of the other girls stepped forwards and placed her hand on the victim's slender waist. The tethered girl looked abjectly at her, her lips trembling, tears pricking her wide fearful eyes but she said nothing. The girl touching her delicately traced the faint red line the whip had left across her back. The bound girl hung her head back, crying plaintively then biting down on her lip to silence herself.

The slender fingers trailing her back turned their attention elsewhere, trailing across her ribs and slim waist and then higher until they stroked under her breasts.

Tanya watched spellbound as the victim's nipples were subjected to the lightest of touches from the other girl's long, aquamarine varnished nails. The helpless victim sighed then groaned faintly as the slender nails toyed with first one nipple and then the other until both stood proudly erect.

'Which girl would you rather be, Tanya?' the man asked in a whisper that was so low it was plainly not intended for the camera.

Tanya glanced sideways at the man then back at the spectacle before them.

'That bit with the whip; that was for real wasn't it?' Tanya demanded.

The man nodded affirmatively.

'I don't believe I'm standing here watching this,' Tanya said, shaking her head in disapproval.

'Oh come on Tanya, what's your problem; all the girls are enjoying themselves including the one tasting the pain. She gets off on being treated like that. Every girl has her own particular liking…'

'I … don't … think…' Tanya bit her lip nervously, her mind racing. Did she really want to get into this? Her mind flashed back to when the four college lads had pinned her squirming body still whilst taking turns with her. That had been so good… maybe being punished would feel as potently satisfying.

'Having second thoughts?' the man asked.

Tanya shook her head. She wasn't going to pass on this opportunity and besides, she reminded herself, think of the money. She could at least give this a go, then if she didn't want to carry on she'd tell them and they'd have to stop……..wouldn't they?

'Well?' the man prompted.

'No. I don't mind trying…' Tanya answered hesitantly.

'Good girl, in which case, we need to get on with the filming then. I want you to pretend to object to what you're witnessing and then to try to leave.'

'Then what happens?' Tanya asked.

'We'll pretend to forcibly stop you and we'll do some impromptu filming. Okay?'

'Yeah... sure,' Tanya nodded, then as the man nodded for her to go ahead she saw the camera was turned back on her and taking this as her cue she announced that she wanted to leave the school immediately.

'You're here because you deserve to be, don't forget that,' cautioned the young man, raising his voice for the benefit of the camera.

'Oh, go to hell!'

'Don't swear at me young lady, not unless you're doing it to provoke punishment. Is that what you'd like? A dozen strokes of the cane perhaps across your pert little arse?'

'Piss off! ' Tanya snarled and turning on her high heels she snatched hold of the door and strode out into the corridor.

'Come back here at once!'

'I'm leaving! If you think you're going to stop me, just try!'

She was half way down the stairs when glancing back she saw the man standing at the top of the stairs looking down at her. The cameraman had followed also and was still filming.

'Tanya, come back before you regret your actions.'

Ignoring the warning Tanya continued down the stairs as fast as her high heels and tight, short skirt allowed.

Reaching the bottom of the stairs she saw the front door just a short distance across the hallway from her. Then came the sound of rushing bare feet hurrying down the stairs after her. Glancing back she saw the three girls, naked except for their briefs and bras rushing down the stairs after her. Tanya ran across the hall and snatched at the front door thinking that unless the girls were quick she could have escaped and then she guessed they'd have to carry on filming outside. As it was though although the handle turned in her grasp the door refused to open. Feigning frustration, she turned to face her pursuers.

Tanya was dragged by the arms, kicking and screaming away from the front door, across the hall and down a corridor. Two of the girls had a hold on her arms, each pulling viciously in opposite directions until the pain in her shoulders was enough to make her eyes smart. Tanya made a show of kicking out at the girls and promptly the third girl ducked behind her, snatched hold of one of Tanya's ankles and yanked her off her feet. Dangled now between the three girls like some game trophy Tanya was carried into a room, whose door was marked "Medical Room."

'There's no point in struggling you dumb bitch, unless you enjoy it!' laughed one of the girls.

'So what do you think of the Rutherford, so far?' laughed one of the other girls.

'Get your hands off me!' Tanya protested as she was dragged across to a broad, leather couch.

'So, we have a new recruit have we?'

Tanya glanced sideways to see a woman in a nurse's uniform sitting at a desk, look up from where she was writing. She smiled and watched as the three girls hauled Tanya onto the couch and then pinned her down on her back.

'She's struggling rather a lot Miss Black. You couldn't calm her down a bit for us could you?'

The young nurse made eye contact with Tanya and gave her an apologetic smile.

'Of course girls, just keep her still for a few moments…'

Tanya shook her head, writhing urgently against the three pairs of hands that held her down. Two of the girls each had a hold of her wrists and had her arms bent back over her head and pinned down against the soft leather whilst the third girl immobilise Tanya's writhing legs by grasping her ankles and pulling her legs taut.

Tanya saw the nurse turn her back to them as she opened the doors of a wall-mounted cabinet. When she turned back to face Tanya, she was dribbling a few droplets from a glass container onto a large strip of cotton wool. Tanya stared in alarm, suddenly wondering whether the container held merely water or really did have some drug in it. From the doorway of the room the man with the camera was still filming and Tanya told herself that was no real cause for alarm, this was after all just acting as the woman dressed as a nurse advanced to in front of her brandishing the pad of cotton wool.

Though young and pretty, with silvery blonde hair, the woman posing as the nurse looked a thoroughly vicious piece of work. Her blue eyes seemed to sparkle with cruel amusement at Tanya's predicament and as Tanya caught the first whiff of some heady chemical she knew that the cotton wool wadding had in fact been impregnated with more than just water.

'Come on now you silly little girl… you can't do anything to stop this happening,' the nurse admonished as Tanya jerked her head back in objection to the cotton wool pad over her face.

'Let me go! No…'

Tanya twisted her head from side to side in a futile effort to resist.

The powerful chemical smell wafted up her nostrils, a sudden terror gripping her and she struggled urgently in the determined grip of the three girls. She glimpsed their faces, gleeful, excited… the nurse, smiling triumphantly. There was nothing she could do to stop them and suddenly giddy and faint; she could only sigh in protest now as the wadding was held under her nostrils.

'Come on now, don't be coy,' the woman laughed softly.

The smell was invasive and potent. Tanya turned her face upwards gasping for pure air but her nostrils were full of the chemical and a wave of drowsiness came over her.

'Stubborn little thing aren't you?' scoffed the young woman. ' Well you have to learn that here you don't have any choices in what happens to you. So if I say that you're going to sleep, then you're going to sleep...'

The young nurse placed the pad of cotton wool over Tanya's nostrils and with her other hand smothered her mouth.

'It's quite harmless. Just the thing though to make troublesome little girls easier to discipline.'

Tanya tried twisting her head away but all her strength had evaporated from her body.

'Feeling sleepy are we?' the woman gave a self satisfied smile, lifting away the pad of cotton wool as Tanya went limp under her hands. All the strength had evaporated from her body. She gazed up helplessly, drowsy... too tired... too tired to do anything to object as her limp, drugged body was lifted easily and turned face down on the couch.

She felt something being wrapped around one of her wrists and tightened. She sighed, tried to open her eyes, tried to resist but it was too much of an effort. Her arms were drawn above her head and the softness of the restraining hands was replaced now by the firmness of broad leather wrist cuffs. A pair of catches was then released and the rear section of the couch was lowered to an angle of ninety degrees, leaving Tanya bent at the waist over the contraption and her feet now just brushing the ground.

'What... are... you... doing... to...me?' Tanya sighed.

Her only answer was to feel the softness of the cotton wool pressing once more gently against her nostrils and the warmth of a hand covering her mouth. Made docile by the drug she'd been forced to inhale, Tanya could only sigh in despair as her tormentors proceeded to strip her clothes from her.

'Okay girls, get her skirt and pants off and get those nice legs well spread.'

CHAPTER TWO

The leather cuffs tight were tight around her wrists, pinning her arms down above her head.

'What are you going to do to me?' Tanya sighed, pulling weakly with her arms against the restraints that held her face down over the couch while her legs were spread and bound.

'Do with you? My dear Tanya, we're going to teach you to be a good girl and do what's asked of you.'

'This isn't fair... damn it... let me go!' Tanya jerked her arms hard but the leather around her wrists was tight and the cuffs were clipped to rings at the corners of the couch so however hard she struggled her arms remained held down either side of her face. Just as the girl getting whipped had been for real, Tanya realised that she really was unable to break free from the restraints they'd bound her with. In truth she was secretly thrilled to have been plunged into such a situation as she now found herself in, though she had no intention of letting on to her tormentors that being subjected to such treatment was satisfying some deep, dark craving for such sexual subjugation.

The couch had been lowered at the rear so that she was now bent across it at the waist with her feet left touching the floor and supporting her weight. Her ankles were bound like her wrists and try as she might she couldn't pull her legs free from where they'd been spread and secured to the lower corners of the couch. Though they had left her high heels on, her skirt and briefs were gone and she felt acutely vulnerable bent face down over the bench. The three young girls had gone now but the man with the camera was still there, calmly filming her. Her predicament was potently arousing and her mind raced with what might happen next but despite her eagerness she felt compelled to continue her pretence of outrage at being treated in such a fashion.

'You bastards! I didn't agree to this! Let me go!' Tanya

swore, the effect of the drug fading now and some of her strength returning along with a rising sense of nervousness at her predicament. The man with the camera switched the machine off and eased its weight from his shoulder.

'I'll edit that bit out.'

'You'll have to edit the rest out as well, because if you think I'm going to do what you want you can sod off!'

'We'll see about that,' answered the young man named Miles.

Tanya glanced over her shoulder at him just in time to see him gesture to the nurse. A second later and the chloroform soaked cotton wool pressed against Tanya's nostrils and the nurse's soft hand was smothering her mouth. Tanya shook her head, gurgling in protest.

The chemical was ruthlessly effective and in seconds Tanya's head was slumped on the leather couch and once again she was struggling to remain conscious.

'Uhhh...don't...make...me...'

Even as she tried to object to what they were doing to her, a pair of hands firmly took hold of her chin and encouraging her jaws apart they forced into her mouth what felt and tasted like a large rubber ball.

'Nuhh...'

'Keep still now, there's a good girl.'

The chloroform soaked cotton wool was held under her nose again. Tanya sighed weakly.

'Feeling sleepy are we?'

Her eyes fell heavily shut and Tanya sighed as sleep took her forcibly. Whether she was unconscious for a few seconds or many minutes she had no idea.

Opening her eyes the first thing she took in was that the cameraman was filming again, this time from directly in front of her and looking at the glass of the camera's lens close before her she saw her face reflected, a red rubber sphere protruding from between her forcibly parted jaws, leather straps tight across her cheeks and even as she watched the nurse was fastening the straps at her nape.

'Nuhh!'

'You'll have to learn Tanya, that unless you can control that tongue of yours, you'll be kept silenced. The choice is yours,' Miles cautioned.

'Some more restraint would be a good thing I think,' said the young nurse picking up several long leather straps.

Tanya shook her head, groaning through the gag in objection as a leather strap was wrapped around her thighs, close up under her buttocks then pulled tight and fastened, forcing her legs close against the bench. She blinked back her tears, the last of her courage evaporating as another strap fell over the small of her back. As it was tightened she sighed, shamefully conscious as it was fastened, how it left her buttocks thrust out over the edge of the leather bench and too her surprise she found she suddenly now felt aroused by what she was being subjected to.

As if reading her thoughts a hand briefly caressed her rump and she screwed her eyes shut in humiliation.

'I shouldn't be surprised if you get to learn to enjoy this, Tanya,' the young man laughed softly. She felt his hand linger against the curve of her arse then move lower. The lips of her sex were wet under his exploring touch. She writhed ineffectually against the straps and cuffs; the sensation of being touched there, whilst she was so defenceless was deliciously arousing.

'The bitch is loving this,' commented the man dryly.

Tanya groaned inwardly as she heard the man's comment. Of course they could sense how she was responding and for a brief moment she felt ashamed of being so aroused by being put in such a position.

Another strap, high over her back, was pulled tight pinning her shoulders down against the bench and squashing her breasts under her. Tanya grunted through the gag and now try as she might she could hardly move. These people certainly knew what they were doing. Tanya gazed at the camera lens close before her and saw again her reflection and the ball gag protruding from her forcibly parted jaws, her lips curling over it in a painful grimace as her mouth was held achingly wide. Experimentally Tanya screamed for them to let her go but her words were nothing more than a faint moaning, so ruthlessly effective was the gag.

'She's not going to be able to do anything to object now, irrespective of what we do to her,' the nurse ran her fingers along the edge of the broad leather strap, feeling Tanya's muscles straining underneath it. Tanya sighed, writhing a little as the man's fingers brushing her sex lips slid inside her, twisting and pushing deeper.

'Give her an introductory lesson in the art of discipline then would you nurse?'

The fingers withdrew from her sex, drawing a gag muffled groan from Tanya. To her shame and surprise, what she was being subjected to was potently exciting. Thankfully she was gagged otherwise they would have heard her cry of pleasure as the man thrust his fingers into her pussy.

'Time for you to learn some manners young lady: do you know what this is?'

Tanya gazed at the young woman now standing before her, a short leather strap cut into half a dozen thick strands in one hand.

She had imagined that the man was going to fuck her and though she might have pretended to object she wouldn't have minded. Now though, the realisation that she might be subjected to some pain, made her jerk her arms and legs urgently against the straps that held her down. The man grinned with amusement at her efforts to extricate herself.

'Not a hope, darling; you're just going to have soak up the pain and accept that we're going to do to you just whatever pleases us.'

'Nnnhh!'

'You can shake your head all you want,' admonished the girl dressed in the nurse's outfit, 'but you'll have to learn to take your punishment.'

'Doesn't she look good struggling so hard. Nothing like smooth bare skin glossy with perspiration to arouse the senses.'

As the man spoke he stroked Tanya's bare back and drew his fingers teasingly down her ribs close to but just avoiding her breasts that were squashed under her against the bench.

'This is called a tawse and I am sure it'll help you to become a more civilised young lady who knows her place and who knows what is expected of her.'

The woman swung on one heel and walked down the side of the couch.

The next seconds passed with agonising slowness. Tanya began shivering uncontrollably. She buried her head against the leather of the couch and held her breath. This was for real and it was being filmed! They were going to whip her and film her suffering! There was a deliberate pause and the tension was too great. Tanya shook her head, looking up, eyes wide with alarm, then just at the moment she gazed into the camera she felt the leather crack down against her exposed rump.

Thwack!

'Nuhh!'

The pain was sudden, sharp and strangely sweet. Tanya felt herself wanting to cry; she sighed through the gag, gazing at her reflection in the camera lens. Strands of her long honey blonde hair fell across her face; other strands were caught in the leather straps that hugged her cheeks. Between her generous, soft lips the rubber ball protruded and seeing herself gagged was deeply arousing.

When the boys at the university had gagged her, forcing her own panties into her mouth the sensation had been as potent as if someone was teasing her clit. The feeling of losing control and being dominated had been strangely and headily arousing. Deep down though Tanya had known that if she'd really wanted to she could have torn herself free from Julian's hand that pressed down over her mouth and she could have screamed at the top of her voice for help. She knew that someone would probably have heard and more than likely the boys would have quickly let her go. They were after all friends and she had deliberately egged them on and they all knew it. Despite her protests that she didn't want a fuck, they and she knew that she was really willing for them all to enjoy her body and her struggling was just a show. The excitement of her protesting and the lads taking her by force had added to the pleasure of the experience for all of them.

Now though, there was no way on earth she could extricate herself from her bondage and there was certainly no way she could free herself from the gag they'd subjected her to. The rubber ball was just soft enough to sink her teeth into fractionally but far too firm to squash. It filled her mouth completely and held her jaws wide enough to be uncomfortable. Even if the ball wasn't held firmly in place by the leather straps that were tight across her cheeks she doubted that she could have expelled it from her mouth without using her hands. That option in any event was denied her since her hands were held down a little above and to either side of her face. She gazed at the leather straps that bound her wrists. They were broad and supple and well used. The wrist cuffs resembled dog collars and were fastened in just the same manner except that the leather cuffs over-lapped each other. There were thick cords like heavy bootlaces tied to metal D rings which were fastened to the wrist cuffs and the cords had been pulled taut and secured to the corners of the couch. What they were fastened to Tanya couldn't see since the cords ran over the edge of the padded couch but jerking her arms against the restraints the cords came taut and no amount of effort would pull them loose or allow her to lift her hands anything more than a fraction from where they were held pinned. Well, she reflected, there was certainly no way she could get free and no way that she could tell them to stop. She was completely at these people's mercy. The thought should have made any ordinary girl terrified but whilst Tanya was certainly alarmed at the prospect of what she might be subjected to she was also excited by the possibilities that lay ahead.

The tawse came down again against her bare rump.

Thwack!

'Uhhh!'

Tanya jerked her arms desperately against the tight leather. Sweat glistened in the valley of her collarbone as she lifted her body, straining to pull herself free. The first blow had been exciting, arousing, but perhaps quite enough. Now after the second her bottom stung painfully and she knew, or imagined, that she couldn't bear very much more of such pain. She blinked back the tears that had welled in her eyes after the second blow and for a brief moment she was allowed to focus on the sensation of the painful heat of the tawse striking her bare bottom. The pain radiated outwards, from her rump and seeping into her sex or so it seemed. Her thighs quivered, her chest heaved as she panted and mingled with it was the feeling of the leather, uncompromisingly tight around her ankles and wrists as she was held down, all too helpless and utterly vulnerable for whatever lay in store.

'Nuhh…'

Tanya gave a plaintive cry and looked about her. She saw smiling, grinning faces and knew that they had no intention of letting her go yet. This was just the beginning, she realised and the thought went like a dart from her brain to her sex and made her sigh into the gag, as her pussy grew moist at the thought of what might lay ahead.

Thwack!

This time the tawse was delivered with a little more force and the pain made Tanya jerk urgently against the restraints. She felt the straps tight across her back and realised that she was utterly helpless.

Thwack!

She strained against the leather belts but she couldn't lift her back, couldn't close her legs. Her bottom throbbed now with pain and she wanted it to stop or at least for them to let her rest for a moment.

Thwack!

She writhed and twisted as the whip goaded her. The leather restraints creaked dully but held her fast. This was too much, she was sure she couldn't take anymore. She looked urgently about, tears misting her eyes. They had to stop, they really had to, she thought, desperate now to be shown some mercy.

'Dear me, is something the matter?' taunted the girl, delivering the strokes.

'Does that feel a little tender now?' The man stroked over the swell of her arse making Tanya flinch and sigh. She felt his fingers slide between her buttocks and then his fingertips were stroking her sex and it was too much for Tanya who groaned into the ball gag, tossing her head from side to side.

Her already swollen clitoris was lightly caught between finger and thumb and squeezed then pulled a little. Tanya gave a plaintive sigh. A finger slid slowly into the moistness between the folds of her sex. Tanya whimpered pathetically and found that she was silently begging, imploring the man to finger-fuck her and make her come. She was achingly in need of an orgasm and she felt feverishly aroused.

'She needs more pain, nurse; if you would be so kind,' said the man, matter of factly, then he withdrew his touch and for a few long seconds there was only the feel of cool air against Tanya's bare arse.

Thwack!

Again the tawse bit against the already stingingly sore skin of her bare arse. Frantically, Tanya shook her head in objection. They were taking this too far, she couldn't take any more pain, they had to stop!

'How are we feeling now Tanya?'

The man gazed down at her, smiling smugly. She looked up at him, panting hard and glaring angrily. The bastard had to make the bitch with the whip stop; she was being too hard on her.

'Oh dear, poor Tanya, are you crying?' the man smiled apologetically and he delicately wiped the tears from her cheeks with his thumb.

'Is this all a little bit too much for you?'

His patronising tone was infuriating but Tanya could do nothing: she couldn't speak, she couldn't move. She was forced to take whatever punishment they fancied subjecting her to and the truth was she couldn't bear the thought of being whipped much more, her body felt awash with pain already. Abjectly she gazed up at the man, realising that anger and indignation were getting her nowhere. With her pretty blue eyes wet with tears, wide and sorrowful, she silently begged the man to show her some mercy. As if sensing her thoughts, he nodded sympathetically.

'Feeling contrite already?' he asked, smiling down at her.

* * *

Miles had walked around to where he had a good view of her face.

He liked to see their pretty faces become contorted with pain and humiliation. After half a dozen strokes every girl began to cry or plead. This one though had started off gagged so of course she couldn't beg them to stop, she could only suffer in silence. He knew enough about the randy little bitch to know she deserved plenty of this treatment. And if she found this too much then she was in for a surprise, this was just a taster of what they had planned for her. Her Godfather had taken the trouble to photocopy numerous pages from her diary and Miles, grinning to himself, had enjoyed reading them. The young bitch had come to the right place to fulfil her fantasies; that was for sure.

Miles stroked her hair from the girl's face. She tried pulling back but couldn't so he took further advantage, letting his hand caress her cheek as the nurse smacked the leather down again on her rump.

Thwack!

Unable to resist the urge to drag her arms against the constraints even though she could see how useless her struggling was, the girl writhed frantically. Miles watched her struggling with amusement and mounting excitement.

He'd seen plenty of young girls lured by the film company's rewards of lucrative payment and he had lost track of how many girls he'd seen in similar positions to the one Tanya now found herself in. She was though, easily one of the most desirable girls he'd encountered. Physically she was all too fuckable; slim, generous tits, narrow waist and slender long legs with nice firm buttocks and thighs. She had the body of a model; not a fashion model with legs to her armpits and small tits; Tanya had the body of men's magazine model; shapely legs that you could imagine slithering across the bed sheets and with breasts that provocatively taunted by their size and perfect shape. More than that though Tanya had an impish, mischievous smile and her blue eyes sparkled with the promise of what she'd been willing to do. There was something about her expression that seemed to say she would be a good time girl for any man who had the balls to take control of her.

From the moment Miles had met her, he had determined that he wanted to fuck Tanya and to fuck her senseless. Before that though he wanted to tame her and recognising that she was deep down another naturally submissive girl, he knew his first task was to break her to the rein, like a wild filly. He would then make her submit to the whip and finally he would mount her and force her to accept him as her master. Bringing Tanya to rein had been all too easy; the dumb blonde had all too unwittingly played right into his hands. Now she was learning to respond to the whip. Having read her diary, he knew just how he needed to train her and he felt confident that it was just a matter of time before he had her completely under his control.

'Does that feel a little too persuasive for you, Tanya? Are you thinking that you should maybe be saying sorry to your teachers for the way you spoke to us earlier?'

Tanya looked up into his face, her ball gag spread lips trembling, her pretty blue eyes moist with tears. He could tell that already she'd had enough. She'd not lasted as long as he'd imagined she might. She obviously didn't like the taste of pain quite as much as some. But then in her diary she hadn't fantasised about being on the receiving end of such punishment. She had though confessed to fancying being forcibly taken by a group of men and she had described in vivid detail an episode when she'd deliberately got drunk with four male students and then egged them into subjecting her to a gangbang. Her Godfather had thoughtfully photocopied much of her diary and Miles had been afforded a chance to read it. They'd agreed that Tanya was, though just nineteen more than ready to experience what the film company could offer her. In fact having read the lurid details of some of her fantasies, they had no qualms about giving her the lead part in the next film where she'd be playing a poor teenage girl subjected to all manner of torment from the owners of the private school in which she had been incarcerated.

Miles had already decided that he'd make sure Tanya got what she wanted as far as her diary was concerned and more besides, if he was given the chance. The bitch had made it crystal clear what she craved and he would be more than happy to make sure she was satisfied.

* * *

Dear Diary Monday June 13th.

Well, after the episode with Julian and his mates I have

spent the whole week day-dreaming during lectures about what I could do this weekend that would be more scintillating than getting gangbanged by Julian and his friends. I was quite tempted just to ring him up and ask him if he was up for it again but I think he might have been a bit embarrassed by the episode after he'd had time to sober up and to reflect on what we'd all got up to.

Anyway I found myself fantasising about what it would have been like if it had been with four blokes who I didn't know. What would it have been like if they'd held me their prisoner for longer than just an hour or so? On Thursday afternoon I was sitting in a History lecture daydreaming about being abducted by four guys whom I'd bumped into in a pub and who then had followed me home. Whilst I was supposed to be taking notes on the Macedonian and Punic Wars I was sketching in my mind images of me being stripped and gangbanged by four meaty, anonymous blokes. On Thursday night I went to bed and continued my fantasy, on Friday I dressed in my favourite black mini skirt and tank top and went to some of the pubs where students don't go, on the rougher side of town. I returned home alone that night but resolved to make another foray on the Saturday night. I woke up on Sunday morning in some guy's bed with a bit of hangover and a vague recollection that we'd had a decent shag but I went back to my digs on Sunday in the early afternoon feeling ravenous. I had missed breakfast and lunch and I was in urgent need of a gangbang!

I fell asleep on my sitting room sofa after a Chinese takeaway and a few glasses of wine and had the most delicious dream. I imagined that I met this muscled hunk, mid-twenties who took me back to his home on a housing estate on the south side of town to meet some of his mates and to teach me pool after I had expressed an interest, having chatted him up in a pub where I'd watched him playing pool. Back at his place, he showed me his pool table, which was set up in his garage. He called some of his mates on his mobile and they came round for a game. Well, it didn't take long before I realised that the game was "let's strip and fuck the girl senseless". Of course I tried to get out of the garage but they quickly cornered me at the far end against the up and over door which they pulled down and as soon as I started shouting for help they pinned my arms behind my back and smothered my mouth with their hands. I writhed like mad but two of them were holding me still and whilst one of them began to discard his jeans the fourth one got some duct tape from a work bench, cut off a strip and they pressed it across my mouth, gagging me.

They then dragged me kicking and struggling across to the pool table and forcing my waist up against the edge of the table, two of them got my wrists and pulled my arms outstretched from the far side. My mini skirt was hoisted up around my waist and my G-string was impatiently pulled aside. I cried out for them to stop but the tape muffled my pleading and the next thing I felt was someone behind me coaxing my thighs apart and then a cock was driven into my pussy.

When I woke, saw my empty takeaway boxes and unfinished glass of wine all I could do was to sit up from where I'd fallen asleep on the sofa and rub my stiff neck and resolve to clear up the lounge, brush my teeth like a good little girl and go to bed straight away and hope that I could carry on with my delicious dream.

* * *

Miles nodded to the girl dressed in the nurse's uniform who was waiting on his authorisation to continue delivering the punishment. For a moment he had wondered whether their victim had suffered enough but then, remembering her lurid dreams that she'd recorded in her secret diary, he had no trouble in convincing himself that Tanya was desperate to experience as much torment as he could mete out to her. He gave his accomplice a tacit nod and watched as she brought the tawse down again on the tethered girl's naked and now crimson bottom.

Thwack!

The tawse cracked against the bare rump again. The skin was already streaked red and Miles watched as Tanya renewed her efforts to extricate herself from the restraints. She was a seriously fit bitch, her slim body well toned and she was putting up an impressive struggle to free herself. Her desperate efforts to escape would certainly make good viewing, he mused, watching her writhe and twist frantically against the restraints they'd fastened upon her. Her bare arms and legs were glossy with perspiration and she was breathing hard. Struggle all you want, little girl, Miles thought to himself, you'll not get free from those cuffs.

Thwack!

Tanya gave a gag muffled cry of anguish, tears began to run down her cheeks and she shook her head despondently. Miles stroked her bare legs where they were shiny with sweat around the inside of her shapely thighs. Her tight T-shirt was damp across her back. She looked in a pleasingly sorry state already and they'd hardly even begun. He stroked his fingers through her tousled hair and tightening his grip amongst her blonde strands he forcibly drew her head up so she had to meet his gaze.

'This is your own fault,' he smiled apologetically, 'and it's so un-necessary really. Why don't you just say how sorry you are? Admit to me that you're a bad little girl and I'll take care of you.'

Tanya gazed up at him; he could read the pain and distress washing through her in her wide, pitiful eyes. He nodded again to the woman.

Thwack!

The tawse cracked against Tanya's buttocks. She gave a long, anguished groan.

'Don't you want this to stop?' Miles crouched in front of the girl, releasing his grip on her and lifting strands of blonde hair clear from her face. She was panting hard now, perspiration running down her cheeks and neck.

'Now be sensible and tell us how sorry are for your bad behaviour.'

Miles crouched closer to her face, wiping the tears from her cheeks. She opened her eyes and looked imploringly at him.

'This will go on until you say sorry.'

'She's a stubborn little thing,' said the woman, wiping the beads of perspiration from her own brow.

'Well, she's got to learn to say sorry and mend her ways,' said Miles, ' let's have a look and see what condition her pretty little bottom is in.'

His hands ran over the swells of her buttocks, gently drawing her mounds of flesh apart and massaging them at the same time. The tethered girl struggled weakly. The cameraman moved down the side of the couch and the camera was swung in and focused on Miles as he examined the bound girl's rump.

'Silly girl, you can't do anything, you'll just bruise your wrists, keep still while I just look...'

Miles put the fingers of one hand into the crease between her taut buttocks. Tanya squirmed ineffectually. His fingers moved down to her soft slit of flesh. Tanya shook her head, whimpering through the gag as his fingers opened her up and calmly invaded her body.

'Very warm and damp aren't we?'

'She's stopped struggling, maybe she likes that,' suggested the woman scornfully.

'I think this little girl is enjoying our punishment, that's why she doesn't want it to stop,' said Miles sliding two fingers further into the defenceless girl's exposed sex.

'You like that don't you?' Miles gently demanded, letting his fingertips just lightly brush over the girl's swollen sex lips, 'You want me to do this to you, don't you? You're enjoying this punishment aren't you?'

Tanya groaned through the gag. Weakly she lifted her head from the couch and shook her head.

'Well Tanya, if you don't want this treatment to continue, you have to say how sorry you are for your bad behaviour. Well, what have you got to say for yourself?'

Straining to look back over her shoulder so she could make eye contact with the man, Tanya gazed abjectly at him, gurgling incoherently through the gag.

'Let's see what you've got to say for yourself.'

Unbuckling the strap at Tanya's nape he eased the hard rubber ball from her mouth. Immediately Tanya was blurting out breathlessly in earnest protest.

'Somebody help me! Please...let me go, I don't...uhhh...'

Jamming the ball gag back into her protesting mouth Miles silenced her once more. Desperately trying to resist the gag Tanya shook her head urgently but it was easy for him to pull the straps taut across her cheeks and a second later he had the strap fastened snugly at her nape.

'Well Tanya, if you don't want this treatment to continue, you have to stay how sorry you are for your bad behaviour. Are you ready to apologise?'

The girl glared up at him and shook her head negatively.

'Very well; nurse, give her another six of the tawse.'

Stepping back, Miles watched with self indulgent relish as the young girl posing as the nurse brought the leather tawse down across Tanya's arse.

Thwack! Thwack!

Tanya gave an anguished cry, shaking her head urgently but the ball gag effectively muffled her objection.

'On her back.'

Thwack! Thwack!

Miles watched with amusement as his tethered victim tried to buck under the blow but the strap across her back prevented it.

'Thighs,' Miles ordered.

Thwack!

Thwack!

Tanya's slender legs jerked urgently against the restraining cuffs.

'That's enough for the moment,' he ordered.

Tanya was panting rapidly now and Miles, who had practised this torture so often, had got it down to a fine art. This time when he fingered her sex she was slick and hot to his touch and from her gag muffled sigh he knew she was on the brink of an orgasm. However much they might hate the pain, this situation, being bound and treated like this invariably would make the right sort of girl come. They just needed the right treatment. Of course this was just the start. Once they had been trained to get off on a judicious mixture of pleasure and pain they were given other even more viciously stimulating treatments. And even if they didn't enjoy what they were subjected to, they had no say in the matter and it made for equally good film material.

'Is that feeling good... you like that don't you? Come on Tanya... time to come...'

He stroked her slowly, skilfully, he'd had plenty of practice and then when he judged she was getting close to her climax he fingered her deeply, pressing his thumb at the same time against her swollen clitoris. Familiar with the routine the cameraman had zoomed in as obligingly Tanya's slender body shook and writhed against the restraints as she was brought to orgasm.

'Now Tanya, I wonder if you're ready to confess to being such a bad little girl?' Miles asked withdrawing his fingers. The girl looked up desperately at him.

'Nurse; the tawse again please; on her rump.'

Thwack!

The girl jerked under the blow, her eyes smarting with the pain.

Miles stroked her arse, making her flinch as he traced the red lines left by the leather tawse.

'Again.'

Thwack!

Tanya jerked her arms and legs, writhing urgently, tears now running down her soft cheeks. Her pretty, blue eyes gazed up forlornly at him, begging him to stop the punishment.

'Again.'

Thwack!

Her eyes screwed shut, her straining body taut against the straps; Tanya's hips ground urgently, her neck arching back as she writhed frantically. Through the ball gag he could hear her muffled cry. The bitch had come again! So she was the type that really did like being treated like this, he mused. Well, she'd get all she could take, that was for certain.

'Well Tanya, this punishment will go on unless you're ready to say how sorry you are for your bad behaviour. Do you want to tell us how sorry you are?'

The girl nodded and Miles grinned with satisfaction at having broken her spirit of defiance. Unfastening the gag's strap he eased the ball from her mouth.

'Now, apologise like a good little girl,' he ordered.

'I'm sorry... please don't punish me anymore...'

'Well done Tanya. I think Scawder School is going to make you an obedient young girl, after all. Don't you?'

Tanya gave a consensual nod and Miles grinned, stroking her tousled hair affectionately.

CHAPTER THREE

Tanya lay passively as the man unclipped the wrist cuffs from the corners of the couch and then unfastened her legs.

'There, that wasn't too bad was it?' Miles grinned at her.

'You bastard…how dare you treat me like that?' Tanya gasped, still breathless and in shock from what she'd been subjected to. Her poor bottom throbbed but as the man loosened the restraints from her limbs she began to realise that there had been something about the whole ordeal she'd found intensely stimulating. So stimulating in fact she'd come repeatedly. The thought made her cheeks crimson.

'Let me help you up.'

'I can manage, get your hands off me!' Tanya glared daggers at the man as she stumbled to her feet. Dazed and breathless, wearing only high heels and her T-shirt, she gazed around her. The other girls and the woman dressed as the nurse were all watching her, waiting to see how she would now react. The man with the camera had stopped filming. Tanya couldn't believe what had happened to her and how her body had responded. Despite the pain of the tawse, or maybe because of it, with little effort the man had brought her to several exquisite climaxes just by fingering her pussy. There had been something powerfully erotic for her about being tied down and although it had scared her, the thrill and satisfaction had been worth it.

'Had enough already? You can go home now if you want or stay and do some more work?'

This was work! Tanya smiled inwardly at the thought. The throbbing pain across her buttocks was fading already but the memory of how it had felt being tied down and between the blows, feeling a stranger's fingers exploring her pussy was still vividly fresh in her memory.

'Well, have you had enough or are you game for some more filming?' Miles questioned.

'I don't know…' Tanya looked uncertainly around her at

the others. Surely with the other young girls on the film, nothing too serious could happen? After all, it was a film she was making, so what could they do to her that was so terrible?

'If you're scared about not being in control Tanya, let me explain how we can work. We need the scenes to look and feel real; your struggling and all that. It's best if you don't know what is going to happen then you'll genuinely looked more alarmed or frightened at what is unfolding. Understand? However, I'll give you a safe word. If at anytime you want us to stop all you have to do is say that word; alright?'

'Okay then, I'll do it,' Tanya agreed.

'Great stuff: just remember you can scream and beg for us to stop and we won't unless it suits the film. If you really want us to stop just say an agreed word. Got that?'

'Like what?'

'You choose.'

'Chocolate,' said Tanya.

'Right, "chocolate" it is. Happy now?'

Tanya nodded and repeated the word to herself. She immediately felt much more confident about everything now.

'Excellent, let's get on and shoot another scene then. Come on Tanya, it's time for a change of scene.'

Still only in her high heels and wearing only her T-shirt, Tanya was taken a short distance down a corridor and led into a room full of props and equipment. She still felt a bit groggy from the chloroform and weak from her struggling against the straps they'd tied her down with but with the thought of the money she could make uppermost in her mind and feeling more relaxed now she knew she could stop proceedings if she wanted to, she was eager to find out what they expected from her next. The young woman dressed as the nurse produced some clothes for her to change into and Tanya dutifully did as she was asked. Ten minutes later and dressed in what resembled a school uniform Miles led her to the next shoot.

He gestured for Tanya to sit in the chair facing the desk and he closed the door. The cameraman was already in the room filming their arrival.

'You asked to see me Headmaster,' Tanya said demurely, reciting verbatim the line that she'd been instructed to repeat just before Miles had opened the door and pushed her ahead of him. The Headmaster turned around, smiling disarmingly. Tanya had seated herself, crossing her legs; acutely conscious that the little dark blue skirt she'd been given barely covered her briefs so short was it. The white blouse she'd been given was also a size too small so that her breasts seemed to jut out from under the thin cotton and the lace of her half-cup bra was clearly outlined. A pair of high-heeled shoes, some eye shadow and pink lipstick completed her "school uniform" and her long, blonde hair had been plaited into a ponytail.

'Miles tells me you took it into your head to try to leave the school without our permission?'

'I'm very sorry Headmaster. Really.'

'Good, I'm pleased to hear that you are.'

Picking ice cubes with silver tongs shaped like a birds talons and dropping them into two tall glasses he regarded Tanya thoughtfully for a moment.

'I know I've been bad sir, but I won't do it again.'

Tanya found herself repeating the lines Miles had given her as he had led her down the corridor.

'Well, if you take it into your head to behave like that again be certain that you'll be even more severely punished. However, if you want to make you time at Scawder more, what shall we say… pleasing for yourself then all you need to do is make sure that you behave in a way that pleases me. You're a bright young girl Tanya, perform as expected and I'll make sure you're rewarded for your efforts to please.'

'I'll do my best to please you, Headmaster,' answered Tanya demurely.

Miles gestured to the cameraman and the filming was stopped.

'Well done Tanya, you got your lines right on the first take. Keep up that sort of performance and you can expect to get a bonus when we're finished.'

* * *

The girl that Tanya had watched being chased and then whipped in the games room she was to find out was called Jezra and like Tanya she had come to Scawder eager to make some quick money. At eighteen, she was a year younger than Tanya and had come from Greece to Britain to spend the summer working and improving her English. For the last four days she had been at the remote hunting lodge filming. The other three girls, all a few years older had come from London and it seemed they were all hired and paid to act in the films like Jezra but they were never subjected any of the punishments that Jezra had been subjected to. The oldest girl, Sasha, the petite Greek girl warned Tanya, was especially sadistic and revelled in tormenting her. Tanya was hesitant to ask Jezra if she too had been given a safe word; if she had then she could hardly complain at what she was subjected to but if she hadn't or the other had chosen to ignore it then that put an altogether different complexion on proceedings.

The morning's filming completed, Tanya and Jezra were left in a small bedroom where a tray of sandwiches and crisps and a jug of orange juice had been left for them. Miles had escorted Tanya to the room where Jezra was already sat on a bed reading a magazine.

'We'll be filming again in an hour or so and I want to keep you in character, you'll give a better performance that way,' Miles announced as he held the door open for Tanya.

'What do you mean?' Tanya asked.

'I'm locking you in. Have a rest and I'll be back for you in a while.'

'But...'

The door was pulled abruptly shut and Tanya heard the man turn a key in the lock. She looked over her shoulder at the other girl.

'The bastard's locked us in!'

'You may as well get used to it.'

'This is ridiculous!'

From the window, Tanya could glimpse a bend in the drive between the high rhododendrons but the window had recently been fitted with two iron bars so any thought of escape was immediately quashed.

'They have let me out for exercise and walks but never alone.'

'You mean you don't go home at the end of the day?'

'No, that's part of the contract.'

'Shit!' Tanya stared sullenly out of the window. So how did you end up here?'

'I responded to an advert; it was pretty ambiguous but reading between the lines I guessed it was to do a porn film. They were offering good money and I thought I'd have a go. I thought it might be fun. I'll tell you what though I reckon what they're making is for strictly private sale,' Jezra suggested.

Tanya, who was staring out of the window, glanced over her shoulder at her companion. Jezra, she thought, was incredibly pretty. A little shorter than Tanya, she had chestnut brown skin, smooth, almost glistening. Her long hair was as black and shiny as a raven's wing; she had slender fingers with long, perfect nails and captivating, large dark brown eyes.

'So how long have you been held here Jezra?' Tanya asked, refilling her glass with orange juice and offering the last packet of crisps to the other girl.

'Just four days... four painful days,' Jezra forced a smile.

'Could you tell me what I can expect? Would you mind?' Tanya asked.

'No, you may as well know what'll probably happen to you then at least it won't be such a shock for you,' said the Greek girl, settling herself back against the pillows of one of the two single beds that were in the little room. Tanya slumped herself down in the only armchair in the room, yawning and glanced at the window, wishing she could open it. The room was hot and stuffy and she felt in need of some fresh air, she felt so lethargic.

'Are you going to tell me then?' she asked, looking at Jezra who had leant her head back against the pillows and closed her eyes.

'Mmm... sorry? I was nearly falling asleep there,' Jezra opened her eyes, smiling apologetically.

'You were going to tell me about what to expect?' Tanya prompted.

As she waited for the other girl to talk, she sipped from her orange juice. Her eyelids felt so heavy she knew that despite all the excitement of the day when she was allowed to sleep she'd be out like a light. She stifled a yawn and put aside her glass, worried that she'd drop it, she felt so tired. When she looked expectantly at Jezra though, she saw that the other girl was in fact asleep. That's just how I feel, she told herself and curling sideways in the chair she closed her eyes for what she told herself would be just a few moments.

'Had enough to drink have you?'

Tanya flicked her eyes open and saw Miles grinning down at her, saw her arms drawn down onto her stomach before her, leather cuffs binding her wrists together. There was another man kneeling before her and when he stood up she saw he had fastened leather cuffs around her ankles and these were clipped together with a bulldog clip that prevented her separating her legs.

'Bring her along then,' Miles ordered.

The other man hauled Tanya from the chair and tossed her over his shoulder. She was far too sleepy to make any objection and only as the men carried her from the room did she realise that the food or drink she'd been given must have been drugged.

'Where are you taking me?' Tanya asked sleepily.

No answer was forthcoming and it was all Tanya could do to keep awake as she was carried from the room along the corridor and into another room that was set up as a dormitory. The three other "sixth form" girls were all there, each sat, semi-naked on one of the row of single beds and the men with the cameras were there too as was Campbell and the girl who acted the part of the school nurse.

'Get her clothes off then and get her ready,' Campbell ordered.

Tanya was tossed down onto one of the single beds and the leather cuffs and her clothes, except for her briefs were pulled from her. She felt too sleepy to resist and looked bewilderedly at the other young girls as they watched her being undressed by the men.

'Right, put the duvet over her and let's get shooting.'

Encouraged to lie down, Tanya felt herself quickly drifting into sleep and she was dreamily wondering how long the drug might take to wear off when she was vaguely aware of someone calling out: -

"And action!"

The three girls all rose from their beds and stealthily closed around the bed where Tanya lay. Sasha, the tallest and oldest of the girls moved swiftly to the head of the Tanya's bed. She was naked except for a simple white thong. In one hand she held a stocking. Her skin was deeply tanned and her breasts, which were large with wide, dark areolae, glistened where she'd massaged baby oil over them. Her short hair was heavily gelled and combed back so it shone in furrows and the subdued light they were filming with glinted off the silver belly stud and silver chain necklace she wore.

Dropping the stocking she held on the pillow above Tanya's head, she stroked with one hand over Tanya's exposed shoulder then drew Tanya's hair clear of her cheek and circled it around her ear. With one fingertip she traced a line over Tanya's lips, then she thoughtfully sucked on her finger, her long, dark purple varnished nail contrasting with the gleaming white of her own teeth.

'Are you asleep Tanya?' she asked, softly.

'No... nearly...' Tanya sighed dreamily.

Sasha turned to one of the girls, nodding at her accomplice.

'It's time for you to undergo your initiation ceremony into the Scawder sixth form, Tanya,' Sasha announced, smiling reassuringly as Tanya sleepily looked up at her.

Simultaneously one of the girls tossed aside the duvet that was covering Tanya and caught hold of her ankles whilst the other girls snatched hold of Tanya by the wrists.

'Right, fasten her wrists and ankles to the corners of the bed,' Sasha ordered.

'Let me go!' Tanya objected as the girls forced her arms above her head and bound her wrists with more stockings to the corners of the metal bed frame. Her legs were then spread and tied fast with cotton belts taken from towelling robes

'Feeling comfortable?' Sasha grinned down at Tanya as she tested the ties the girls had pinned her down with. They were just as effective as the leather wrist and ankle cuffs the men had earlier used on her. She glimpsed the cameraman filming her and shook her head despondently.

'Please, what are you going to do?' Tanya looked up, wide-eyed with alarm at Sasha who stood over her, grinning maliciously.

'Right, soften her up.'

Gazing up forlornly at Sasha, Tanya gasped as one of the other girls drew apart the globes of her upturned arse and poured baby oil between her legs.

'Mmmm..' Tanya sighed; unable to deny the pleasurably arousing sensation the oil gave her.

'Ever enjoyed one of these before, Tanya?'

Tanya looked up to see Sasha holding quite the largest vibrator she'd ever seen.

'Just the sort of thing to give a sex starved girl a nice intense orgasm,' Sasha laughed perching herself on the edge of the bed and stroking between Tanya's spread legs with the tip of the device.

'Uhhh…mmm…' Tanya sighed, writhing against the restraints as she felt the dildo teasing her sex lips.

'How deep would you like it Tanya?'

The vibrator, slick with baby oil was slid effortlessly into her pussy and quickly pushed deeply into her drawing a gasp from Tanya.

'Enough… please…' Tanya groaned, shaking her head urgently as the device was pushed still further inside her. As the sensation of penetration quickly grew too intense she twisted frantically against the ties that held her arms and legs.

'Does that feel good, Tanya?' Sasha grinned with satisfaction as she saw the expression on Tanya's face and then she switched the vibrator on.

'Uhhh…too much… stop…' Tanya tossed her head from side to side; gasping feverishly as the powerful device plunged inside her and propelled her startlingly fast towards an orgasm.

Sasha knew from her own experience the intense feeling of being filled that the vibrator produced; ten inches long and with powerful vibrations once switched on to 'high' it was more than enough to satisfy most girls. Tanya was jerking and twisting against the ties and her panting gaps and sighs told Sasha that her victim was very soon going to come.

'Uhhh…yes…mmm…' Tanya sighed, closing her eyes, her back trying to arch against the restraints. Moaning softly, she came, a long, shuddering orgasm that left her almost breathless.

'Now let's turn the vibrator up to high.'

'No… please…' Tanya shook her head, groaning as an even more intense vibration rippled through her. Pressed against the bed sheet, her pussy throbbed and as the sensation got too much Tanya struggled against the restraints but that just served to heighten her arousal and a moment later she climaxed again and even more intensely.

Urgently Tanya jerked her legs against the bindings around her ankles.

'Enough…please…no more…'

The camera was close before her now, focusing on her face, as she tossed her head from side to side in ecstasy. Hands stroked over the swell of her buttocks. It was all too much for Tanya and with a choked cry she came again.

'I think that's enough for now.'

Weakly, Tanya lifted her head and saw Miles standing regarding her.

'What would you like done with her now, Deputy Headmaster?' asked Sasha.

'Bring her to my study.'

'Very good, sir.'

The vibrator was prised from Tanya's throbbing sex. Sasha and one of the other girls each unfastened a binding around her wrists and then they pulled Tanya's arms up behind her back and used the stockings to bind her wrists together. A voice called from the camera to "cut" and more lights were switched back on.

'Right, get her to the next set.'

CHAPTER FOUR

Tanya sat alongside Sasha and the two other girls who'd tormented her, watching while the cameras prepared to film once again. They had moved to a large drawing room on the ground floor, half of which had been set up to look like an opulent study. Campbell was sat in a director's chair running his eye over pages of directions, whilst the girl who was dressed as the nurse was applying make-up to Tanya. Her job finished, she stood up. She was wearing a dark blue little skirt and a white blouse that contrasted with her tanned skin. Campbell signalled for them to start filming. Reluctantly, Tanya stood up and crossed over to where they had told her she had to stand.

'Settling in are we?'

'Yes, thank you Headmaster.'

The man acting the part of the Headmaster stood facing an opened French window, his back to Tanya.

'Sasha says that you are trying hard to be a model pupil.'

'Yes Headmaster.'

Tanya watched him close the window and lower the sunblind.

'It would be preferable that being a model pupil was something that came naturally. It worries me that it is something that you have to try hard to accomplish. Are you naturally a bit of a wild thing, I wonder?'

'No, Headmaster,' Tanya answered, then she quickly added, 'I hope not, sir.'

'The Head Girl tells me that you were masturbating in bed last night and when she told you to stop you refused.'

'That's not true,' Tanya objected.

'You're lying Tanya and the punishment for such disobedience is the cane. Go and stand over there by that chrome rail on the wall.'

Tanya reluctantly obeyed, glancing around to see the Headmaster opening a roll top bureau.

'Headmaster, I'm really sorry, I didn't mean to...'

'Be quiet Tanya, speak only when spoken to. I knew you'd be a bit of a challenge but I'm surprised to find you trying to step outside my rules so soon and so blatantly.'

Tanya bit her lip apprehensively as he marched across the room to where she stood anxiously waiting. She had been told to act scared but that was hardly necessary. She had no desire to feel a cane cracking down across her bum but she knew she'd have to go through with it if she wanted them to continue to employ her. She told herself that the money was her incentive for putting up with such treatment but in truth she was already getting addicted to what her alter ego, Tanya the schoolgirl, was being subjected to. For a moment she felt guilty for admitting this to herself and she wondered whether she shouldn't try to quit the place now whilst she still had the strength of will to refuse the deliciously wicked pleasure playing the submissive schoolgirl offered her.

She doubted now that her Godfather had any intention of returning at the end of the day's filming to collect her. The bastard had more than likely been paid to deliver her to these people and she was now effectively their prisoner until it suited them to release her. Of course theoretically she could walk out and even go to the Police but she had signed their contract and of course they could say that she had been willing all along to act her part. On the one hand she found being drugged disconcerting but on the other hand she couldn't even prove that they had drugged her and so far they hadn't forced her to do anything that she hadn't coped with, so maybe she was worrying unnecessarily.

'Hold onto the rail with both hands apart and stand with your feet behind that line on the floor.'

'I'll fall over,' Tanya objected.

'Of course you won't, just hold the rail, feet back, that's it.'

Tanya had to bend from the waist to keep her feet behind

the line and not let go of the rail. She looked over her left shoulder. The man dressed as the Headmaster was standing right beside her and now he reached for her skirt and pulled it up her thighs and bunched the material around her waist. She was wearing just a thong, which conveniently left her buttocks exposed.

'Six strokes of this and you can consider yourself let off lightly.'

At that moment there was a knock at the door, or more accurately Miles, already standing inside the room watching the filming, rapped his fist against the back of the door.

'Come in.'

At the signal two of the other girls entered.

'You wanted us, Headmaster?'

'Yes girls, come here both of you.'

Tanya saw the Headmaster open a desk drawer and hand each of the two girls a leather wrist cuff just like the ones that had been used on her in the medical room, except that these had short leather straps dangling from them.

'Girls. Her wrists.'

The two girls slapped the leather over her wrists, deftly slid the buckles home then looped the leather straps around the chrome pole, pulling them tight then binding them fast.

'Time for some Scawder discipline Tanya, six strokes. I'll be lenient.'

Crack!

The cane snapped down over her rump and Tanya yelped. One, she counted to herself.

Crack!

The second blow was in exactly the same place. Tanya bit down on her lip.

Crack!

She gave an anguished cry and shook her head.

'Stop... please...hurts too much...'

She had been told to beg them to stop after the fifth stroke but already after three blows to her buttocks the stinging pain had brought tears to eyes.

Crack!

She tightened her grip on the chrome rail, screwing her eyes shut.

Crack!

The fifth blow was delivered intentionally harder than the previous and the sharp pain was too much.

'Ow! Fuck!' Tanya swore.

'Six more strokes for swearing and one more for speaking without permission: that means eight more!'

Tanya bit back the urge to swear again. They hadn't told her this was to happen!

Eight to go, just eight, you can take eight Tanya, she told herself.

Crack!

The cane slapped down again on her rump. She whimpered in protest but managed to keep her mouth shut. Seven left. She sighed. The next blow was lower, harder, Tanya yelped in pain.

'I'll consider that noise as talking so eight still then.'

Crack!

This time the tip of the cane was flicked cruelly high between her thighs and Tanya cried out, retreating towards the wall and closing her legs defensively together.

'One more for speaking; still eight then. Back to the line and spread your legs girl.'

'No!' Tanya shook her head in refusal, dragging her arms back angrily, but the cuffs

around her wrists held her fast, pain lancing into her shoulders as she pulled ineffectually against the restraints.

'Oh dear, that means another one for talking; that's nine now. Helen, fetch two thigh pulls from the wardrobe.'

The two girls, faces gleaming with satisfaction, gleefully fastened broad leather belts around each of Tanya's thighs. Tanya gazed down at her thighs; the sight of the black leather tight around her legs was deeply arousing, a molten heat poured through her loins at the thought of what was happening to her. She watched speechlessly as leashes were then clipped to steel rings sewn into each belt and pulling on the leashes from opposite sides of her, the girls forced Tanya's legs backwards away from the rail until she was struggling to keep hold of the chrome.

'Uhhh.... no more...' Tanya gasped.

'Good. Just pull her legs a tiny bit farther apart. Excellent. Now Tanya, nine more strokes and we're finished.'

Crack!

Tanya kept her jaws firmly shut, tears rolling down her cheeks but determined not to cry out and thereby extend her suffering.

Crack!

Glancing to one side she saw the cameraman focused on her. She gazed ahead of her at her outstretched arms, leather cuffs tight around her wrists and bound by black leather cords to the gleaming chrome pole. She imagined what it would be like watching a film of this...

Crack!

Against the tender inside of her thighs the cane tip struck, viciously sharp, stinging... she knew the pain now, knew how long the throbbing lasted before it diminished and just the dull ache remained like after one had burnt oneself.

Crack!

Her thighs felt like jelly now, the muscles trembling from the repeated blows. She glanced down at the broad leather binding her thighs, the leather straps running from the thigh bindings to the girls, one on each side of her. They smiled cruelly as she glanced at them in turn, both relishing her suffering.

Crack!

The pain made her pussy throb expectantly. Maybe the men would fuck her after it was over. She wanted that, she realised, shamefully.

Crack!

The pain was like a drug now that washed through her, encouraging her pussy to ache with longing: ache with the need to come. Her cheeks burnt with guilt as she realised that part of her was enjoying being subjected to this torment.

Crack!

The tip of the cane smacked against her thigh, so high and skilfully aimed this time that the very tip momentarily embedded into the flimsy white cotton of her thong where it caressed her sex. The sensation for Tanya was like an electric shock.

'Uhh!'

'I think that counts as speaking so another stroke to be added to your total Tanya.'

'That's not fair! You bastard, I didn't say anything!'

'Oh dear, another six for swearing; that makes eight still to go.'

'No... please... I can't take anymore... really!' Tanya sobbed.

'Well, what can you suggest as punishment instead Tanya? How do you want to show your contrition? What can you offer me in return if I waive your punishment?'

These were the lines that Miles had told her about and to which she had been given specific answers. Now Tanya needed no encouraging: she was more than willing and doubtless the continued caning had been designed to ensure that her tone would be one of genuine desperation at appeasement.

'If you let me off the rest of my punishment Headmaster I'll show you how grateful I am,' Tanya pleaded.

'And how will you do this?'

'Let me kneel before you and serve you Headmaster the way a bad girl should.'

'Very well.'

The bindings were released from the chrome pole and her arms promptly drawn behind her back. She stood trembling and passive as the leather cords were then laced together, pinning her wrists close to each other at the base of her spine. Leaving the leather belts still fastened around her thighs, she was encouraged to kneel. The man stood over her, smiling expectantly. One of the girls unbuckled the belt of his trousers and pulled down his trouser zip. Tanya watched, silent, as the man's trousers and pants were drawn down his legs. His cock was hard, the tip already shiny with pre-come fluid. Tanya's breathing quickened. She'd done this plenty of times but she'd never been forced to do it. She sensed the camera filming her every move and imagined the film being watched by men, each fantasising that she was actually performing this on them. She suddenly wanted to show them how accomplished she was: how well she could satisfy them.

Leaning forward she lowered her head and gave the swaying cock shaft a tentative lick. The man caught hold of her by her tousled hair and encouraged her. Tanya drew the tip of her tongue slowly against the underside of the cock, then bathed the swollen purple head with a long continuous lick until she drew a contented sigh from the man and he eased his hold on hair.

'Is that good Headmaster?'

'You can do better than that Tanya, come on girl, put it in your mouth.'

Tanya drew back and looked up with wide eyes remembering what Miles had told her to do. The camera was there filming; she gazed at the swaying cock and suddenly longed to have it rammed into her pussy. Maybe she should really refuse, maybe then he'd fuck her as a punishment? She had been told she had to pretend to object.

'Come on girl, put it in your mouth.'

Tanya leaned forwards and gave the tumescent head another lick then drew back.

'I can't do it sir, it's too big, I don't want to, I'm sorry,' she looked abjectly at the man, thinking to herself that they had to be pleased with the way she was performing her part.

'Don't be a bad girl, Tanya.'

The man tightened his grip on her long blonde hair and with one hand up against the back of her head forcefully drew her close against his shaft.

'No...please... don't make me...'

'Girls, help her,' the man ordered.

One of the girls crouched beside where Tanya was knelt and caught hold of her head to stop her pulling away. Tanya whimpered and twisted. There were fingers pressing into her cheeks then her mouth was encouraged open. What happened next took Tanya completely by surprise. She had been told that she would be coerced into giving the man a blowjob but she was in no way prepared to feel something hard and metallic forced into her mouth. A second later and Tanya's jaws were forcibly driven widely apart.

'Uuhh!'

Tanya shook her head wildly but she couldn't dislodge whatever it was they'd put in her mouth. A rush of panic filled her and she tried to get her hand to her mouth to pull the foul thing out but her hands were bound behind her back. As she struggled to stand up the two girls forced her back down into a kneeling position and the man took hold of her hair using it like a rein to control her.

'Relax Tanya... it's just a little something to help encourage you.'

'Nuuhh!'

In the lens of the camera close before her, Tanya glimpsed her reflection. Polished steel rods protruded from her mouth, joined and crossed as if hinged and she realised with dismay that she was now utterly unable to close her mouth again unless or until they chose to remove the device from her mouth.

'Now then Tanya...'

The man drew her head forward and his cock was slid between her widely parted lips and she felt it brush her tongue.

'Now lick and suck it Tanya or there'll be worse than this for you.'

'Uuhh...'

The cock was pushed deeper into her mouth. She tried shaking her head, tried pulling back but it was no good, there were three of them holding her and the cockshaft was filing her mouth making her want to gag.

'Good girl... now suck, come on!'

Tanya obeyed as best she could.

'Helen, you know what to do now girl.'

One of the two girls reached under Tanya's chin and caressed the man's balls, rolling them in his scrotal sac, toying with them, coaxing the man swiftly and skilfully towards orgasm.

'Yes... very good...good girls.'

Tanya felt the man's cock twitching more violently and then he came, copious amounts of semen splashing against the back of her mouth and trickling thickly down her throat.

The man stepped back and affectionately ruffled Tanya's hair as she was forced to swallow the last of his come.

'Good girl, Tanya, I think you're learning what's expected from you at Scawder, aren't you?'

'Right, cut; that'll do for now,' Campbell ordered.

Tanya was hauled to her feet. The cameras stopped filming and the men in the room exchanged knowing glances whilst the two girls who had been holding Tanya smiled at each other conspiratorially. The device that had pinned her jaws open was removed from her mouth.

'Come here Tanya,' Campbell ordered.

Leather belts still snug around her thighs and her arms still tied behind her back, Tanya walked hesitantly across to where Campbell sat, a clipboard on his knee, a tumbler of Scotch in one hand.

'So how are you enjoying the film world, darling?'

Tanya looked indignantly at the silver haired man.

'I don't appreciate being forcibly prevented from leaving here and I don't think you've any right to drug my food!' Tanya demanded hotly.

Campbell smiled, took a leisurely sip from his Scotch and looked her up and down.

'No-one is stopping you from leaving if you really want to. Only your schoolgirl persona is being held here against her will. You signed a pretty interesting contract Tanya; you're getting well paid and you're doing all this of your own free will.'

'Paid? Free will? Contract! Like hell I've agreed to being treated like this!'

'Your Godfather gave me your bank account details and you'll find a wire transfer from an overseas account was made today into your account. The contract you signed was witnessed. Now by the end of the week's filming you'll have made a very tidy sum. Of course if you want to break your contract now... we can demand the money back we have advanced you and you can leave here now. It's your choice?'

Tanya glowered at the men; her mind was racing. Was she over reacting? Just think of the money, she told herself and bedsides, the truth was every scene was a turn on for her and why not enjoy a climax from being caned as a change from enjoying a climax from being shagged?

'Okay, I guess I'm over-reacting to getting treated like this.'

'Well, didn't Miles give you a safe word so you could have us stop if things hurt too much?'

'Yes, he did,' Tanya admitted sheepishly.

'Tanya, the first day is always the hardest. We're finished for today and you've been great. Take the evening off, have some drinks and get a good night's sleep and if you're still unhappy about things you can finish work tomorrow. Fair enough?'

'Thank you,' Tanya agreed. She already knew though in

her own mind that she would be ready and willing for more "work" tomorrow. The sexual torment and punishments she'd been subjected to were too intoxicating for her to refuse more of the same. She was already longing for the next session.

CHAPTER FIVE

'How do you think she's shaping up?' Campbell asked.

'Pretty good; the first day is always the challenge and we've pushed her as far as any girl before so I'd say she's going to be just what we wanted,' Miles answered.

The two men were in the dining room, the polished oak table was strewn with papers, half finished mugs of coffee and a couple of whisky glasses and a half empty bottle of Scotch. It was a little before midnight and in the privacy of a small sitting room they had watched the unedited filming of Tanya. Both men were more than satisfied with how the day's work had turned out. Their new recruit not only looked young enough and sexy enough to take the lead part in the current film but she had responded excellently to the punishments they'd subjected her to.

'Have you finished reading that copy of her diary her Godfather gave me?' Campbell asked.

'Yeah, it makes for a good bedtime read, doesn't it?' said Miles.

'I would have thought Miles, that with Sasha sharing your bed you wouldn't have had much time for late night reading.'

'To be truthful, she's beginning to bore me. She's willing enough for anything I suggest but that's the thing, I feel like starting again.'

'Breaking in a new recruit? Bringing a new slave to heel?' suggested Campbell.

'Precisely.'

'Now let me guess; you fancy trying your hand with Tanya?'

'Wouldn't you?'

'My dear chap, I'm too old for all this energetic stuff: just give me a girl willing to suck my cock as often as it pleases me. I have to say that young Tanya did that job pretty well today.'

'Yes… she certainly looked good.'

'So what's your plan, Miles? I know you'll be up to something with our new employee soon enough. You never can restrain yourself from treating them to that jumbo cock of yours for very long can you?'

'I take it you have no objections?'

'How could I if I don't know anything about it?'

Campbell gave a conspiratorial nod and poured them both some whisky.

'I was thinking that the least I could do for her,' said Miles, ' was to bring to life one of those fantasies she's written down in that smutty little diary of hers. And perhaps I could add a few touches that she's not even thought of?'

'So which did you have in mind exactly? I don't suppose it would be her craving for a nice hard gang bang, would it?'

'I have found a couple of willing volunteers.'

'And will you give her the option of exercising her safe word if your little game gets too much for her?' Campbell asked.

'I might tell her at the outset that she can use it,' Miles grinned mischievously.

'But?'

'But of course once she's allowed herself to be gagged then, well…' Miles smiled and left his sentence unfinished.

'My dear chap, you have a cruel streak you know. What if the poor girl really wants to stop playing your game before it's over? Surely you'll respect her wishes?'

'I think we both know what the randy little bitch wants and deserves. Well, first thing tomorrow morning she's going to get it.'

'I shall be out walking tomorrow morning.'

'How convenient.'

'Just make sure none of the other crew hear her screams.'

'Don't worry, no-one will hear anything.'

CHAPTER SIX

The next morning Tanya was woken at nine and given a breakfast tray of cereal, juice, toast and coffee. She warily sniffed the orange juice and coffee for any unfamiliar smells. They seemed okay. She had been given a small single room up on the top floor and when the previous evening she had asked if she couldn't share with Jezra she was told that the other girl was still working. Adjoining her room was a little walk-in shower with loo and wash hand basin. There were clean towels, soap, shampoo and in the bedroom a chest of drawers containing a handful of clothes her size. The young woman who was dressed as the nurse had brought her breakfast tray and she pulled some items of clothing from the drawer and told her to wear them for the morning's filming.

Her bedroom had not been locked during the night and the previous evening she had been able to relax watching a small portable TV that was in the room and had enjoyed a supper with a couple of chilled lagers that they'd given her. As expected there had been no news from her Godfather.

After showering Tanya dried herself and pulled on the clothes: a lacy thong and matching half-cup white bra, a tight white tank top and black Lycra mini-skirt. She was halfway down the stairs when she encountered Miles.

'I was coming to fetch you, we're ready to start.'

'I'm ready,' Tanya smiled.

'So are you enjoying your new job then Tanya?'

'It's okay... what about you Miles? I bet you enjoy watching new girls get put through the ropes?' Tanya glanced at the man's crotch and grinned, ' I suppose the only hardship for you is having a hard-on all the time?'

Miles laughed at her comment and looked her up and down lasciviously.

'You're a right little cock tease, aren't you Tanya?'

Tanya stood one stair above him and provocatively licked

her lips then idly flicked her hair clear of her face.

'What if I am? Would you like me to tease your cock, Miles?'

Tanya grinned mischievously at him and in response felt his hand on her exposed thigh.

'You'd like that would you, Miles?' Tanya asked, widening her eyes and allowing the tip of one finger to settle against her lips.

Miles slid his hand higher up thigh, under her skirt, his fingers curving around the swell of her buttock.

'You little flirt.'

'What do you think you're doing?' Tanya looked reproachfully down at him as she felt his exploring hand find the lace of her thong and his fingers sliding underneath the delicate material.

'You're desperate for it Tanya, aren't you?'

'Uh huh…' Tanya sighed appreciatively as the man eased his thumb up the crease of her pussy. She was already a little slick with arousal and when she felt his thumb brush against her clit she had to hold onto the banister to steady herself.

'Who gave you permission?' she asked, her voice husky and her breathing ragged as she felt his thumb stroke against her clitoris. Fighting down the urge to push her hips forwards she shook her head admonishingly.

'I haven't given you permission Miles… if you want to play with me you have to play on my terms.'

'Okay Tanya, whatever you want.'

'If you're very good I might just let you fuck me. Would you like that?'

'What do you think. Now come with me!'

Without waiting for her response Miles jerked her by the wrist and obediently Tanya allowed herself to be led by the hand down the stairs.

'Where are we going?' Tanya asked.

'Somewhere nice and quiet.'

Miles took her to a big old-fashioned bathroom. Two of the other men were there but there was no camera to be seen. Tanya was led by the wrist into the middle of the room and behind her she heard the door closed and a dull click as the old key in the door lock was turned.

'Get your clothes off Tanya,' Miles ordered.

'Where's the camera?' Tanya asked, glancing around her. The other two men grinned, Miles caught hold of the Tanya's crop top with both hands and dragged it up her body and as Tanya backed away from him the skimpy garment was pulled over her slim arms then tossed aside.

'Come here.'

'This isn't part of the film is it?' Tanya demanded, ' What do you want? Tell me what you want me to do?'

Miles advanced to in front of her and when Tanya tried to take a cautionary step back he caught hold of her wrist to restrain her.

'Relax Tanya, you're going to enjoy this.'

'But why are they here?' Tanya glanced at the other two men and licked her lips nervously.

'Why do you think?' Miles answered enigmatically, grinning as he fingered Tanya's skirt.

There was the faint metallic rasp of the zip on her mini skirt being pulled down then with both hands on her waist Miles pushed the lycra skirt down over her hips and the material slid to around her knees.

'Take it right off.'

Tanya did as Miles ordered, her heart hammering now with anticipation of what she might be letting herself in for. Discarding her skirt without removing the high-heeled shoes she looked expectantly at Miles as he savoured her near nakedness. She was trembling a little from nerves and the cool air but she had no intention of admitting to him that she was scared as well as excited at the prospect of getting a shafting from one man whilst two others looked on. She guessed that they in turn might well want a go and the scenario reminded her vaguely about one of her fantasies. She glanced at the locked door and her heart skipped a beat.

'Turn around.'

She did as instructed. Immediately Miles drew her arms behind her back and broad, soft leather wrist cuffs were fastened around her wrists. Glancing over her shoulder she saw each leather wrist cuff had a bulldog clip fastened to a metal D ring and as her wrists were held close together Miles deftly clipped one to the other.

'Enjoying yourself, Tanya?' Miles asked.

'Of course, no complaints so far,' Tanya answered as flippantly as she could. In truth she was already feeling a trifle anxious and found the other two men standing watching more than a little disconcerting but then, she reassured herself, all that was going to happen was that Miles was going to give her a fuck and if he wanted to bind her before he shafted her, she didn't mind at all, it would only serve to heighten the experience for her.

'What do you want to do Miles?' she asked, trying to not sound at all nervous but her voice trembled a little and sounded thin and timid in the broad emptiness of the large tiled bathroom.

Miles caught hold of her with one hand by the chin and pressed a finger against her trembling lips encouraging her to be silent.

'Be quiet darling, there's a good girl. Now tell me, how does that feel?'

Miles moved his hand to the swell of her breast, curving his palm over the gossamer veil of lace that just covered her tits.

'Nice...mmm...'

'Good girl; now keep still.'

Tanya did as she was told, concentrating on trying to control her breathing as the caress against her breast grew firmer as her nipple was rubbed through the lace until, aching pleasantly it swelled and stiffened, making her wish that Miles would stimulate it even more, so enjoyable was the sensation.

'Cuff her ankles.'

Tanya opened her eyes even as one of the two men appeared crouched beside where she stood. She watched him slip leather cuffs around her ankles and fasten each one tight. Tanya gazed down, watching mesmerized as the broad leather cuffs were drawn snugly around each of her ankles and buckled firmly closed.

'Okay Tanya, it's wish fulfilment time.'

'What do you mean?' Tanya stammered, nervous now as she sensed a change in Miles' tone of voice.

'On your knees baby, there's a good girl.'

The men encouraged Tanya to kneel, hands pushing down on her bare shoulders then they pulled her face down onto the tiled floor. The coldness pressed against the bare skin of her legs and her breasts were squeezed under her. All three men were gathered around her now. One of them held a rope.

'Just relax Tanya, we're going to give you a good time; you want to have a good time don't you?'

'Sure… and you want me tied up, I should have guessed.'

Tanya tried to sound flippant but whilst the idea of being tied up was admittedly erotic she was a bit anxious about just what exactly the men had in store for her.

They bound the rope first around one of her arms above her elbow and then around the other arm. When the rope was pulled taut, Tanya's arms were drawn close together behind her back, pushing her shoulders forwards and making her grunt in discomfort as the rope was then knotted tightly so that she was left barely able to move her arms at all.

Craning her head she saw Miles walked across to the big, old enamel bath and opening the taps fully, a cascade of water began pouring into the bath. Only when Miles glanced back and grinned at Tanya did it suddenly dawn on her what his intentions were.

'No way! Let me go!' Tanya demanded. Her words were all but drowned out by the sound of the water roaring from the old brass pipes and tumbling into the bath.

'Keep her still, it'll only take a few minutes to fill.'

'Let me go! Please!'

Her squirming body was kept pinned down against the tiles until the bath was filled, upon a gesture from Miles the two other men pulled her legs together, clipped her ankle cuffs to each other, effectively hobbling her, then dragged her by the ankles across to the bath.

Galvanised by the sound of running water, Tanya struggled frantically but her efforts were useless. Glancing sideways she saw Miles standing beside the bath, water gushing from its big, old brass taps. He grinned at her triumphantly, testing the temperature of the water before turning off the taps. Even as he silenced the taps though he gestured to the two men crouched over where Tanya lay tethered and one of them clapped his hand across her mouth.

'I'll tell you what Tanya, if this session gets too much for you, I'll allow you to use your safe-word,' Miles ruffled her hair affectionately and smiled reassuringly at her.

Tanya swallowed nervously. She knew what they were planning but now her panic was quickly subsiding as she reassured herself that if it got too much she could just shout "chocolate" and the session would be stopped. Knowing that, the idea of what she was about to be subjected to was giddily arousing.

'Alright?' Miles prompted.

Tanya nodded affirmatively.

'Right, get her in the bath.'

Miles gestured to the other men who promptly caught hold of her from both sides and lifting her by her bound arms, she was hauled face up against the side of the bath.

'Promise me if I say "chocolate, you'll stop?' Tanya demanded.

'I promise,' Miles smiled reassuringly.

The next second hands caught hold of her by her thighs and she was upended, her face and shoulders sliding down into and under the water.

Tanya just shut her mouth in time as the warm water enveloped her. She kicked and struggled to get her head above the surface, nearly made it then felt a hand against the back of her head forcing her down. She thrashed her head; the pressure from the hand eased and her eyes then nose broke the surface and then her mouth and chin were out of the water. She just managed to take a gasp of air before her head was forced back under the water, warm water rushing down her windpipe, bubbles rising in front of her face. They hadn't given her enough time to get her breath properly! Thankfully though a hand grasped her hair and quickly hauled her head upwards and air rushed into her lungs.

Miles was smiling at her, the fingers of his hand meshed in her hair, holding her head just clear of the water. Tanya gazed dazedly at him, her lungs heaving, her whole body trembling with excitement and exhaustion. Her protest was cut short as her head was forced back under the water. Of course, Miles would only stop if she used her safe –word, "chocolate", she realised. She felt the hand release its grip from her hair and using her tethered legs and arms as best she could, struggled frantically to get her head back above the surface.

'Choc…uuh! '

Before she could even get out the word out Miles pushed her head down enough for her to be forced to take in a mouthful of water. Tanya felt his fingers tighten their hold on her hair and her head was quickly lifted up again, air rushed into her mouth, she was coughing uncontrollably and then before she could clear her throat her head was forcibly submerged yet again.

For how long this treatment was kept up she had no idea.

First, she'd be held down under the water until she imagined she couldn't last any longer and then he'd allow just her nose to break the surface and she'd deliriously pant oxygen before being submersed once again.

After maybe half a dozen times she was so exhausted and breathless that she gave up struggling. She had to say her safe word, "chocolate", but each time she was given a little air it was only through her nostrils and her mouth was always kept under the surface of the water. She gazed pitifully up at Miles trying to communicate to him with her eyes that she really had had enough now. The man regarded her calmly, a faint smile on his face then he edged her head back under the water once more. This time Tanya felt too weak to even struggle and sensing her energy was now all spent the men hauled her from the bath and deposited her on the tiled floor.

Tanya gazed dazedly at Miles who was crouched grinning at her. Her body felt utterly drained of all its strength. Giddily faint, she could do no more than lie weakly panting while Miles, kneeling over her, smiling with satisfaction at her condition. For a moment she was too dazed to even realise that she should blurt out her safe word whilst she had the chance.

'Hush now Tanya, there's a good girl...'

A hand caught hold of her chin. Before she could react, a soaking wet face cloth was forced into her mouth. Gurgling in protest, Tanya shook her head ineffectually whilst one man held her head still while Miles fingered the drenched cotton into her mouth. A hand firmly held under her chin to prevent her opening her mouth, a towel was then used to wipe her cheeks dry and before she could try to expel the waterlogged material from her mouth a broad strip of adhesive tape was applied across it and smoothed across her cheeks. Tanya shook her head in distress, tears welling up in her eyes.

'Something the matter sweetie?'

Tanya gave a gag muffled groan of despair.

The men all laughed.

'Get the hose from the locker and we'll get her washed out. Drag her over to the shower, we'll do her in there.'

The men caught hold of Tanya by her tethered arms and slid her across the tiles and into a broad shower cubicle. One of the men produced a long length of what looked like garden hose and fastened one end to one of the bath taps. With what effort she could summon, Tanya tried weakly to haul herself away but it was hopeless and a moment later, easily held still by one man, the other used a bar of soap to lather between her bound legs.

'Unclip her ankle cuffs, she's too exhausted to give you any trouble now.'

A second later and hands encouraged her legs apart so that the soap could be more efficiently applied into the crevice between the firm globes of her buttocks.

'Now keep still Tanya, there's a good girl.'

The cold, firmness of the hose end was abruptly pressed against her anus and before she knew what was happening she felt the hose being forced into her rectum.

'Right, switch on.'

Tanya shook her head, groaning through the gag as a jet of water was delivered into her rear passage.

'Keep still Tanya... there's no point in struggling we're nearly finished.'

The hose was promptly withdrawn. Hands pinned her still. The soapy sponge was pushed against her anus and then it was being forced inside her. Too exhausted to struggle, Tanya lay passively as she felt the sponge expanding inside her rear. As they then pulled it from her she whimpered plaintively through the gag. Once more the hose was inserted into her rear and switched on. Someone caught hold of her by the hair and pulled her from under the shower just as the hose was removed and the shower switched on.

Tanya was dragged into the middle of the tiled floor and the three men stood looking down at her. She was too dazed now to move and lay panting through her nostrils breathlessly. She looked up with wide, sorrowful eyes at Miles as he stood over her, leisurely unfastening his trousers.

'Hook her up against the back of the door.'

Too weak to offer any resistance, Tanya was dragged across to the closed door by which they'd come into the room. There were two large coat hooks fastened to the back of the door. Removing the rope that was bound around her arms and separating the cuffs that bound her wrists, her arms were stretched above her head and drawn out to either side, the men slipping the D-rings fastened to each wrist cuff over the two hooks so that Tanya was left stretched, her nipples grazing the door, her feet just brushing the floor. Naked except for her T-shirt that clung damply against her body, she gazed up at her outstretched arms as the men proceeded to unbuckle her high heels. When her shoes were pulled from her, her bare feet were almost left dangling, her toes barely scraping the tiles below her.

Tanya looked over her shoulder, her eyes wide with alarm as Miles stroked one hand down her back and then over buttocks. In his other hand she saw a bottle of baby oil, which a moment ago had been amongst the items on a shelf alongside the bath. She shivered nervously as cool droplets were dribbled between the crease of her buttocks and ran in rivulets over the tight crater of her anus.

'Right then darling, I've read that secret little diary of yours,' Miles told her, his mouth close against her cheek, 'it's time for you to get the gang-bang you've fantasised about so just relax and enjoy it...'

Tanya twisted by her outstretched arms as the man's fingers glided over the oiled skin between her buttocks and his fingertips brushed tantalisingly over the lips of her sex.

'You can manage to service three of us can't you?'

Tanya stared wide-eyed at the man, panting hard and

unable to respond thanks to the face cloth that filled her mouth. Miles smiled with satisfaction at her helplessness as he stroked her tousled hair clear of her face.

'Now let's make sure you're nice and welcoming for us.'

More droplets of baby oil were dribbled between the crease of her buttocks and Tanya sighed through the gag as Miles began to rub his thumb against her anus.

'Does that feel good? Looking forward to a nice, hard anal shafting are you, Tanya?'

Tanya shook her head urgently, looking over her shoulder imploringly at the man, her eyes wide with alarm as she suddenly realised what was going to happen to her. The bastards were going take her up the rear, she hadn't expected this and it was something she'd never experienced before. She whimpered nervously through the gag as hands drew apart the globes of her rear and then the man was massaging the oil into her sphincter until it softened enough for him to push his thumb easily inside her. Tanya shook her head vigorously in protest.

'Come on sweetie, you know you want it.'

'Nnhh!' Tanya shouted the word "no" but it came out as nothing more than a muffled grunt and Miles just laughed. The other two men stood watching, clearly amused to see Tanya's anguished expression as she suffered Miles' thumb forced inside her rear. Squirming as she hung helplessly suspended Tanya could do nothing as Miles eased his thumb from her rectum then pushed it back into her. Repeating the action half a dozen times her anal muscle was softened up enough for him to then penetrate her with two fingers together.

'Nnnhhh...' Tanya twisted against her outstretched arms, shaking her head and trying to say "no" to what she was being subjected to.

'Good girl...'

Miles withdrew his fingers grasped her hips with both hands and pulled her backwards. Tanya felt the hardness of his cock slide between her buttocks and press up against her anus. For a second there was a pause, Tanya could hear her own ragged panting, she could feel the man's warm breath against the back of her neck. Slowly Miles pushed himself forward, driving his engorged shaft into her rear. Tanya groaned through the gag as the cock filled her, withdrew and was then driven back into her, mercilessly hard and right to the hilt.

'Uhh!'

'Does that feel good? A bit harder, maybe?'

Gazing up at her outstretched arms, Tanya hung helplessly, too weak to struggle after her ordeal in the bath as the man rammed his cock back into her rear.

CHAPTER SEVEN

Tanya grunted through the gag. He was being too hard on her; he was penetrating her too deeply! Surely he knew she couldn't take him inside her like this! The cock eased out from her rear and was driven back in. Tanya shook her head, groaning through the gag as the man proceeded to anally fuck her. Tears pricked her eyes as the man's shaft withdrew and was then rammed back into her. As long as she remained gagged, she couldn't stop them. The thought poured through her aroused body like a liquid fire and she writhed feverishly as an intense climax whipped through her. The sensation of being penetrated this way though shamefully pleasurable was physically so intense she hoped it wouldn't last too long. She hung, gazing at her outstretched arms, the leather snug around her wrists as the man pumped his cock repeatedly into her rear. She moaned into the damp material filling her mouth and knew that she was about to come again and for a moment the pain was obliterated by the exquisite pleasure that washed through her tethered body.

Miles was already so aroused that he came quickly but even as Tanya felt him withdraw from her, she glimpsed over her shoulder one of the other two men step forwards, his jeans and pants discarded, his cock ramrod hard and ready to enjoy her defenceless body. She glanced at Miles, the man's spent cock was enormous, no wonder it had felt as if it was more than her lithe body could accommodate. Though the other man was more normally endowed the thought of another shafting was too much for her and Tanya shook her head in protest. This wasn't fair; she couldn't take anymore!

Summoning all the strength she had, Tanya struggled desperately to stop the man using her body as his colleague had. The experience though intensely arousing had been intensely painful. Her body throbbed in the after shock of being penetrated. Groaning in protest through the gag she twisted and writhed frantically, managing momentarily to evade a repeat of the merciless shafting she'd been subjected to but then, impatient to have her and irritated by her stubborn refusal to submit to them, the men decided on another strategy.

'Fetch a clothes peg from the laundry cupboard, I think she needs calming down a bit.'

Tanya watched helplessly as one of the men crossed the room, opened a cupboard door and then marched back across the bathroom.

'Hold her head still.'

Tanya would have begged them not to but with her mouth filled by the soaking cotton face cloth and her lips tightly sealed by the broad strip of heavy adhesive tape her pleading amounted to no more than an incoherent muffled groan.

'Give it to me and watch,' said Miles, 'pin it from below like this and it won't come loose... now lets see her struggle.'

The inoffensive clothes peg was slid up around her nostrils and the next second they were pinched tightly shut. Tanya shook her head urgently but the peg held fast. When she tried desperately to brush it off against the door someone caught her hair and pulled her head back, laughing.

'No you don't, that's cheating Tanya.'

Her mouth taped and her nostrils pinched shut, in no time Tanya was writhing feverishly as she felt herself suffocating.

'A few more seconds and she'll be fine...doesn't she look a picture? Feeling sorry for yourself now, Tanya?'

Tanya gazed plaintively at Miles as he controlled her head by grasping her tousled hair, calmly watching her as she struggled desperately.

The blood hammering in her temples, her back twisting and arms pulling in one last effort to get free, Tanya looked imploringly at the man who just smiled sympathetically

Groaning through the gag she felt herself growing increasingly giddy.

'That should do the job…'

The peg was released from her nose and at last she was panting air again into her deliriously weakened body.

'She'll be nice and docile now.'

Before she'd even begun to recover, hands grasped her slender waist and the hardness of a cock pressed against her anus. Too exhausted to resist she hung passively as the man speared his cock into her rear and proceeded to shaft her.

Tanya groaned through the gag as the anal shafting got under way once more. The sensation, however painful, combined with being tethered and gagged was so arousing she was quickly brought to an intense orgasm. The anal assault continued though, painfully deep and hard. She shook her head weakly, tears blurring her eyes. Feebly she tried to pull her aching young body away from the man but he had his hands firmly around her slender waist and her efforts were hopeless. Tanya shook her head, crying out through the gag as the anal fucking continued relentlessly: the cock pumping into her tender rear with a determined ferocity. For a moment she imagined herself passing out, for a brief second the man paused, pulling her head back by her long, tangled hair until dazedly she hung breathlessly as he calmly regarded her. Satisfied that she wasn't unconscious the man rammed his cock back into her now agonisingly tenderised rear passage. The minutes dragged past until eventually the man came with a satisfied grunt and pulled his spent cock from her exhausted body. For Tanya it had been a shamefully pleasurable, albeit painful, experience. Thank heavens it was over though, she thought, just one more man to go and her ordeal would be over. She was two-thirds of the way through her initiation into anal sex, if she could just cope with one more shafting…

Sure enough no sooner had the second man withdrawn his cock from her than the third man stepped forward, grinning at her dismayed expression. Pleading with her tearful eyes, Tanya shook her head, silently begging the man not to use her. Her young buttocks were grasped and drawn apart and her tender anus was once more penetrated. Painful though it was in no time at all Tanya was groaning through the gag as her body trembled with another orgasm. The man rammed his cock back into her making her back arch. Groaning through the gag, Tanya struggled frantically but hopelessly as the cock was repeatedly ploughed back into her. Her head was turned sideways, a hand under her chin. Miles smiled at her sympathetically, stroking some strands of perspiration-soaked hair clear of her face.

'Tell the truth now Tanya, there comes a certain pleasure with the pain, doesn't there?'

Tanya nodded weakly in admission. Miles grinned and stepped back, letting his friend continue to shaft her.

'I think when you're done with her I'll have a second helping.'

Tanya gazed at Miles, saw him idly caressing his scrotum, his flaccid cock starting to thicken again as he watched her distressed face and she shook her head despondently. The bastard was going to subject her again to that enormous cock of his and now after three fuckings her poor rear was achingly tender.

The man shafting her quickened his pace then ramming his cock into her one last time he came. For a brief moment there was a respite from the torment. Tanya hung tethered against the door, forced to watch despairingly as Miles coaxed his giant cock back to a state of full hardness with one hand whilst with the other he stroked her hair clear of her face.

'You don't mind if I have a second helping, do you?' Miles asked sarcastically.

Tanya looked balefully at the man then glanced over her shoulders at the other two men.

'Come on Tanya, we know you want it,' Miles smiled, stroking his cock, which was now fully erect once more.

Tanya hung her head back as he slid his hand between her legs and stroked her sex. She was shamefully wet with arousal and come juices and the touch was exquisite, drawing a gagged whimper of appreciation from her as he stroked her throbbing clitoris and swollen vulva.

'You dirty little girl, you're really enjoying this aren't you?'

Tanya closed her eyes and shook her head in denial but the truth was that a part of her was relishing being subjected to the sexual demands of the men.

'Come on Tanya, admit to me that you've enjoyed getting butt-fucked and I'll be kind to you.'

Tanya blinking back the tears that misted her eyes looked sorrowfully at the man as he stroked her sex. It was all she could do not to writhe and sigh in ecstasy.

'I can be kind or cruel, the choice is yours but if you want me to be kind, admit that you've enjoyed getting taken like this?'

Panting breathlessly Tanya glanced down over her shoulder. The man had his arms slipped around her hips and his hands were between her legs, one hand stroking her clit, the fingers of the other were embedded a little way into her pussy. After the mercilessly hard anal shafting, the softness of his touch against her sex was more than she could stand and even as he held her she felt herself about to come again and her hips began to rock against his touch.

'You like that don't you? You see I can be kind as well as cruel,' Miles laughed softly then took his hands away leaving Tanya frustrated.

'Now,' he said, 'if you want me to be kind, tell me the truth, you enjoyed getting butt-fucked didn't you?'

Tanya nodded, desperate for the man to resume playing with her pussy.

'Good girl,' Miles smiled victoriously, 'in which case, the kindest thing I can do for you is to give you another dose.'

She felt the man's hands on her arse, her pert buttocks being eased apart.

'Nnhh!'

Tanya cried out through the gag, shaking her head despondently in protest as the man's cock nudged against her anus. Her sphincter muscle was now so weakened he penetrated her easily and now her body had become accustomed to the demands of the men, it was as shamefully pleasurable for her as it was painful. Tanya gave a long groan as she felt the man's enormous cock fill her rear once again.

'Hush now Tanya…keep still, there's a good girl.'

The cock eased from her aching backside then ploughed back into her. Tanya dragged her arms against the wrist cuffs that held her hooked up against the door. Her rear passage was so sensitive now that each time the man withdrew his cock and rammed it back into her, it forced a gag-muffled cry from her. Whether it was the exquisite pleasure or the acute pain that made her cry out, Tanya no longer knew or cared. The ruthlessly effective gag silenced her protest almost completely.

'Let's ungag her and see how she's feeling.'

The sticky tape was peeled loose from one cheek and pulled away from her mouth. Fingers coaxed the soaking cloth from out of it. Breathless, Tanya hung, gasping air and gazing at Miles, blinking from the tears that filled her eyes.

'Do you want me to stop?' Miles demanded

Tanya gazed at the man, too breathless for a moment to answer so she just nodded affirmatively as her aching body hung weakly and she panted air gratefully.

'Well?' Miles asked, smiling as he watched her, 'if you can't take anymore you'd better say stop then hadn't you?'

Tanya was too intoxicated and dazed by the ordeal to realise that the man was giving her a chance to say her safe word "chocolate". The thought of the anal shafting by Miles continuing was more than she imagined she could cope with and all she could think of was that he'd offered her a chance for her ordeal to end.

'Please stop,' Tanya begged, looking pathetically at the man regarding her. ' I can't take anymore...' she sobbed breathlessly.

Miles nodded understanding and smiled reassuringly at her.

'Poor Tanya, there now... it's okay, relax...'

With a sigh of relief that her ordeal was over at last Tanya closed her eyes.

Grinning with satisfaction, Miles promptly caught hold of her jaw with one hand and before she realised what was happening he had pushed the soaking cotton between her protesting lips.

'Nuuhh!'

As the damp material was fed back between her lips, past her teeth and into her mouth Tanya felt her stomach churning, knowing she was to be subjected to more torment. She felt the warm water trickling down her throat; the thick cotton filling her mouth and with what strength she had left she writhed against the leather cuffs that held her by the wrists helplessly outstretched up against the door.

Miles coaxed her jaws together with one finger under her chin. Tanya shook her head vigorously in objection and in response to her struggling, hands quickly held her still.

'Well sweetie I did you give you a chance to use your safe word,' Miles laughed admonishingly.

Tanya gazed at him, wide eyed with despair and her cheeks moist with tears. Miles grinned with satisfaction as a fresh strip of the heavy adhesive was smoothed back over her mouth and cheeks.

'You only need to say the word "chocolate" and we'll stop,' Miles told her, a broad grin on his face.

Tanya glared at the man, straining with her jaw muscles to prize the sticky tape from her lips. Miles smiled smugly as he watched her. Twisting her head to one side she dragged her mouth against her outstretched arm and felt the tape against her skin. Repeatedly brushing her mouth with her arm as best she could she at last felt a corner of the tape come a little loose from her cheek.

'Got something you want to tell me, Tanya?' Miles taunted. Tanya groaned through the gag as she strained once again to prise her jaws apart. This time she felt the tape had been loosened and a surge of determination filled her as she realised that she would be able to get the horrid stuff off her sealed lips given enough effort and time.

Miles gestured to one of the other two men who quickly went and retrieved the roll of sticky tape from where they'd left it. In the time it took the man to get it Tanya had prised loose a corner of the tape and by repeatedly opening and closing her jaws as best she could the whole strip of tape that covered her mouth was gradually becoming weakened and looser.

'What's the urgency Tanya, stop exerting yourself so much... relax.'

Tanya paused for a second from her labour to free herself from the gag and stared at Miles as he calmly regarded her, a smug smile on his face. A noise behind her made her turn and as her outstretched arms twisted against the wrist cuffs she glimpsed hands to either side of her face and then a fresh strip of sticky tape was being stretched across her still sealed lips and this time the tape was drawn right across her cheeks. Another pair of hands lifted her tousled hair clear of her neck and she felt both ends of the tape being pressed down firmly around her nape.

'Nnnnhhh!'

The end still attached to the roll was pulled back around from her nape, back across her cheeks and once more across her mouth before it was cut with scissors and the end smoothed down around her nape.

'Well as you've got nothing to say for yourself Tanya, I

take it you don't mind if we carry on where we've left off?'

'Nhh!'

Once more Tanya felt the man's cock forcing an entry into her tender rear.

'That feels just so good,' Miles laughed then he pushed his cock into her as far as the hilt, eased it out and calmly drove it back into her again. Writhing against her restraints, Tanya could only cry into the gag as she was shafted mercilessly yet again until Miles came with a satisfied grunt. Tanya closed her eyes, allowing the feelings to wash over her exhausted body then she looked around expectantly, anticipating that the men would now unhook her from where she hung, securely tethered. When she gazed around at the men's faces though her pretty blue eyes widened with fear and dismay as she realised that they hadn't yet finished with her.

'You don't mind if my friends have a second helping each do you?' Miles asked, laughing scathingly as Tanya shook her head, tears filling her pretty blue eyes before she hung her head back and looked up despairingly at her bound wrists and outstretched arms. Her body ached so much now she was desperate to rest. She looked pleadingly at Miles but he just grinned at her abject expression then turned to one of his accomplices.

'Get the leg spreader.'

Tanya gazed down, watching helplessly as the men caught hold of her ankles, clipped each ankle cuff to opposite ends of a steel rod and thereby forcibly held her legs spread vulnerably wide. Miles stroked her cheek sympathetically and whispered in her ear.

'Should have said your safe word darling when you had the chance.'

Stepping back from her Miles smiled apologetically before turning to the other men. To Tanya's dismay both now sported heavily engorged and hardened cocks once more and she knew with certainty that they too were going to use her aching body yet again.

'Okay, fuck the bitch senseless.'

Tanya gazed despondently up at her outstretched arms as she felt one of the men grasp her hips and her drag backwards until the thickness of a hardened cock slid between her buttocks. I can't take anymore anal shafting, Tanya thought. For a second she held her breath then gave gag-muffled cry of despair as her anus was forced to widen yet again as the man's cock ploughed mercilessly into her rectum. Tanya shook her head, crying out through the gag as the anal fucking was resumed. Despite the agony of what they were subjecting her to, she came and it was the most prolonged orgasm she'd ever had. To her shame she realised that such merciless treatment was satisfying some sexual craving in her for being subjected to such forced submission. However pleasurable it was though it was now utterly unbearable and as the man continued to shaft her Tanya shook her head writhing frantically as the sensation of the man's cock pounding her arse quickly became too much. She strained to pull her lips open, desperate to cry out her safe-word but the broad strip of adhesive bound repeatedly across her mouth held her ruthlessly silenced. She cried out through the gag for them to stop but the water soaked face cloth that filled her mouth muffled her cry almost completely. Someone caught hold of her hair, subduing her thrashing head and looked into her tearful eyes.

'Enjoying it, Tanya?' sneered Miles.

Trying desperately but scarcely able because of the firm grip Miles held her in, Tanya shook her head as best she could, gazing pitifully at the man whilst his accomplice continued shafting her rear. The renewed anal fucking was too much, her poor body felt mercilessly abused. Tanya sighed plaintively through the cruelly effective gag. Miles grinned, tightened his grip on her long hair with one hand and drawing her head back with his other hand he stroked her cheek sympathetically as tears coursed down Tanya's distressed face.

'Is that a little too much for you? Would you like us to stop?'

Whilst forced to listen to Miles' teasing words, Tanya had to suffer the other man's cock ramming back into her, ploughing into her aching rear right up to the hilt, balls slapping against her arse. Time and time again the cock penetrated her rear, relentlessly hard.

'Good girl... not much more...'

Out as far as the engorged head the cock withdrew then back it was driven into her painfully tenderised rectum. The sensation brought a fresh wave of her orgasm and she imagined herself fainting. In and out of her aching rear the man's shaft pounded her relentlessly. The assault went on until the man finally came and then his place was taken by the third.

Tanya looked balefully at Miles; her pretty cheeks wet with tears. A fresh pair of hands caught hold of her waist and once more she felt the engorged head of a cock nudge against her trembling body. Tanya groaned as the man promptly drove his shaft into her rear passage. Grinning with satisfaction Miles reached in the pocket of his shirt and produced a small bar of chocolate. Tanya gazed at the chocolate, pleading with her tear filled eyes. Miles grinned at her and smiled understandingly. Biting off a square of chocolate he smiled at Tanya.

'Beginning to wish you asked for something earlier when you had the chance?' Miles smiled, then drew some strands of perspiration-soaked blonde hair clear of Tanya's face. Tanya nodded affirmatively and Miles smiled sympathetically.

'I did give you a chance you know,' Miles shook his head reprovingly. 'Well, this'll teach you what happens to sexually greedy young girls. It's your own fault Tanya, you'll have to learn to control that appetite of yours and if you will keep a diary of your sexual fantasies you should be grateful when someone takes the trouble to give you some wish fulfilment.'

As the anal fucking continued relentlessly, with tears rolling down over the tape smoothed tightly across her mouth and cheeks, Tanya had to admit that she'd brought this upon herself and Miles was right. When the cruel shafting of her slender young body eventually stopped and Tanya was unhooked from where she'd been stretched up against the door, she knew that Miles had probably given her no more than she'd secretly craved. Lying flat on her back, she lay passively as the men removed the leg spreader and then the cuffs from around her ankles and wrists. She gazed up at Miles as he stood over her and as much as she hated him she had to admit that she felt almost slavishly devoted to him now for the torment he could give her.

CHAPTER EIGHT

The filming at Scawder lasted five days. For five days Tanya's pert arse was thoroughly caned and she grew used to the feel of leather restraints tight around her wrists and ankles. Five days' filming, eight or nine hours a day to make a film that lasted just ninety minutes. By the end of it Tanya found that she could actually orgasm by just being caned as long as the strokes were delivered with appropriate skill. Being tied down, helpless and subjected to such sweet pain as a well directed slender cane could deliver, she came repeatedly and to the delight of the film's director. Though the film contained plenty of action to Tanya's surprise there was no penetrative sex and this, she was told, was because the film was aimed for a specialised market, men and women who liked to watch young girls suffering corporal punishment. So for five days unusually for Tanya she didn't get screwed once, except of course for the merciless session Miles and his accomplices had subjected her to in the bathroom.

Though she wished she could hate Miles for what he'd subjected her to, she was unable to deny how deeply satisfying the ordeal had been. From that time onwards she found herself almost craving his attention and she was able to only hold out for a day and a night before she begged Miles for a fuck. He refused, though he was more than happy to have Tanya look after his physical needs in other ways and this suited Tanya who decided she would curry favour with Miles because when the filming was over he'd intimated he might be able to find other more exciting work for her and for Tanya this was too much of an opportunity to let slip through her grasp. Besides, Miles was physically very well hung and she was sure that she could persuade him to fuck her, if she persisted with her pleading.

The Victorian greenhouses were neglected and overgrown, largely forgotten behind a wall of thick rhododendrons at the far end of one of the lawns that surrounded the isolated hunting lodge. After days of heavy rain the skies had cleared and a warm sun had beckoned Tanya outside during the last afternoon at Scawder. The filming was over and in a few hours she would be leaving. Already the film crew were packing up, props were being loaded into a transit and the girls were relaxing outside on the terrace with beers and cigarettes.

The greenhouse door stood jammed half open, wedged between a rusty old wheelbarrow that lay overturned and a gnarled vine that had grown unchecked and had crept out through the doorway and spread across the mossy panes of glass and become tangled in an enormous old hydrangea that covered one corner of the greenhouse. Inside it was hot and humid, the air rich with the smell of peat. Tanya, wearing cut off jeans and crimson bikini top, could feel the heat of the sun through the glass against her bare back. Her knees sunk into the rich earth as she knelt facing Miles, fingering the zip of his trousers and looking up at him with an impish smile.

'So can I come with you, can you find me a decent job then?'

'Get on with it Tanya.'

Miles caught hold of Tanya's long blonde hair with one hand and drew her head back.

'Ouch... hurts...'

The grasp on her hair eased a little.

'I don't know whether you're up to what I have in mind.'

'What is it? Tell me.'

'First things first Tanya, I really need to come, so get on with it darling.'

'Sorry.'

Tanya eased the zip down and unfastened the belt of Miles trousers then slid his trousers down his thighs. She could see a damp patch of cotton where his erection pressed against his tight sports hipsters. Though she'd felt Miles cock twice up her arse she'd never really seen it that first time in the bathroom though she could still appreciate its size and now as she stroked its outline through the tight black material she had to admit that amongst the many men she'd had, this guy probably had the thickest and longest cock of them all. She smiled as Miles sighed, his grip on her hair easing, he leant back against the wall, legs planted well apart as Tanya slipped her fingers under the waistband and slid his pants down his thighs. His cock was already rock hard. Seeing it sway before her, dark crimson, the purple head swollen and seeping pre-come fluid, she longed to feel it filling her pussy but knew for now she had to wait. She glanced up to see Miles watching her expectantly.

'Get on with it Tanya, there's a good girl.'

'Say "please",' Tanya demanded petulantly.

'Please,' sighed Miles, his impatience evident in his tone.

'You do look very sticky… I think you're going to come for me quite quickly, aren't you?'

Without bothering to wait for an answer, Tanya lightly furled her fingers around the swollen shaft and guided the bulbous head to her lips. Her first explorative lick with her tongue drew an appreciate gasp from the man. Taking her time, Tanya took the engorged cock head into her mouth and forming a seal around it with her lips she sucked deeply once then even as Miles gave a shuddering groan in response she drew her tongue over the cock head before drawing back her lips and letting the edges of her teeth find and lightly pull against the ridge of the cock head. Miles gave a shuddering sigh and she felt his body tensing as he was propelled rapidly towards ejaculation.

'I think it's time for you to come for me, Miles,' Tanya cooed, her head now drawn back from his swaying cock and the fingernails of both her hands stroking up his shaft from base to head. Miles groaned deeply and Tanya smiled with satisfaction.

'How many spurts can you give me this time, Miles?'

Tanya questioned, the fingers of one hand now furling around the man's swollen balls and trapping them within her grasp she then constricted the sac of flesh between the man's cock and balls with her other hand so the latter were held as far apart from the man's cock as was possible.

'Not yet Miles... not yet...'

Tanya applied a little more downward pressure with one hand until she was satisfied that she couldn't coax Miles' balls any further from his cock. Ignoring Miles gasping, she held him in such a state for a full thirty seconds knowing well that it would delay and intensify his orgasm once it came.

'I think you're ready to come now aren't you?'

Releasing her grasp on his testicles, Tanya gave the head of cock another lick of her tongue and then with both thumbs she began to massage it where the engorged head was joined by a bridge of skin to the shaft. Once Miles' breathing was coming in urgent enough gasps to make it evident he was about to come, Tanya once more took the head of his shaft in her mouth and sucked and licked until she felt the man's cock throbbing and twitching uncontrollably. Withdrawing the shaft from her mouth Tanya now lightly stroked with her fingertips below the man's balls and against the base of the shaft with one hand whilst with the other she slid one fingertip up against his anus and only slightly penetrating him she repeatedly pressed her fingertip until with a shuddering groan Miles' cock erupted with a spray of milky come. Quickly drawing her fingertips over his balls, Tanya furled her hand lightly around his shaft and with a pumping action encouraged his orgasm, smiling as half a dozen more spurts of semen were coaxed from his pulsating cock.

* * *

Whilst Tanya had journeyed north by a slow and crowded train her journey back south was in marked contrast. Miles powerful sports saloon ate up the winding roads south and after stopping in Perth for lunch at a riverside bistro they picked up the motorway and by early afternoon were past Edinburgh and by early evening were in Yorkshire where they stopped at a secluded country house hotel.

Though Tanya was still wearing just her cut off jeans and a bikini top the liveried staff at the Virginia creeper clad mansion house hotel were too tactful to even raise so much as an eyebrow as Miles and Tanya were shown to a suite of rooms. Whilst Miles unpacked his suitcase, Tanya lounged on the antique four-poster bed reflecting that this was more the life she'd imagined than three years academic slog with no guarantee of a decent job at the end of it. When they had stopped at Perth she had gone to a hole in the wall at a bank and checked her account and as assured by the film director, her overdraft was now gone, replaced by a tidy sum that she couldn't have dreamt of earning by working the whole summer in Oxford had she opted for the usual summer student jobs.

'You do rather well from your work, don't you Miles?'

The man was half way through hanging his Italian suits and silk ties in a large walnut veneered wardrobe.

'No complaints,' Miles replied, allowing himself a self satisfied smile. ' You should be happy too with what you've just earned, aren't you?'

'I should say,' Tanya slid from the four-poster bed and promptly shimmied out of her cut off jeans. 'So have I time for a bath?'

'Time before what?' Miles asked.

'Before we have a fuck. Wouldn't you like that?'

'You're an impatient little thing, aren't you? I think you'll be perfect for the job I have in mind. Ever fancied a bit of travel?'

'Stop being enigmatic and tell me about this job,' Tanya demanded petulantly.

'Okay but first I want you to turn around and bend face down over the end of the bed.'

Tanya did as she was instructed, obligingly first discarding the thong she was wearing and then spreading her slender legs a little.

'Randy little bitch, aren't you?'

'Are you complaining?' Tanya grinned as she glanced over her shoulder as Miles stroked his hands appreciatively over the curves of her exposed bottom. Not a trace of cellulite, generous but firm and delightfully peach shaped, Tanya knew that such a sight as her wiggling rump was like a red rag to bull for any man given half a chance and she was giving Miles more than half a chance. Without any hesitation or prompting she felt the hardness of his cock rub up against the slit of her sex. Tanya sighed encouragingly.

'Please, stick it in me, I can't wait,' she begged.

Obligingly Miles eased his cock into her already slick pussy and Tanya's fists tightened their grasp on the duvet and she buried her cheek against the silk as she experienced the delicious sensation of feeling the thickest, longest cock she'd ever enjoyed sliding deeper and deeper into her sex.

'Never mind directing porn films Miles, you should be starring in them,' Tanya sighed.

'How do you think I got into them you dumb girl?' Miles laughed then he eased his cock completely from her sex before ramming it into her anus with enough speed and force to make Tanya cry out.

'You bastard!' Tanya cried out in anguish.

'Did you really think I'd do what you wanted?' Miles laughed scornfully.

'Not so hard... please... you're too big,' Tanya protested.

'Doesn't that feel good? Don't you like feeling it as deep as this?'

'Uhhh... please Miles, really...you're too big for me...gently...'

There was no sign though that Miles was going to be any easier on her and unable to cope with the intensity of such deep anal penetration, Tanya made to crawl away over the bed but before she'd scarcely got one leg onto the bed a powerful hand against her back pushed her face down onto the silk covered duvet.

'Come on now Tanya, where do you think you're going? You've been desperate for me to shaft you for the last week. We can't disappoint each other now, can we? Besides, you were begging for it just a minute ago.'

'Alright but really Miles… your cock's too big for me…please…'

Tanya's attempt to persuade Miles to demonstrate some restraint was never finished as the man clapped his hand over her soft mouth and then she felt the cotton of her own freshly discarded thong being forced into her mouth.

'Stop it Miles… you don't have to…uhhh…'

Even as she tried to dissuade him he proceeded to finger a silk handkerchief between her jaws as well so that soon her mouth was filled with material that made her protests quite incoherent and effectively muted the volume of her objection. Once he climbed astride her waist and pinned her to the bed with his weight, Tanya could do little more than thrash her arms ineffectually as the man drew a silk tie between her jaws, pushing the now damp fabric of his handkerchief and her thong well back into her mouth. As Tanya shook her head and gurgled in objection the tie was drawn around her nape and knotted tightly.

'I should have known that you like to be rendered helpless before you get shafted, don't you?'

'Nuuhhh…lemme guhh…lemme guh!'

'Something that matter, Tanya? What are you trying to tell me?' taunted Miles.

Tanya repeated her demand for him to let her go but in response to her continued struggling she saw Miles reach inside the pocket of his shirt and produce a slim transparent case not more than half the size of a cigarette packet. Tossing the little box onto the bed he flicked open the lid and Tanya saw half a dozen damp balls of cotton wool and immediately the plastic package was opened she caught the unmistakable whiff of chloroform.

Urgently shaking her head in protest, Tanya struggled to prise her arms free from where Miles pinned them under him.

'I think you're getting too excited at the prospect of a nice hard anal shafting Tanya, best if we calm you down a little I think.'

'Nuhh!'

Tanya gave a gag muffled cry in objection as one moist ball of cotton wool was pushed into one of her nostrils and a moment later a second was inserted into her other nostril and the chemical smell assailed her senses, quickly making her body weak then drowsy.

'It's just to make you nice and relaxed Tanya. You'll find you can just about breathe enough fresh air through your gag to stop you losing consciousness. This way you can enjoy everything I've got planned for you without you getting yourself over excited or disturbing the other hotel guests.'

'Nuuhh…'

Tanya shook her head weakly as she felt the man now ease himself from astride her and then pulled her by the wrists into the middle of the bed.

'Doesn't it excite you Tanya, knowing that there are probably people in the rooms either side of us and maybe walking past the corridor and they'll never even know what's happening to you? Now I think, just to make things easier…'

The sensation of something slipping around her right wrist and then tightening drew Tanya's sleepy gaze. The bastard had knotted another of his ties around her wrist and tied it to one of the posters of the bed. Tanya pulled with what strength she could summon but her efforts only served to tighten the silk knots.

'Don't be a silly girl now…'

Miles was standing on the other side of the bed, her left arm was pulled sideways and Tanya gazed despairingly as her other wrist was dealt with in similar fashion.

Now she was effectively tied to the bed she could do nothing but watch as Miles took his time to discard his clothing and then go to his suitcase from where he produced a roll tape of black tape and scissors. Weakened by the chemical soaked cotton wool inserted in her nostrils Tanya had no energy to put up anything more than a half hearted struggle whilst Miles bound one of her ankles repeatedly with the tape which adhered to itself and then dragging her leg to almost full stretch he bound the tape around one of the bottom posts of the antique bed. Repeating the procedure with her other leg Tanya was left bound spread-eagled and face down on the bed.

'Exciting isn't it Tanya, knowing that you're going to get a nice hard anal shafting and however intense it gets, however much you want it to stop, you haven't got any say in the matter. You see, I know that that's how you really like it, so as much as you pretend, I have no qualms about seeing those pretty eyes of yours filling up with tears as you shake your head, desperate for it to stop.'

'Nuhh...'

Tanya shook her head, groaning through the gag in protest as Miles coaxed apart her pert buttocks and speared his shaft into her rear.

'Is that good? Is that deep enough to satisfy you? Bit harder maybe?'

'NNHH!'

Tanya shook her head vigorously, gurgling in protest as she felt the man ramming his enormous cock repeatedly back and forth into her aching rear. For a moment there was a merciful respite but it was only so that Miles could untie the knotted silk tie that gagged her and use it to fill her mouth even more completely before he finished the gag once more by repeatedly binding the black tape across her mouth and around her head. Once he'd finished Tanya knew that even if she'd screamed she'd not be heard if someone was walking right past the door. There was something potently arousing about being so helpless, she thought as she felt the man once more grasp her hips and drive his shaft into her aching rear.

Feeling increasingly weak and drowsy Tanya could do no more than cry into the material that filled her mouth and ruthlessly silenced her. Of course now that the tape effectively sealed her lips, she could only breathe through her nostrils, so with each breath she continued to drug herself. The weaker she felt herself becoming the more urgently she panted for breath and this served simply to make her even more helpless. The anal shafting continued relentlessly and Tanya could do no more than writhe weakly against the restraints Miles had used to control her young body and with each thrust of his enormous cock Tanya could only groan and sigh, tears pricking her eyes as the man took her at his leisure until with a satisfied grunt he came.

* * *

The next couple of days passed in a bit of haze for Tanya. After the cruel anal shafting he subjected her to at the hotel he plied her with champagne, a room service dinner and afterwards a long, hot bath infused with essential oils and eventually Tanya began to forgive him for being so hard on her. Besides, the simple truth was that the experience had been powerfully arousing and she'd enjoyed a heady climax long before Miles had satisfied himself.

The next day Miles took her to the boutiques of York's cobbled lanes and bought her more designer clothes than she'd had all year. After lunch in a fashionable restaurant, wearing some of the new clothes she'd been given, Tanya spent the afternoon dozing in Miles' car whilst he drove them back down to London and to his Docklands penthouse apartment.

The next day, after a night in Miles' bed, most of it spent fucking like rabbits, they went to meet the business associate Miles had offered to introduce Tanya to with a view to some work for her. Frederick Sturmberger's office was in one of Docklands' newest prestigious office apartment blocks. The German's business, passed, he explained, down three generations was freight shipping. The walls of the opulently decorated suite of offices showed framed photographs of numerous container cargo ships and Sturmberger explained to Tanya that he now controlled the transport of nearly twenty percent of all South American exports to Europe. Tanya, sensing that this was something the German was clearly incredibly satisfied with, looked duly wide-eyed with admiration. Over lunch in a private dining room Sturmberger wasted no time in explaining to Tanya just what sort of a job offer he was making to her.

'The sea journey for container ships from South America to Europe is very slow and I believe that it is very important to keep good crews: this means contented crews who will not slacken and will do their jobs properly.'

'Of course, absolutely,' agreed Tanya, between a mouthful of chilli salt deep fried baby squid and a large mouthful of Chablis Grand Cru. Sturmberger glanced at the waitress who was serving them and immediately she drew the bottle of wine from its ice bucket and replenished Tanya's glass then the German's.

Sturmberger was to Tanya's surprise only in his twenties. He had recently inherited the business from his father. He was very tall, slim and wore black Armani jeans and a black Polo neck sweatshirt under a dark blue double-breasted blazer with large silver buttons each bearing the same crest, an anchor and a dagger that Tanya saw was discreetly everywhere in the office complex from the letterhead paper on the man's desk to being monogrammed on the damask napkin she had draped over her lap. Sturmberger waited until the waitress had resumed her position standing almost to attention a short distance from the table before he resumed the conversation. Miles, the only other person lunching with them at the polished mahogany round table that would easily have seated a dozen people, was being noticeably quiet whilst Sturmberger spoke.

'A lot of the cargos that I transport are low value bulk commodities but some are very valuable and I have to ensure that they are properly cared for; that means having crews that I can completely trust. Good men deserve good rewards and often the thoughtful measures can be worth a great deal.'

Sturmberger gestured for the waitress to clear their starter plates. Tanya watched him whilst he carefully dabbed at his mouth after his last mouthful and watched the girls serving them. I bet, thought Tanya, he doesn't miss a thing. The young German's gaze was intent, his eyes almost unblinking when he looked at Tanya as he spoke. He had Slavonic good looks, a strong almost stern face and what made him especially striking was the fact that he was completely shaven headed, his eyes were a piercing blue and his right cheek bore a long scar. The moment the waitress had left the room Sturmberger resumed his conversation.

'I have a prize ship, Tanya, that I use to transport my most valuable cargoes. The ship was commissioned to my design and launched only two years ago. The crew had the best of facilities and get the highest rates of pay but I determined to give them even more rewards for their service and as a way of passing the time on such a long journey I have given them some additional entertainment.'

At this point Miles gave the merest cough to clear his throat and took a sip from his wine glass. Sturmberger pressed on, leaning forwards a little and focusing intently on Tanya as he spoke.

'Men will be men and weeks away for land can deprive them of much; I have had incorporated into the ship a games room for them where they can play with a young girl willing to amuse them throughout the journey. You understand?'

'Yes, I think so...' Tanya answered.

'Of course I pay the girl very well and she is properly looked after and discreetly guarded but as far as the crew are concerned she is there for their pleasure and amusement. My good friend Miles thinks that such a position would appeal to you.'

'I'm not sure...'

'I can pay you more for eighteen days, the duration of the journey, than that girl serving us just now will earn in a year.'

'That's quite a lot for a few weeks' work... what would I have to do?' Tanya asked.

'Keep twenty-two crewmen amused. You will be their pet to play with; there is a lot of equipment I have provided for them to use on you and you'll be subjected to whatever pleases them. Of course they are under orders not to physically hurt you more than in a playful way and you will have the appropriate protection from the ship's captain. You will be paid in full into your bank account on the day the ship sets sail and when the ship reaches South America you can choose either a paid return flight to the United Kingdom or take a second term of employment and make the return journey by ship under the same conditions. I have a very detailed contract of employment for you. We'd both be bound by it once signed. Because you will be at work at sea we can avoid the problem of certain countries' laws on certain, how shall I describe them? services provided, I think is perhaps one suitable expression.'

'Can I have time to think about your offer please?'

'Of course, you can have until we finish coffee, that should give you at least an hour.'

CHAPTER NINE

'And this is the games room, through here.' The man gestured for Tanya to go through the door that he had just opened for her. Stepping into the room Tanya caught her breath and behind her she heard the man give an amused laugh.

'Impressive isn't it?' the man suggested, now walking past her and into the room. Impressive was not the first adjective that had sprung to Tanya's mind.

The room was located in the lowest deck of the enormous ship and long before reaching it Tanya had already become bewildered and disorientated by the numerous floors and rooms that she had been shown. It felt as if the ship must have miles of corridors and they all looked the same and few rooms had signs on them identifying what one would find behind one of the dozens of anonymous steel doors. The main hold of the ship was stacked with sealed containers, literally dozens of them each one the size of an articulated lorry. There were also two other holds used for holding loose materials and these she was told would be filled with either hardwood from the South American rainforests of with coffee beans or rice or some other commodity that also served as ballast for the return journey.

The room she was now standing in was unlike anything she'd seen anywhere and suddenly the full realisation of what she had embarked upon dawned on her. The room was windowless, the walls metal, painted a pale blue. A dark blue carpet covered the floor of the room, which was about thirty feet by twenty. At the far end of the room was another door and also at the far end was a double mattress covered in black vinyl, which had black leather straps and buckles sewn to each of the four corners. There was a full length couch, whose aluminium legs were bolted onto the floor and again from its corners Tanya could see trailing straps and from its sides dangled, broad leather belts. Above the couch screwed to the low ceiling was a large mirror and dangling from the ceiling not far from the couch were several lengths of chain each ending in collar of broad black leather with stainless steel rimmed eye holes and a stout steel buckle. There was a long green baize covered table which sported numerous lengths of coiled multicoloured nylon rope, several plaited leather riding whips and three large aluminium cases, the contents of which Tanya could only guess at. Opposite the door by which they'd entered there was a dark red vinyl covered and padded cross whose base and top were bolted to the floor and ceiling respectively.

Tanya made a hesitant circuit of the room. Unable to resist the temptation to discover the contents of the three cases on the table she lifted the lid of one. The collection of gags, masks, shining steel clamps and coils of slender black leather cords were too intimidating and Tanya quickly closed the lid.

'You weren't meant to look in those,' the man warned.

'Don't worry, I've no intention of looking in the others,' Tanya answered petulantly. She looked across to the man who stood leaning in the doorway. Unlike most of the crew who wore jeans and T-shirts this man was dressed in pressed white cotton trousers and a starched, short-sleeved shirt with black epaulettes. Also, unlike most of the crew, who spoke at best only a few words of fractured English with heavy foreign accents, this man spoke fluent English with only a hint of an accent that Tanya guessed to be German.

Tanya had left England two days earlier and after taking a car ferry as a foot passenger to Ostend she had been collected by a driver and taken to the Arhaus freight shipping harbour where she saw for the first time the ship that she was to work on for the next eighteen days and nights.

'What's through the other door?' Tanya asked the man watching her.

'That is your bedroom and your private area. I'll show you.'

The man crossed the room and after keying in an access code to a wall mounted security panel the door slid open revealing a simply furnished ship's cabin complete with bunk bed, a small television, shower cubicle and toilet, a narrow desk, one upright chair and a clothes locker. This room also had a porthole and on closer inspection under the bunk bed Tanya saw there was a small fridge and alongside it her bag that she'd brought which had been taken from her on arrival and which had been stowed for her.

'This is your room, only the ship's officers have the access code to this room. When you're not working you'll be able to rest in here. You will work mostly daylight and evening hours. You can take meals in your room or you can join the junior officers mess table for dinners if you'd like some company. There are four junior officers, two are German but they speak English, one, our Chief Engineer is Norwegian and he also speaks some English and the ship's Quartermaster who is Indian speaks better English than the other three put together. Have you any questions?'

'Do I get to know the code for the door as well?'

'No.'

'I somehow guessed that would be the answer,' answered Tanya.

'We set sail tomorrow at 04.00 hours, all the crew will be working until we are well out into the English Channel. You will not be required to start work until 09.00 hours. That gives you about twelve hours to relax, eat and sleep. There are some videotapes in the locker if you want to watch TV. You'll not get a picture for watching live TV but there's satellite sports and entertainments channels in Spanish; most of our crew our South American you see.'

'Could I get something to eat then?' Tanya asked.

'Sure, I'll have a meal brought down for you. There are drinks in the fridge, which will be re-stocked for you as often as needed. I have other matters to attend to now, so you will excuse me.'

Without waiting for a response the man left, the sliding door closing behind him and Tanya found herself alone, staring out of the porthole at the lights from another container ship in a neighbouring berth and wondering if this was really such a good idea as it had seemed when Sturmberger had sold her the idea over Chablis and seafood a week earlier.

* * *

Finishing their dinner with coffee and two glasses from a decanted bottle of Taylor's 1963 Vintage Port, Sturmberger dismissed the young woman who had waited on them and he and Miles withdrew to the television lounge of Sturmberger's Mayfair house. Whilst Sturmberger switched on the television and slid a video into the player, Miles retrieved the decanter of port from the dining room and their glasses.

'Take a seat,' the German gestured to Miles who eased himself into one of the leather Chesterfield armchairs.

'We've had a message to say that Tanya is safely on board, so here's to another profitable trip.'

'Would you like to see one of the films of the last one? Hans has edited it down to three hours and mixed the different camera shots to very good effect,' said Sturmberger, as the television screen flicked on and with the remote control he switched on to play the video he'd put into the machine.

Sturmberger had fitted concealed cameras into the fittings of the games room on his newest container ship. Only two of the ship's officers knew of these and the rest of the crew were ignorant of the fact that when inside the games room enjoying the girl that Sturmberger had provided for their amusement he was in fact filming all that went on. The resultant films were sold by Sturmberger's contacts to wealthy buyers around the world. Given the nature of what the films showed, Sturmberger was able to charge a handsome price for each film and as each seaward journey produced enough material for half a dozen films, the returns not only paid the wage of the girl but also turned Sturmberger a very tidy profit. Since most of the wealthy buyers from around the world all spoke English as a second language Sturmberger had decided that it would be best if the girls were English. Then when they were begging and pleading for mercy, there was no need for subtitles. Miles, in exchange for a cut of the profits was providing Sturmberger with a steady stream of suitable girls.

'This is the second film, Miles, using material mostly from days five to ten of the journey. We made four films from this girl. The last of course is the best, as always.'

On the screen a lithe, tanned girl, naked except for thigh high leather boots and a black thong sequined with diamonds was struggling urgently in the grip of two men who dragged her across to a padded cross. As the girl's attempts to break free from the men's grip grew more urgent a third man stepped forwards and the girl was held struggling against the cross by two of the men whilst the third bound each of her wrists in turn against the arms of the cross so that she was soon held, arms outstretched whilst the men then wrapped rope around her waist, pulling it tight and pinning her body against the cross.

'I'll fast forward it a bit,' said Sturmberger.

A moment later and the German pressed the play button once more. The girl was now to be seen writhing frantically against the ropes that bound her, tears coursing down her cheeks, her long hair tousled about her pretty face. Dangling from the erect nipples of her breasts were small, steel alligator clips and from these dangled fine cords hung with weights.

'A lot of breast work on this one by a particular group of the crew; look at this.'

Sturmberger fast-forwarded the tape once more.

The girl was still bound to the cross but now the clamps

and weights had been removed and as the girl begged between choked sobs for the men to stop, a nylon rope was bound in a figure of eight around her young breasts so that they became two trapped cones of swollen flesh that turned purple as they were cruelly constricted still further by means of binding yet tighter two fine cords around them. By now the girl was shaking her head vigorously and pleading desperately for the men to let her go. The men's laughter could be heard and then one of the men caught hold of the girl by her hair with one hand and holding her chin with his other hand held her still whilst his friend inserted a hard rubber ring gag between her jaws and then whilst her head was dragged forwards and downwards by one man the other wrapped the straps of the gag around the back of her head and secured the buckle. When the girl was allowed to lift her head back, her mouth could been seen, jaws forced wide, saliva trickling out over the black leather ring jammed in her mouth as her pleading was reduced to an incoherent gurgling cry of anguish.

'Would you like to see some of the third or fourth films?'

'Sure,' said Miles, replenishing his glass from the port decanter.

Sturmberger switched tapes and pressed the play button again.

The film started with the same girl being dragged, kicking and screaming across the room to the bench by three men and a dark skinned young woman. Held down on her back, the girl struggled desperately as the four accomplices set about restraining her with the straps hung ready from the sides of the bench.

'It was a clever idea not to allow them access to the cases with the best equipment until the last days of the voyage, that way the most enjoyable watching is kept until the last film,' said Sturmberger.

'And of course you release the films one at a time at intervals, encouraging everyone of your clients to eagerly buy the next film, knowing that it should offer even more rewarding viewing,' concluded Miles.

The German nodded affirmatively, smiled with satisfaction and fast-forwarded the tape.

Strapped down on the bench, the naked girl was blindfolded with a black scarf and whilst the three men stood watching, the young woman with them was stroking the tethered girl's thighs which were pinned and spread by four leather straps, two just above her knees and two more as high up her thighs as was possible. The camera filming the scene was switched to one that was located almost directly above the bench and was zoomed in more closely. Stroking the tethered girl's sex lips with one fingertip the young woman, herself striking pretty and wearing tight jeans and an even tighter white T-shirt, smiled with satisfaction as her blindfolded victim was soon tossing her head from side to side with arousal.

Holding open a small black case one of the men, tall and broad shouldered, grinned with cruel amusement as the young woman took from the case some slender plastic coated wires whose exposed copper ends were fastened to small, serrated edged metal clasps. The young woman bent at the waist over her victim and lovingly kissed the tethered girl between her spread and tethered legs. She then drew back a little and whilst whispering something to bound girl she eased one of the serrated clasps over the girl's labium, which she held proud from her sex between a finger and thumb. Slowly releasing her hold on the clasp the tiny metal jaws clamped shut around the distended flesh of the girl's aroused sex drawing a plaintive cry from the victim. When the second clasp was fastened to the other of her outer sex lips the blindfolded girl gave a gasp of alarm and then began to whimper nervously as the young woman stepped back to regard her victim's condition.

'Is this the third or fourth film, Karl?' Miles asked, hardly able to take his eyes for a moment from the screen before him.

'This is the fourth but it's only the beginning, by the end the girl's in a pretty sorry state.'

'What was her name, I forget.'

'I don't know, Amanda, Anna, something like that,' answered Sturmberger, ' she was the one who tried to escape, remember?'

'And tried to cause us trouble when the ship reached South America, yeah, I remember having to arrange some Police bribes to smooth things over,' said Miles.

On the screen before them, the girl's arms and legs were twisting and straining urgently against the straps that held her down as the young woman stood over her flicked on and off a switch on a black box from which trailed the wires that were now clamped to her pussy. Between each brief electric shock that the girl was subjected to the woman torturing her would stop to finger the girl's sex, making her cry out in tear choked gasps, pleading for her to stop and let her rest. After half a dozen short, sharp shocks the girl was sighing and tossing her head from side to side as this time when the woman masturbated her she was brought to a climax that made her tethered body strain against the straps.

'I take it the electric shocks from that thing aren't anything too serious?' asked Miles.

'No, of course not,' answered Sturmberger, ' enough to make the girl struggle but mild enough to not really hurt. Anyway Miles, take the tape home and enjoy it... the poor girl has so many orgasms I quite lost count. There's some good viewing later... the girl is a natural for the camera, her face is very expressive... pity she wasn't up to making the return journey. What did happen to her in the end?'

'The Police Chief at Santiago del Feunta took her as sweetener for his kind adjustment of our paperwork for the special consignment we got through last month. When I last saw her she was in a Police cell being serviced by four of Rodriguez's men.'

'I dare say she'd have enjoyed that,' Sturmberger suggested with more than a trace of irony.

'I think she was wondering how she had gone from trying to press charges against us to being charged with smuggling in the space of twenty-four hours,' said Miles, ' it didn't take long for her agree to drop her charges against the ship's Captain and crew and to sign an admission of guilt to petty smuggling charges statement in exchange for not spending six months in a prison cell awaiting trial.'

'I take it she signed that before she knew the local Police were going to keep her in their jail overnight?' said Sturmberger.

'Of course, that was the threat that finally persuaded her to sign the statement.'

'But the Police Chief still held her overnight?'

'Of course... still I dare say the silly girl has learnt a good lesson.'

'Including to check the small print on her contract of employment with Sturmberger Shipping!' Sturmberger gave a short laugh as he refilled their port glasses. 'Do you realise that out of the eight girls so far only one has read the contract carefully enough to realise that they she would only get paid the full amount if she agreed to make the return journey under the same conditions?'

'Yes... I've been quite surprised by that, I guess that must be quite a blow to the ones that really needed the money.'

'Miles, my dear friend,' said Sturmberger, ' you mustn't worry about taking advantage of these girls' natures. They want to be treated like this; deep down they enjoy it, that's why they sign up. The money is secondary. All the girls you have found me are naturally submissive... some stern discipline, a little tormenting, a judicious mixture of pain with the pleasure we give them, this is what they crave.'

'Except perhaps for Anna or whatever her name was?' Miles suggested recalling the last time he had seen the girl and the plight she had ended up in.

Shut in the cell of a remote little Police station in a shanty suburb of one of the big ports that Sturmberger Shipping used, Miles had watched as the four Policemen had stripped her of her clothes and then dragged her across a rough wooden table. As the girl had looked beggingly at Miles to intervene, handcuffs had been used to fasten her wrists to the far legs of the table as she was forced to bend over the table. With her bare feet scraping and scuffing the concrete floor two of the men pulled the belts from their trousers, each looped a belt around one of her thighs and from opposite sides of their victim they then jerked on the belt ends dragging the girl's legs apart. Another of their number stood behind the girl and with the minimum of fuss, even as Miles watched, unzipped his flies and speared his engorged cock into the girl's exposed sex.

Assured by the Police Chief who was also watching that she wouldn't get

harmed and that she'd be released the next morning, Miles had left the building and walked briskly up the muddy road until he caught the attention of a rusting old taxi that he flagged down and had drive him back across town to his hotel. In the hotel bar he settled his nerves with a couple of large gin and tonics and then went to his room to shower. Outside the humidity and heat combined was oppressive in the extreme but at least the hotel was air-conditioned. Stepping into the marble tiled walk-in shower he stood under the refreshing jets of water and recalled the fetid atmosphere of the police cell.

If only the stupid girl hadn't caused such a fuss when they'd arrived then she could have been on plane home by now, he had thought, remembering the dismayed expression on her face as she gazed forlornly up at him from the table she was held down over whilst the four Policemen took it in turns to enjoy her defenceless young body.

After that he had resolved to make absolutely sure that any girls he recruited for Sturmberger were totally right for what was expected from them. He was almost a hundred percent certain he'd made a good choice with Tanya. From the way she'd responded to the filming sessions in the Scottish highlands he was confident that she'd get to enjoy her time on Sturmberger's prize container ship as on-board entertainment. Of course, the sessions in the ship's games room would get pretty hard on her over the eighteen days she was subjected to the regime but Tanya seemed to be just the sort of randy submissive who'd secretly revel in such a situation.

CHAPTER TEN

The ship's second mate and quartermaster using short crowbars levered the wooden box open.

'Did the boss tell you what was inside?'

'No, he only said it was some new equipment for the games room and that the Englishman, Miles, isn't to be told about it either. Herr Sturmberger says that the Englishman has got a soft spot for the girls and he might object. The Englishman thinks that the electrocution box and some of the other hard torture stuff is restricted to being used on the girls for just the last few days of the trip.'

'But it's on the films? How can the Englishman be so stupid?'

'Herr Sturmberger edits the films so that the best stuff is only put on what he calls the third and fourth films, irrespective of when it was really filmed, so that the Englishman thinks that the girls only get subjected to the hardest sessions in the last few days.'

'So what's the point in not telling the Englishman about this new equipment, he'll see it in use on the films?'

'The boss is going to keep it secret and just put it on a separate fifth film.'

'So the Englishman will never even know, what a shame! Well, let's see what it is.'

The two men finished prizing open the small wooden crate and then pulled away the packing to reveal what inside. When they saw it their eyes widened in surprise and then one grinned in amusement.

'I've seen pictures of these on the Internet, this new bitch we've got on board is in for a hard time, that's for sure.'

The man picked up an instruction manual and flicked it open. A couple of simple black and white drawings demonstrated quite graphically the purpose of the machine and passing it to his colleague he gazed at the chrome, steel and rubber contraption.

'So in principal it is just like a piston really that could be used to power a propeller.'

'Or in this case to drive a rubber phallus rapidly back and forth into whoever is put on the receiving end!'

'And look at the size of some of those things!'

'I've seen our pretty little new recruit, this machine is going to bring tears to her eyes!'

'Listen to these instructions in the manual: it says that adequate lubrication must always be used, the recipient must be introduced gradually to the fastest speeds and that the two largest heads should only be used on the slowest speed and that they are unsuitable for anal penetration.'

'So do you think we should leave these instructions for the crew to read?'

'There's no point, they'll be too excited to bother to waste time reading all this.'

'But don't you think some of the men may think this is all going a bit far? What is the Captain going to say when he finds out about Herr Sturmberger's latest toy? He's never been very happy about the last lot of equipment for the games room, never mind this new machine. I'm just waiting to see what happens when he finds out the games room has got hidden cameras and Sturmberger's making a bundle of money by making films from what goes on in that room.'

'No-one knows about the cameras apart from you, me and the boss and the Englishman and no-one is else is going to find out.'

'But this new machine, the men will talk, the Captain will get to hear of it and...'

'The men won't talk about it because they'll never know about it, no-one is going to know about it except for Tony's gang of four. Sturmberger wants them to use it on the girl then we hide it away under lock and key.'

'But all the crew share the room and have access to the equipment, how...'

'We let Tony in to use the girl at night when she's supposed to be off duty and sleeping. They get to enjoy her and we get some really good action for the fifth film, the Englishman knows nothing, the Captain knows nothing, the rest of the crew know nothing.'

'But the girl might talk?'

'None of the crew speak more than a few words of English, the officers who do don't use the games room.'

'But at meal times she could speak with any of the other junior officers, if she…'

'She has said that she wants to have all her meals in her own room.'

'Has she?'

'Of course, she told me herself.'

The two men grinned conspiratorially at each other.

'We'll drug her meal or drink then once she's eaten and fallen asleep you and I can move her into the games room and we leave her for Tony and his gang to enjoy. They'll not say anything, so everyone else will be none the wiser.'

'So when does this happen? The girl will say what's happened to someone just as soon as she gets a chance. Isn't Herr Sturmberger taking an unnecessary chance? There was nearly a load of trouble with that Anna girl, remember?'

'The boss has worked out all the details, don't worry. On the last night before we reach port, you and I are ship's duty officers for the night shift. We'll be the only people to see Tony and his friends go into the games room. We'll have the new girl waiting for them and we'll move the machine in ready for them when no one is around beforehand. We film the action and once we've got enough the girl gets a few sleeping pills and she'll be out of it until we're docked. We keep her sedated; I say she's sick and offer to escort her ashore and to her hotel where a doctor is called to check her out. The doctor has already been bribed to give her some pills that will keep her feeling ill and in bed for a few days. We tell her that Sturmberger is paying for her to rest in the hotel for a week and that she has a ticket for a return flight. The ship reloads and sails out. The hotel has been told that she is to pay her own bill there. As she won't have any money she'll most likely get thrown in jail. The airline ticket she has got, if she does manage to get to use it, is on an internal flight into the jungle to a backwater, logging township. If she arrives there, it's safe to assume that she'll not last long enough to make it on the once a week flight back to the coast. The area is thick with bandits, natives and drug smugglers. One way or the other the boss has made sure that we'll not be troubled by Tanya once she's served her purpose.'

CHAPTER ELEVEN

Tanya woke up feeling as if she'd drunk too much and was for a moment too drowsy to realise what had happened. She had a vague recollection of having eaten some of the pizza that had been brought to her room for her and she'd had a couple of drinks from the fridge. She'd had a shower then, feeling tired had lain down on her bunk. Quite suddenly she'd felt exhausted, almost as if the eighteen days of hard physical work she'd been subject to had finally all caught up on her. Never mind, she thought, she'd done it, she'd given the crew what they'd wanted from her, she had a few sore muscles and aches and pains from struggling too hard against some of the restraints they'd bound her with but she'd coped pretty well, she congratulated herself. What's more, she'd been fucked enough times to last her a month of Sundays! There had been some times when she'd really felt she'd bitten off more than she could chew but somehow she'd managed and at least now it was all over.

Trying to focus her senses now though Tanya had a strange feeling that all was not right. In fact something was seriously wrong. For a start rather than waking up in her bunk she found that she was now lying face down across the double bed that was in the games room. Lifting herself up on one elbow, she rubbed the sleep from her eyes and saw that she was not wearing the baggy T-shirt that she had gone to bed in but her slim body was dressed in some of the skimpy underwear that she'd brought with her.

What the hell is going on, she wondered, rolling onto her back and drawing the fingers of both hands through her long hair to clear it from her face. From the corner of her eye she glimpsed the large mirror fastened to the ceiling above the bench where she'd spent many hours over the last couple of weeks being tied down and tormented. As if she hadn't given them enough of a good time for her money, someone must have decided that on her last night she'd be made to endure one last session of sexual subjugation. Somehow they must have drugged her food or drink and moved her into the games room. The bastards...

Rubbing the sleep from her eyes, Tanya sat up and looked around her and then she saw that she was not alone. Stood over the table of equipment just a short distance away from her were three men and a young woman all of whom she recognised. The men, seeing she was now awake, said something to each other in a language that Tanya didn't understand but guessed was Spanish. They were young, lean and well muscled with tanned olive skin and dark hair. Had Tanya encountered the men at a nightclub or bar she would have been thrilled to see them now move swiftly towards her, smiling. However, right now, Tanya felt far from confident that she was ready to deal with what was about to be thrown at her.

These guys had spent more than their share of time during the last fortnight enjoying her body and whilst many of the crew were content simply to give Tanya a good shafting these lads enjoyed tormenting her as much as she could cope with. The girl had joined them for several sessions and though she'd skilfully masturbated Tanya repeatedly making her climax she'd also subjected her to some moments of torment that had made the tears roll down Tanya's cheeks.

'What a minute guys... I feel a bit dizzy, sorry...'

'It'sa no problem, you just stay there.'

Even as they spoke to her, one man dropping to his knees on the bed beside her, Tanya felt a strong hand snatch hold of her wrist and draw her arm behind her back.

'Please...not yet...'

Ignoring her protest the men pushed her face down onto the black vinyl and both her arms were pinned behind her back and a pair of leather wrist cuffs fastened upon her, leaving her hands trapped together at the small of her back. The two young men then discarded their work overalls and leisurely stripped off until they stood over Tanya, both quite naked and each displaying a rock solid erection as they looked down at her.

'Pretty girl... what's your name?'

Until now the men had not spoken a word of English and they hadn't spoken to Tanya throughout the days that they'd frequented the games room. One of the men knelt beside her and stroked his hand down her bare back.

'Tanya.'

'Okay Tanya, my name's Antonio, you can call me Tony. You pretty girl, very pretty...'

'Thank you, Tony,' Tanya answered, trying not to sound as nervous as she felt.

The young man smiled sympathetically and gestured to one of his friends who went back over to the table and returned with two more leather cuffs.

'Very sexy clothes, you feeling sexy yes?'

Without waiting for an answer the man's fingers slipped under the waistband of the lacy white briefs Tanya had found herself wearing and a second later they were dragged down her legs and discarded. Tanya felt the cool suppleness of soft leather being wrapped around her right ankle and then the binding was pulled tight and buckled snugly against her skin. Her second ankle was likewise bound, the cuffs around her wrists were then separated from each other and Tanya was made to lie on her back.

'Now pull your legs up Tanya, there's a good girl.'

Encouraged by the men's hands Tanya obligingly drew her legs up until her ankles were pressed up against the back of her thighs. She had become almost conditioned over the last couple of weeks to submit to the men's demands and besides, what was the point of resisting, she was one girl against three men?

Simultaneously pulling on her wrists the men drew her arms down until her wrists met her ankles and promptly the bulldog clips dangling from the leather wrist cuffs were fastened to the bindings around her ankles, leaving her pinned in position.

'Very good... now you ready for good fuck, yes?'

Yes, thought Tanya, gazing down at her helpless position, legs pulled up and eased apart, her pussy nicely exposed, the lads had obviously done this a few times, she thought, sighing uncontrollably as Tony eased himself down over her prone body and without any further preamble sank his cock into her pussy, drawing a gasp from Tanya.

After the leader had satisfied himself they took four slender red ropes from the table of equipment and binding one around her left ankle they drew it down to the left corner of the bed fed it through a canvas loop and pulled it tightly back up to her ankle and bound it several more times around her before knotting it firmly in place. Having then dealt with her other ankle in the same fashion two of the young men settled themselves either side of where Tanya's head and shoulders rested against the black vinyl.

'Very nice... very firm...'

As Tony caressed one of Tanya's breasts with his hands, she gazed sideways at him, sighing in response to his touch.

'Okay baby... you gonna like this...trust Tony.'

Tanya glanced up at the young woman who was stood watching. Her dilated, dark eyes showed her arousal and she smiled when she saw Tanya looking at her. Tanya watched apprehensively as the young man turned away from her for a moment and fastened one end of another of the red ropes to the canvas loop sewn to the top corner of the bed. Pulling the rope taut with one hand he gave an order to his friend who reaching across Tanya's chest, cupped her breast with both hands and lifted it up into a cone of flesh between his hands. As he did so Tony drew the rope under and around her breast, looping it fully once around her breast before drawing it back to the top corner of the bed and feeding the rope through the canvas loop he drew it taut. Tanya, panting hard, tried to wriggle herself higher up the bed to ease the pressure the rope had applied on her breast but the ropes they'd bound to her ankles prevented her gaining more than a fraction of an inch and the sensation of her breast being bound so cruelly was making her whimper plaintively.

As the men bound her other breast in a similar fashion, she knew that this was just the beginning of a session as cruel as any she'd been subjected to so far. Gazing down at her breasts, held firmly proud of her chest by the red ropes, she sighed despondently as the men now dangled two long bootlaces before her.

'Oh God... no, please...' Tanya shook her head, gazing pleadingly at the two men who were now grinning with delight at her expression of discomfort. Whilst one man held each of her tits in turn the other bound one of the bootlaces tightly around the trapped cone of flesh until that part of her breast which was left exposed above the repeated binding swelled out, purple and painfully distended.

'Feels tender, yes? If I touch you like this?'

'Uhhh...please! Hurts!'

'Silly girl, there's no good with you struggle like that, you not get away. You stay like this long time yet. Now, let's feel some more...'

'UHH! The cords are too tight, please... loosen them just a little, please!'

The men ignored her. Gazing up through tear blurred eyes Tanya could see that Tony, now stood looking down at her with a satisfied smile, was hard once more, his thick, circumcised cock, glistening with her pussy juices and the cockhead heavily engorged and seeping a little lubricating fluid from it's eye-hole as he watched her writhe helplessly.

'Very pretty sight... you have big nipples, you like it if we make you feel good, yes?'

What Tanya might have wanted was irrelevant and if she thought that her poor breasts had suffered enough tormenting already, she realised with dismay, she was sadly disillusioned.

'No guys... please, don't...' Tanya looked wide-eyed with alarm as Tony produced a small black box trailing a couple of slender plastic coated copper wires.

'Okay Tanya, you know this make you feel real good...trust Tony.'

'No...please, stop...'

Tanya writhed helplessly as her right nipple was caught between a thumb and finger and coaxed into a state of full hardness. With her breast tightly bound, the sensation of having her nipple treated in this way was achingly arousing but there was more to come, much more...

'Good girl, nearly ready...look, see looks good, eh?'

Tanya craned her head forward and watched as Tony wrapped the exposed end of copper wire around her nipple, twisting it snugly tight against her erect teat. Tanya sighed, tossing her head and dragging her arms ineffectually against where they were pinned to her ankles as her other teat was likewise treated.

She had been subject to this shock treatment for the last two days by some of the other crew but she suspected this time was going to be worse. The first time two men had simply attached the electrodes by means of sticky tape to her breasts and on the second time, the men who'd tried out the device on her whilst they had fastened the wires with clips to her tits, they'd only given her one short sharp shock, which had made her come, crying out so loudly that they didn't bother with the machine any more after that but contented themselves with stretching her from the ceiling by her bound wrists and shafting her from behind. Now though as Tanya looked anxiously at her nipples bound tight by the fine copper wire, she knew that she was in trouble. Something told her that these men and the girl weren't acting with the permission of the ship's Captain. It was the middle of the night and Tanya had never had to work at night.

'You pretty wet, you enjoying this... now we make you

really wet. You see.'

'No please... don't,' Tanya begged, gazing down at her tightly bound breasts, her nipples aching from the wire wrapped around their delicate flesh.

The sensation of one of the men stroking her clit was abruptly replaced by a hot, needle sharp sensation shooting from her nipples into her breasts, making Tanya cry out at the sudden intensity of it and though the electric shock lasted but a couple of seconds she was left feeling dazed and breathless.

'Now let's feel, see you like it, yeah?'

The man was fingering her pussy once more and Tanya groaned deliriously as he drew his thumb up the crease of her sex, which was slick with arousal.

'Uhhh!'

Before Tanya had time to recover the man removed his hand from between her tethered legs and another short, sharp shock of electricity was discharged into her tits. The alternating sensations of pleasure and pain were too potent and Tanya knew that she was about to have one hell of an orgasm.

'You gonna come for us now, you see...'

One of the men stroked Tanya's tousled, perspiration-drenched blonde hair clear of her anguished face whilst the other man slid two fingers into her sex, drawing a fevered moan from her before withdrawing his hand and then came another short, sharp and all too exquisite shock to her aching tits.

'No! Please... let me go...uhh...' Tanya sobbed, twisting her arms and legs desperately against the leather cuffs and ropes that held her immobile. A fingertip stroked against her swollen clit then there came another jolt of electricity into her cord bound breasts and the sensation was too much... with a loud cry Tanya came, her orgasm washing over her in waves, making her cry out in sobbing gasps as the exquisite sensation was prolonged and heightened by the men giving her poor breasts several more short shocks as she came.

Dazed, breathless and still trying to recover from what she'd just been subject to Tanya watched through tearful eyes as the young woman knelt down beside her and examined Tanya's throbbing breasts. The rope and cord-bound flesh ached agonisingly and her nipples throbbed madly. Panting hard, Tanya turned her head sideways and looked beggingly at the young woman as she stroked the little of Tanya's tits that remained exposed above the cone of tightly bound cord.

'Please... make them take the cords off... hurts so much...please...' Tanya begged.

The young woman fingered one of her breasts, making her gasp and squirm and fresh tears spill down over her already wet cheeks. The young woman tormenting her turned to the ringleader and spoke with him in Spanish and Tanya, though she couldn't understand what was being said, knew from the man's tone and cruel smile that he was agreeing to some suggestion that the girl was making.

Delicately removing the copper wires from Tanya's still throbbing nipples the girl then stroked between Tanya's tethered legs and teased her sex with her fingertips. Shaking her head with despair as she guessed what was to happen next Tanya was still unable to prevent a sigh of pleasure escalating into a long moan as the girl skilfully played with her sex, stimulating her until Tanya was trying to buck her hips as she was coaxed closer and closer towards another orgasm.

'Oh, no, please...'

Smiling as she worked the girl was binding the exposed ends of copper wire to two small steel crocodile clips.

'No, please, I won't be able to bear it, please don't.'

'Hush, pretty girl...'

'No! You have to stop! You can't...'

The bite of the steel clip upon one of her sex lips was

enough to make Tanya beg with her tormentors but when they ignored her pleading and she felt her other sex lip subjected to the same treatment, Tanya shouted at them to stop and struggled frantically to get free from what she knew would happen next.

'Silly girl... you no escape... too bad you no like, we have many, many hours yet to play games with you.'

'Someone help me! Let me go...'

A firm hand smothered her mouth. Fingers furrowed her tousled hair then twisted, pinning her thrashing head still. Tanya glimpsed another man stood over her a something dangling from a rubber strap in his hand.

The men were speaking to each other. One bent down beside her on the bed where she was struggling against the ropes that held her. He had another rope in his hands. Tanya shook her head but couldn't pull free from the hold Tony had on her and his hand remained pressed down against her mouth.

'Okay, let's see if you like this.'

The hand covering her mouth was abruptly withdrawn and fingers and a thumb pressed into her cheeks coaxing her jaws open and before Tanya could react a rubber ring had been jammed into her mouth pinning her jaws wide. As she gurgled in protest and tried shaking her head a thick rubber strap was dragged around her cheeks and jerked tight and buckled fast.

'Nuuhh!'

As Tanya shook her head, crying out incoherently through the ring-gag for them to stop, the men calmly took another rope, fed it behind the small of her back, bound it tightly around one of her arms then drew it back behind her and pulled it tight around her other arm and tied it leaving her arms now all the more firmly pinned against her sides. Looking up at the men and the girl and dragging her wrists and ankles ineffectually against the tight ropes, Tanya felt a surge of fear but also a rush of excitement as after all the experiences of the last couple of weeks she realised that she was in store for some even more demanding time at the hands of these people. The piquant bite of the steel clamps on her labia was as tormenting as it was painful and a dark voice in her head was already urging them to flick on the switch that would send a jolt of electricity into her pussy. The thought alone was almost enough to make her come. Panting hard through the gag she looked at the faces around then realised that she'd stopped trying to scream and shout for them to let her go.

When the first short, sharp shot came it was like a dart that seemed to shoot from her pussy straight to her brain and made her cry out as best the gag allowed. With the second shock Tanya came and as she lay breathless and basking in the after glow of her orgasm, she saw the leader of the gang watching her closely then giving an order to one of the others, the rubber gag was removed, Tanya was left free to speak once more.

'Uhhh!'

The next shock made her writhe helplessly where she lay tethered but other than crying out at the intensity of what she as being subjected to, Tanya made no protest. She tried to convince herself that this was because she knew they wouldn't free her but she knew deep down it was because she was now helplessly aroused and deeply enjoying being forced into such a state of helpless submission and then tortured in the way these people were.

'You want more?'

Tanya turned her head to see the young woman questioning her. Dreamily she nodded affirmatively. The woman smiled triumphantly and said something to the men. There was a moment's pause and then Tanya was trying to convulse against the ropes as the searing sensation of the electricity rippled through her naked body.

'Uhhh...God... enough...please...'

The next shock was more prolonged and seemed too much

for Tanya to bear but it had left her pussy throbbing with arousal and very close to coming yet again. Tanya gazed up at the girl, panting hard and whimpering as the ropes bit into her flesh where she struggled so much.

'You had enough?' the girl questioned.

'Make me come... please...' gasped Tanya.

The girl turned to the men and nodded. Two of the men left the bed and turning her head Tanya watched them cross the room to where there was a large box and when she saw what they unpacked she could hardly believe her eyes.

Tanya hoped that they would subject her to the machine straight away, she was so aroused, she was desperate for gratification but her tormentors had other ideas. The ropes that bound her ankles and wrists were all removed and the men hauled Tanya to her feet and dragged her across the room to the padded cross. Her arms were held outstretched to either side of her and bound with ropes against the padded red vinyl. They didn't bother to bind her legs but there was still no way that she could have freed herself and although in moving her from bed to cross the ropes and cords had been removed from her breasts, once she was tethered against the cross the young woman examined her aching breasts and satisfied that they could take more punishment she had one of the men hold each tit in turn whilst she bound it with cord.

'Hurts... stop... please...' Tanya begged, as she watched first her right breast being cruelly constricted with cord. Her pleading was ignored and if the men had earlier bound her breasts achingly tight the girl subjected them to an even more mercilessly tight binding.

With both her tits bound into swollen cones of dark crimson flesh, Tanya could only jerk her arms ineffectually as the tears coursed down her cheeks and she was forced to watch her tits turn from crimson to purple. The young girl was plainly delighted by Tanya's acute suffering and to torment and humiliate her further she pulled her own white

T-shirt off over her head and mockingly caressed her own pert breasts, pulling the cotton of her bra cups down under the swell of her breasts to reveal her tits and stroke and caress them as she stood before where Tanya hung bound by her outstretched arms. Speaking in Spanish she then invited one of the men to sample her breasts and Tanya was forced to watch as the man buried his head in her cleavage before closing his mouth on one of her dark nipples, sucking vigorously until it stood firm and hard, glistening with wetness while the man's mouth roamed from the girl's breast to her neck and then mouth.

After letting the man get himself thoroughly aroused playing with her, the girl then shoved him away and pointed at Tanya. The man grinned lecherously and wiping the back of his hand over his mouth allowed himself a moment to stand and feast his eyes on Tanya.

'Please...they ache so much, don't touch them,' begged Tanya.

Ignoring her pleading, the man caressed each cord-bound orb of heavy flesh with his hands, squeezing them to appreciate their generous weight and jerking a cry of anguish from Tanya. Involuntarily and in response to the pain of feeling her tits constricted yet further, Tanya jerked an unfettered leg up, bringing her knee hard into the man's groin. The man let out a guttural curse, the girl gave a derisive laugh and the other two men shouted something unintelligible to Tanya.

Tanya could then only watch with a growing sense of foreboding as the man stalked away to the baize covered table and promptly returned, a plaited leather riding crop in one hand. For one heart stopping moment Tanya imagined the man was going to be vindictive enough to use the whip on her bound breasts but he had other ideas.

Thwack!

'Oww!'

Tanya let out a yelp of pain as the hard leather crop struck her left thigh.

Thwack!

'Oww! Please, I'm sorry…'

A matching blow to her other thigh left her eyes smarting with the pain. The man grinned with satisfaction and hit her again this time on the inside of her left thigh.

'Ouch! Not Fair! Don't please…'

Thwack!

'Now you let us fuck you or you get more pain, yes?'

'Alright… whatever you want, just please don't hit my thighs again, so sore…'

Tanya blinked back some tears and watched as the man promptly discarded the riding crop and moved close up against her outstretched body so that she felt the hardness of his cock press against the flat of her stomach. Guiding his cock into her pussy, the man used his free hand to grasp one of Tanya's bound breasts. Stifling the urge to cry out as her throbbing tit was held up for the man to suck on, Tanya couldn't prevent a gasp of pleasure as she felt the man's cock slide deeply into her throbbing sex and at the same time her right tit was sucked fully into the man's mouth and she felt the firmness of his teeth against her skin. The combined sensations triggered her climax and Tanya was still gasping breathlessly for air while the man pumped his cock repeatedly into her slick sex until with a satisfied grunt he came.

Tanya was left tethered to the cross, her tits still cruelly constricted by the tight cords, whilst she was forced to watch the young girl now discard the remainder of her clothes and using the bed spend the next fifteen minutes satisfying the other two men. By the time they turned their attention back to Tanya, her arms were aching dully from being held outstretched for so long and her poor breasts throbbed unbearably.

'How they feel now?' the girl demanded, caressing one of Tanya's constricted breasts. Tanya could only whimper and sob as her breast was examined. Then to her complete dismay one of the men produced two large iron ball weights fastened to two sturdy steel pegs. Beg as Tanya might, she was forced to watch helplessly as her nipples were teased to full hardness then pulled taut and the pegs were fastened onto them. The weights dragged down excruciatingly on her tits but the tight cords held them in firm cones of swollen flesh, which now ached unbearably and all Tanya could do was to cry and sob whilst the men grinned at her distress.

After several agonising minutes the girl gave her a sympathetic smile and removed the weights and unwound the cords from Tanya's breasts. By now Tanya was desperate to be allowed to rest but she was given no such chance and no sooner were the cords gone from her poor breasts than the men freed her arms from the cross and marched her to the couch, across which they dragged her, forcing her to bend over it and then be tied face down by the straps that hung ready at the corners. Tanya's legs, her thighs still throbbing, were then drawn apart and they bound her by the ankles against the aluminium legs, which were themselves bolted onto the floor. She was now utterly helpless and could never have freed herself, but for their own amusement the men then took two more straps and used them to bind Tanya's thighs tight against he legs of the couch. Of course the straps were placed across her thighs precisely where she'd been hit with the riding crop and as they were pulled taut Tanya could only sob and shake her head, begging them not to be so cruel.

Gazing over one shoulder Tanya saw with dismay one of the men holding what resembled a gleaming steel hook about a foot or two in size and an inch or more in diameter. Fastened to the end of the hook was a length of thin rope and whilst Tanya was forced to lie helplessly tethered and wondering what purpose was behind the device, the girl came to stand before her and with a bottle in one hand made a show of dribbling a generous amount of viscous liquid from the bottle over her other hand. She then said something Tanya didn't understand but a moment later Tanya knew just what was to happen to her next.

'No... please...don't...'

Tanya squirmed and writhed desperately as the girl's fingers coated in the treacly liquid were rubbed between her buttocks. A second later and Tanya felt the girl finger her anus and then her fingers, slippery with the mixture from the bottle were insinuated into Tanya's rear passage.

'Oh no.... please...stop...'

Tanya gave a gasp as she felt what she guessed were all of the girl's fingers being forced into her anus. The giant hook, which was in fact not pointed at the end but gently rounded, was held before her for her to see. The polished aluminium glistened with liquid, which dripped slowly from its enormous curved shaft. As Tanya gazed in dismay at the device she felt the girl withdraw her fingers and a second later the bulbous curved end of the hook was forced into Tanya's rectum.

'No...too much, take it out! Please!'

The cool metal was guided home into Tanya's arse and the long shaft of aluminium was left resting up Tanya's back from her cruelly divided buttocks to the small of her back.

'Ouuch! Let go of my hair!'

Tanya shook her head in objection but it was too late. Whilst the girl, having caught hold of Tanya's long blonde hair pulled it into a taut ponytail, one of the men had set about binding the fine rope secured to the hook around Tanya's hair. Repeatedly the rope was bound around and around and after each full loop it was knotted fast. By the time they were finished the rope was wrapped around Tanya's ponytail seven times and before the first knot had been applied the girl had pulled Tanya's head tautly back so that when they were finished Tanya was left with her head dragged painfully far and when the pressure grew too much and she tried to lower her head forward to ease the pain on her neck, the hook embedded in her arse was forced deeper still making her howl and curse with impotent rage and all too soon tears were pouring down her cheeks and she was begging then hysterically pleading with her tormentors to free her from the cruel device.

'You enjoy, yes? We give you more fun, you want this don't you baby?' goaded one of the men whilst he stood watching her suffering.

'Let me go! Please! Let me go!' cried Tanya, certain she couldn't bear the torture any longer.

'Keep still baby… we give you good feel now.'

After a few moments agonising wait whilst the men and the girl did something behind her which there was no way Tanya could observe so long as her head was dragged back and held immobile by the rope bound to her ponytail. She could only lie, quietly sobbing and cursing her predicament and wishing that the discomfort of being tethered thus would end.

'UUHH!'

Without warning Tanya was subjected to an electric shock discharged deep into her anus. The swines had put an electric charge to the aluminium hook that was embedded in her rump! The second shock made her howl and jerk like mad but all that did was to increase the pain from her rope bound ponytail that was pulled maddeningly tight.

'Uuhh!'

Another shock was delivered and the sensation however agonising also served to push Tanya to the brink of having an orgasm.

'Please… please…' she begged breathlessly.

Sensing that she was about to come the girl had the wires disconnected from the hook and then the rope binding her hair was unknotted and mercifully the terrible device that was embedded in her now throbbing rear passage was removed.

'Okay, now you get to try new machine.'

'No, please let me rest,' Tanya begged, writhing pathetically against the straps that held her down across the couch. The thought that her pussy was now to be subjected to a mechanical shafting with a massive dildo was heaven sent for Tanya. If there was one thing she could never have too much of it was a decent fuck and the idea of being on the end receiving of the device the men had unveiled sent delicious ripples through her young body. She wasn't of course going to let on to her tormentors though and as they moved the machine to up behind her spread legs and fitted one of the largest heads on the piston shaft, Tanya began struggling and begging for them to leave her alone.

'Okay, pretty girl, let's see how you like this.'

Tanya closed her eyes and tensed herself for what was to come but then to her dismay and to the annoyance of the three men and their female accomplice the ship's sirens sounded the alarm.

CHAPTER TWELVE

Having had a few glasses of wine with lunch, which he was forced to abandon, Miles took a taxi to Sturmberger's Mayfair house, more than irritated at being summoned without any explanation. It was a Sunday and the young German businessman made a rule of never working on a Sunday so whatever it was, Miles reckoned, it had to be pretty damn important. His first thought was that something had happened to Tanya. The city was pretty quiet and the journey from the bistro in Chelsea where he was lunching with friends was managed in nearly half the time it would have taken during the working week.

The electric gates to Strumberger's house were as usual closed but Miles had only a moment to wait before the German's voice answered the buzzer and promptly Miles was let in, the gates gliding shut behind him as having paid off the taxi he walked up the drive and jabbed the doorbell. Sturmberger greeted him, dressed in only a brocade dressing gown. Locking the door behind Miles, Sturmberger looked at his business associate with an expression of complete despondency.

'What the hell is wrong?' Miles demanded.

'My prize ship has been seized by pirates!'

'Pirates? You have to be kidding?'

'A drugs cartel to be accurate, operating with speedboats. They must have known what was in the cargo; less than twelve hours off the coast and they hit it during the night.'

'What was the cargo?' Miles asked.

Sturmberger shook his head and gestured for them to go down the mahogany panelled corridor. Miles followed his business associate into his private study where Sturmberger slumped despondently into a dark red leather armchair.

'There's some twenty-one year old malt in the square decanter, help yourself my friend,' he said wearily.

Miles poured them both a glass and handing one to

Sturmberger took a seat opposite him.

'Well, what was the cargo?' Miles repeated.

Sturmberger gave a sigh, took a sip from his glass and wiped his hand over his face before he spoke.

'Guns.'

'Guns?'

'Ja, ja. I had a good order for a consignment of guns. They were on the ship. Someone must have tipped off these drugs cartel people. They knew what they were after even if the ship's Captain did not even know that he was transporting them.'

'What!'

'It was a secret, it was a private deal, quietly done, you know, no import taxes, no tedious paperwork. Just a healthy profit.'

'How could you have been so stupid?' snapped Miles.

Sturmberger looked indignantly at the other man for a minute then he shook his head and took another gulp from the glass he held.

'It had seemed so easy. They were all in cases labelled machine parts, hardly anyone knew. There has never been a problem before.'

'You've shipped guns to South America before? Who to for Christ's sake?' Miles demanded.

'To some freedom fighters who could pay good money for second hand Russian stuff that I bought from a broker in Ukraine.'

'Freedom fighters? You mean a drugs cartel, don't you?'

'Well, they use the drugs money to finance themselves.'

'And I bet once they knew your shipping schedule they decided to save you the trouble of paying harbour fees!'

'You think this is funny!'

'No, but I think you're stupid. Call yourself a businessman? So tell me just what happened,' Miles demanded irritably.

'There's nothing more to tell; they boarded the container

ship by speedboats. The crew just had time to radio for help and sound the alarm then they were overpowered. An old freighter was brought alongside; the bandits broke open all the crates with the guns and put them on the freighter. They also stole other things that caught their eye as well, I'm afraid Michael.'

'Such as?'

'The girl, they abducted her.'

'Tanya?'

'Yes, our pretty blonde is now the property of some South American drugs cartel. I am sorry…'

'That's not going to be much consolation for her!'

'I was thinking for us, she was employed as one of my crew, her family will have to be notified and they will doubtless want to sue my company for negligence or when her body turns up they'll sue for compensation.'

'All you can think about is the financial aspect of this? What about Tanya? What's going to happen to her?'

'Who knows?' Sturmberger shrugged, stood up and walked across to a door on the far side of the room to that which they had entered by.

'So that's it? There's nothing we can do?'

'Well my dear chap, it's not as if they've asked for a ransom. Anyway I thought you should know what was going on. I interrupted my Sunday so that you might be informed straight away.'

'Thanks, that was very thoughtful of you,' Miles answered somewhat tersely.

Sturmberger pushed open the door, revealing a mirror walled mini gymnasium. Sat astride a weights machine, her bare legs and arms bound to the chrome poles of the machine with silk cords was a young woman. She was naked except for a red leather hood that covered her head completely except for her mouth and nostrils and was drawn tight at the back of her head with laces.

Sturmberger walked into the gymnasium, opening his

brocade dressing gown as he made his way across to where the girl was forced into a kneeling position and tied to the weights machine.

'She can't hear a thing, there's cotton wool; in her ears and the mask is padded. Neither can she see. She is reliant on her sense of smell and of course her sense of taste.'

As Sturmberger spoke he held his semi-flaccid cock close before her nose and Miles watched as the girl who had remained quite still until that moment suddenly stirred.

Sturmberger eased himself a little closer and the head of his cock brushed the girl's lips. Immediately she craned her head forward and licked enthusiastically.

'What a darling little thing she is. She knows that she'll be stuck here until she's satisfied me. See how eager she is to do that?'

Miles watched as the girl eagerly licked and sucked at the offered cock, quickly making it harden and thicken.

'Who is she?' Miles asked.

The girl must have been in her early twenties he guessed. It was hard to tell with the leather hood covering her head. She had pale white skin, a little lightly tanned around her neck and forearms. Her skin was lightly freckled and wisps of russet hair showed from the edges of the leather mask. She had pert, slightly upturned breasts and long, slender legs. Her waist was slim as were her arms, which twisted a little against the silk cords that bound her against the chrome poles.

'Her name's Becky: she answered an advert I ran in one of the fee mags. "Wanted, willing young girl for home help. Smart address, central London, maximum 12 hours a week work in exchange for free board. Applicants should be enthusiastic, fit and eager to please. Photo essential." She only started last week but she's coming along nicely.'

'So I see,' said Miles.

'Would you like a turn?'

'I think I could be tempted.'

'She's really quite good...' sighed Sturmberger his breathing quickening as the girl's mouth closed around his cock and her sucking propelled him now rapidly towards ejaculation.

Miles watched as the German was made to come and then sucked dry. When he pulled himself way from the girl's mouth his pleasured expression was enough to make Miles determined that he wanted to enjoy the services of the girl as well. Holding his whisky tumbler against her lips he watched as her nostrils flared in surprise and then she eagerly tilted her head back allowing him to gently tip the contents of the glass into her pretty mouth.

Unfastening his flies but without bothering to undo his trousers further Miles pulled out his already engorged cock and let the bulbous head brush the girl's lips. Immediately her tongue darted out and gave an experimental lick drawing a sigh of satisfaction from Miles. When the girl furled her lips around his cockhead and her tongue lapped eagerly over the taut skin of his erection, Miles couldn't prevent a groan of satisfaction from escaping him and as she sucked him hard, trying to accommodate as much of his cock as she could in her young mouth, Miles knew that she was going to make him come in almost record time. He gazed down at her tethered body; her limbs glossy with perspiration, straining at the silk cords that held her against the gleaming chrome as she eagerly sucked his heavily engorged and now throbbing cock. With the leather hood covering her face and robbing her of her individual identity she was reduced to nothing more than a sex machine dedicated to servicing the men who employed her and even as the thought occurred to Miles that she would never know who she had just serviced and he might never afterwards see her face or know her, her ardent sucking and licking triggered his orgasm and as the first spurts of semen splashed against the back of her throat he slid his hands around the back of the leather hood and held her head so she couldn't pull back whilst his cock continued to pump milky come into her mouth.

Miles need not have worried that the girl might be reticent about completing the task though. Eagerly sucking him dry and swallowing all that Miles had to offer, she seemed keen to keep his cock in her mouth and to coax him back to a state of hardness immediately.

'A randy little bitch, isn't she?' Miles commented, easing his hold on the girl's head and stifling a groan as his cock was licked and sucked eagerly and he realised that the girl wasn't even going to give his erection a chance to subside.

'Becky has a very tight little pussy, perhaps you'd like to sample her?' Sturmberger suggested.

'I think I could be persuaded.'

The silk cords that bound the girl hand and foot were unfastened and the two men made her stand and then they led her across to the room to where a punch bag dangled from the ceiling. The girl offered no resistance when they tied her wrists together with one of the silk cords then drawing the girl's arms to full stretch they bound the other end of the silk cord around the chain from which was suspended the punch bag. Sturmberger then took another silk cord and wrapped it across the girl's back just below her shoulder and pulling it around the punch bag drew both ends together and with the girl's chest now pressed up against the punch bag he knotted the two ends.

'What are you going to do to me? Please tell me?'

The girl's accent was Australian, her voice pleasingly plaintive, thought Miles.

'Shall we take the hood off?' Miles suggested.

Sturmberger shook his head negatively and grinned with amusement.

'She doesn't mind sucking cock but she'd less keen on getting fucked,' he said.

'Really?'

'Well, last time she complained that we were being too

hard on her.'

'We?'

'I invited some business associates to enjoy her. After half a dozen of them had fucked her Becky was complaining that her pussy ached.'

'After half a dozen I'm hardly surprised. How many more of your business associates were there?' Miles asked.

'There were eight all together and I couldn't possible tell the last two that they would have to miss out, could I?'

'And she wasn't happy, I dare say?'

'She did start to make a bit of a fuss, until we calmed her down. I dare say that the episode has made her a bit wary of being tied like this. I have to say all of the men commented though on how pleasingly tight she was. I can't help wondering in fact Miles, whether you might not be just a little too well hung for her liking?' Sturmberger suggested.

Miles gazed at the tethered girl as she hung from the chain supporting the punch bag and her slender body was pressed snugly against the padding. Unable to see or hear what was going on around her must be heightening her sense of vulnerability immensely, he mused.

'How old is she?' Miles asked, idly stroking one hand down the girl's back and allowing his hand to curve around and appreciate her small, taut buttocks.

'Tewnty-one, I think. A nicely proportioned body wouldn't you say?'

'I prefer bigger tits myself but apart from that, yes, she's just what one wants.'

As he spoke Miles slipped one hand under the girl's arse between her legs and his fingers found the soft folds of her sex. The girl writhed a little, her colt like legs tensing then wriggling as he pushed two fingers into her sex and held them there.

'Please Herr Sturmberger... anything but so many men...my poor pussy was throbbing for days afterwards, don't be so cruel again, please don't!' the girl pleaded.

Miles kept his fingers buried in the girl's sex, which was slick with arousal now and feasting his eyes on her nakedness he imagined sinking his cock into her sex and feeling her writhing under him.

'She's certainly not keen for another gang bang, is she?' Miles commented.

The girl was panting hard now and her slender arms pulled against the silk cord that was tight around her wrists holding them outstretched above her.

'Well, aren't you going to at least see if you can get that all too generous cock of yours into her little pussy?' Sturmberger asked.

Miles didn't need any more encouraging. Drawing apart her pert buttocks with both hands so he had a clear view of her sex he aligned the head of his cock with his target and without giving the girl any warning he shoved the bulbous head of his erection into her sex and even as she gasped in surprise he adjusted his hold from her arse to her hips and dragged her backwards, impaling her fully on his hardened cock and making the girl cry out.

'Please! Too big! You bastards, stop it, let me go!'

Miles withdrew his cock almost completely then sank it back again into the girl's body, driving it home up to the hilt of his monster organ, which if the girl's cries were anything to go by was evidently too much for her accommodate without much discomfort.

'No! Please, too much...'

The angry screams of objection had given way now to a plaintive begging. The urgent jerking of her arms to pull free from where she was tethered had been replaced with nothing more than a half hearted struggling against the silk cords. The poor girl had quickly realised that all the anger in the world wasn't going to help her and no amount of effort was going to allow her to break free from the silk cords that held her victim to the men's cruel whims.

'Well Miles, does she please?' Sturmberger asked.

Miles nodded. The girl did have a delightfully tight little sex hole and her writhing and panting was increasing his pleasure enormously. There was in truth nothing he liked better than to subject a girl to his enormous cock and have her tied before he started so that when she quickly realised it was fast becoming more of a fucking than she felt she could endure, she was in no position to change her mind.

'Please…uhh… can't take much more…'

The young Australian had already had her fill of Miles but he had hardly started and having ejaculated only moments earlier there was no way she'd get a reprieve now by Miles coming. By sucking him dry after she'd given him the blowjob and then sucking him some more so he was kept hard, the girl had sealed her own fate. Miles was now in a position to shaft her for as long it suited him.

'Can't take anymore… stop…please…' the girl begged between breathless gasps as Miles continued to subject her pussy to a merciless shafting.

'Does her pleading detract from your pleasure? Would you prefer it if she was silenced?' Sturmberger asked.

'It doesn't bother me at all,' grinned Miles as he eased his cock from the girl yet again and then calmly rammed it back into her, all the while keeping a firm grasp on her hips so she couldn't pull herself free.

'No more! Let me go, let me go!'

The girl's struggling grew more urgent and her crying more desperate and Miles wondered whether it was perhaps now time to stop.

'I think she's had enough,' he suggested.

'Nonsense,' scoffed Sturmberger, ' she's just playing her part, she's more than happy to be treated like this, trust me.'

'Are you certain?' Miles asked.

'Let me put your mind at rest, come and listen to something.'

Miles eased his cock from the girl's writhing body and

leaving her hanging by her outstretched arms he zipped his flies shut and followed Sturmberger through into his office where he took a Dictaphone from his desk.

'When I interviewed her I took the precaution of recording our conversation.'

Smiling smugly he pressed the play button.

'So let me just recap my dear then; you are more than willing to participate in sex games and to act as a sex slave for my amusement?'

'Sure, it'll be fun. You're happy to pay, I'm happy to play!'

'You've no objection to say...... getting whipped?'

'You promise it'll not leave any marks, right?'

'I give you my word.'

'That's okay then.'

'You can expect to be tied up and subjected to as much sex as I choose.'

'No worries, I reckon it'll be a laugh, right?'

'I may wish to have you service guests I may bring home.'

'Yeah, I get your drift. Listen Herr Sturmberger, I've done stuff in Sidney at a club that sounds like just your scene. You want a randy little slut sleeping in your staff quarters who'll suck your cock just whenever you want, well, I'm your girl.'

Sturmberger switched off the Dictaphone and put it back in the desk drawer.

'Does that reassure you, Miles, my dear friend?'

'Sure does,' Miles nodded. 'In fact it makes me think that perhaps I'm being too gentle on her.'

The two men returned to the gym. Miles smiled as he saw the girl hanging by her outstretched arms, her bare feet just touching the floor, her slim body tied against the punch bag. Having heard the tape, he now had no qualms about giving the girl a proper shafting. In fact, he thought, he felt pretty tempted to teach her a lesson or two.

'You're certain she can't hear?' he asked, standing close

behind the girl but not touching her.

'Absolutely,' answered Sturmberger.

'This room is sound proofed, I assume?'

'No, but there's no way anyone is likely to hear, the walls are quite thick and there are other rooms on all sides. I suppose someone in the library would hear but we're alone Miles, you needn't worry.'

'How long has she been working for you?'

'Just over a week and she's enjoying herself I can assure you. She could have left at any time if she wasn't. I think you'll find all her begging for mercy and pleading is conditioning from her time working in a sex club in Sidney.'

'Well then,' said Miles. 'Let's see just how vociferously she can beg for mercy, shall we?'

'What have you in mind?'

'Have you a butt plug?'

'Of course, there's two or three of different sizes in the cabinet over there.'

'Have you used any on her yet?'

'No, not yet.'

'Well, I think we'll fill up her rear and then her pussy will feel even more stuffed when I shaft her.'

'And you think I am cruel?' the German grinned as he watched Miles return with a rubber inflatable butt plug.

'Uhhh....'

The girl gasped and twisted as Miles rubbed the tip of the rubber plug against her sex.

'A little bit of lubrication... now...'

'UUHH!'

The girl gave startled cry as Miles pushed the bulbous rubber plug into the girl's anus.

'Now, before she has time to think about squeezing it out...'

Miles gave the rubber pump that was connected to the plug by a short length of hose several squeezes.

'No! Stop, please!'

'She'll not be able to force that out now however hard she tries,' Miles laughed and disconnecting the hose he fingered the flared base of the rubber butt plug that was now pressed snugly against the girl's rectum.

'Now it's time to carry on where I left off.'

This time when he slid his cock back into the girl's sex he could feel how much tighter she felt thanks to the expanded butt plug that was also filling her. The girl could evidently feel it too as her writhing, when he got back to work shafting her, was all the more urgent and before long she was struggling desperately to pull herself free from the merciless shafting to which she was being subjected.

'Please! Stop! Too much, too tight! Stop!'

Miles ignored her protest and carried on pumping his cock into the slick

tightness of the helpless girl's sex. She was shaking her hooded head vigorously now and writhing desperately. His cock was heavily engorged and he felt potently aroused by the girl's helplessness but having come so recently himself, he knew with satisfaction he'd be able to shaft her for some time yet before he was likely to come again, by which time the girl would be frantic. He thought of her cheery, almost cocky, singsong voice on the tape that Sturmberger had recorded. Well, the randy bitch had clearly demonstrated that she was eager for it so she had only herself to blame, Miles reminded himself.

'That's enough! Stop… please…uhh… please…'

Miles withdrew his cock completely and stroked his hands soothingly down the girl's naked body. She was trembling uncontrollably and her pleading had turned into desperate sobs. The little Aussie girl had certainly had her fill, Miles thought, grinning with satisfaction.

'Could you find something to gag her?' Miles asked his friend. Sturmberger shook his head, smiling.

'I'm sure I may have something lying around that would suit,' he answered.

With the merciless shafting seemingly at an end the girl was sobbing gratefully, blissfully unaware that as she hung from her outstretched arms, recovering her breath, an inflatable ball gag was dangling just inches from her hooded face.

Miles gave a smile of satisfaction as by stroking the girl's back reassuringly he soothed her into a sense of complacency. When he slipped the small rubber sphere of the gag into her mouth, he took her completely by surprise. Before the girl knew what was happening he had the gag's straps pulled tight around her cheeks and the Velcro ends were fastened at her nape.

'Nuuhh!'

Miles twisted the gag's protruding valve, pursed his lips over it and blew hard. The rubber ball inside the girl's mouth expanded. The girl cried out in protest. Miles blew again. Her next cry of protest was more muffled. Miles blew again then stepped back to regard his victim's condition. The rubber ball jammed in her mouth; originally the size of a golf ball had expanded to twice its size. The girl was shaking her head furiously. Miles applied his mouth to the gag's valve once again and blew into it a couple more times. The black rubber sphere was now so enlarged that it forced her jaws pleasingly wide and the only noise to emerge was a muffled groan.

Taking a hold of the helpless girl's hips Miles dragged her backwards and impaled her on his engorged cock. The girl shook her head vigorously and gave a long cry that was reduced by the gag to nothing more than a faint sigh, hardly audible even to Sturmberger, standing just a few yards removed.

'Nice and tight,' said Miles, 'and she wriggles so obligingly.'

Miles eased his cock from the girl and then rammed it back into her slender body. The girl gave another anguished gag-muffled cry. She was struggling vigorously now but her efforts were useless and served only to amuse the men. Hooded and now gagged she was victim to the men's whims and though she already believed that she couldn't take much more of what they were subjecting her to, she was to remain in the gym as the two men's plaything for the remainder of the afternoon and well into the evening.

CHAPTER THIRTEEN

Tanya was too dazed to at first realise just what was happening. The men that dragged her from the playroom and hauled her up onto deck were dressed in mismatched military clothes and jeans and had scarves covering their faces so that only their eyes could be seen. The powerful arc lights that flanked the ship's principal container hold were switched on and as Tanya lay sprawled, naked and bound with rope on a canvas tarpaulin, she could see a dozen of the crew labouring at gun point to remove wooden boxes from the hold. There were four machine gun armed men standing watching them and shouting orders and there were many more to be glimpsed elsewhere.

For a while Tanya was ignored, though she was left guarded by a young lad, no older than herself, she reckoned. The night air was cold and she was soon shivering uncontrollably and every now and again she'd get the taste of salt in her mouth as the enormous ship was washed by a particularly large wave and a fine spray would drift high enough to be blown over the deck.

On the upper deck adjacent to the bridge the senior crew in their white uniforms were gathered and guarded by several of the pirates and from where Tanya lay she could hear some shouting and raised voice. She could see numerous wooden boxes being forced open and their contents checked and then the ship's crane was used to lower them over the side one by one. Maybe an hour had passed before two of the pirates came over to where Tanya lay bound and they barked some questions at her in response to which Tanya could only shake her head apologetically. It was the young lad who was guarding her who eventually breached the communication barrier.

'What country?' he demanded.

'Sorry?'

'What country you from?'

'I'm English,' Tanya answered.

'You prisoner?'

Tanya was about to answer "no" but then in a flash she saw that perhaps to admit to not being a prisoner yet being found in the situation that she was in could lead her into deep water so she quickly replied that yes, she was a prisoner. The men though looked far from convinced but after a moment's discussion Tanya was hauled to her feet and tossed over the shoulder of one of them. A few moments later and she was being lowered by rope into a large speedboat, one of three that were tied alongside the enormous container ship like limpets on a whale.

The speedboats remained alongside the container ship for a while longer and from where Tanya had been bundled she watched the little boats being loaded with items prised from some of the crates that had been broken open. Maybe half an hour later the pirates all piled aboard their speedboats and made off at high speed. What was in the crates that the pirates had wanted to steal Tanya had no idea. She did however recognise one item that was stolen and deposited into the speedboat where she was held: the stomach-churning machine that she had been about to be subjected to in the ship's games room. As the little boats speed away into the night, Tanya guessed that having seen her strapped down and about to fucked by the machine, the pirates had been unable to resist the urge to add to their booty. Before long the twinkling lights of the container ship were far behind them and Tanya knew that she was now embarked on an adventure far more scary than that which she'd started a few weeks ago.

When dawn came Tanya woke, surprised that despite being forced to lie naked on the deck of the boat, she had actually fallen asleep. The first thing she took in was that her wrists were bound together in front of her with rope, a length of which had been wrapped four times around each wrist in turn in a figure of eight and the ends then knotted repeatedly. As best she could she lifted her arms and dragged her fingers through her tousled hair, clearing her face of her blonde hair so she could better look around.

They were no longer at sea, to either side of them rose a wall of trees, they were travelling up a river, perhaps fifty yards broad. The trees were enormous and came right down to the riverbank and occasionally Tanya would catch a glimpse of a parrot taking flight as the boats approached and its bright red and yellow plumage would be visible for a few seconds before it disappeared into the canopy of green. Sitting upright so she could better look around, a rough woollen blanket of bright colours in an abstract design fell from covering her body exposing her bare skin to the air. Her captives had at least been considerate enough to cover her whilst she'd slept and this small token of thoughtfulness made her hopeful that she might not be too harshly treated.

The air was stultifyingly hot and the men on the boat showed shirts that clung drenched with perspiration to their backs. There was a heavy smell too like a compost heap and gazing at the land on either side Tanya could see clouds of tiny insects. Occasionally she could see where one of the enormous trees had tumbled into the river and its trunk could be seen half exposed, half submerged, the bark covered with moss and trailing green fronds and between the branches there stretched colossal spider's webs that glistened with dew and looked big enough to ensnare birds never mind insects. The only insects that came out over the river though and close to the speedboats were giant dragonflies, emerald and blue that skimmed the above the water. As Tanya watched one a fish leaped from the murky water and its vicious looking jaws snapped shut around the dragonfly and both promptly vanished again below the surface.

There were four men on the boat on which Tanya was held hostage. She guessed the speedboat must have been about thirty feet long and now, heavily laden with booty it sat low in the water as they cruised upriver at no more than a fast walking pace. The crew talked cheerfully amongst themselves and when they saw Tanya was awake she was given a tin mug of strong black coffee, which she managed to gratefully hold between her bound hands. The youngest of the crew who alone spoke some fractured English tore in half a sugary bun of heavy pastry that he was eating and gave half to Tanya who eagerly washed it down with the last of the coffee that had revived her stiff and aching body. After the last session in the games room her arms and legs ached dully from being bound repeatedly into achingly submissive positions. Having finished her coffee she handed back the young lad the tin mug, smiled appreciatively and stumbled to her feet. She was long past feeling at all embarrassed at standing naked before strangers and allowed the men to feast their eyes on her body. In truth she felt proud of how she looked and she knew that she was just what any red blooded male would want to get his hands on given half a chance. The sun was pleasantly hot on her bare skin and she stretched indulgently, grateful to have the freedom to move her limbs. In the last couple of weeks she'd spent hours and hours with her arms and legs tightly bound, her muscles throbbing whilst the crew had taken it in turns to enjoy her defenceless body. At least now she was free to stretch her long legs and slender arms, even if her wrists were bound together. She glanced again at the rope. Whoever had tied her hands certainly knew what he was doing, she mused.

The speedboats travelled upriver for what seemed like hours and during this time they turned first from the main channel and headed up a tributary that was only half as wide and then after what must have been several miles they turned again from this course and navigated a still smaller tributary where the riverbanks were no more than five or ten yards apart and the canopy of trees all but closed over the water and there was so little light it felt as if it were dusk. Now Tanya could hear the noise of the forest all around them, the loudest noise was the screeching of monkeys high above them but nearly as loud was the incessant insect noise. The river twisted and turned repeatedly and narrowed even further until the overhanging undergrowth was brushing at the sides of the speedboats and the crews frequently had to duck against branches overhead, from which Tanya glimpsed on several occasions long snakes that wrapped themselves repeatedly around the branches and seemed to be gazing down at the passing boats.

Just as Tanya was wondering whether there would ever be an end to the river there appeared a wooden jetty and a small clearing in the forest and two thatched huts Mooring the boats here the crews set to work to unload their stolen cargo. Tanya was left on board and her young guard's parting warning was more than enough to convince her to stay where she was.

'No swim: many puraque; no walk many snake; stay here is safe; try escape and you die, understand?'

'I won't move, I promise,' Tanya nodded and for the next half an hour she was all but ignored as the men emptied the three boats of their cargo. When the young man returned to check on her, Tanya was peering down into the murky water that lapped at the side of the boat.

'What are puraque?' she asked.

The youth wiggled his bare arm to simulate what Tanya thought was a fish swimming.

'Fish?' she asked.

'No, they very long, thin, no matter. They kill, you mustn't go in river.'

'Okay, I'll take you advice,' Tanya answered.

After an hour the group of men had cooked themselves a meal and had prepared their booty for transport. From the boat Tanya had watched them. The crates were broken open and emptied. Smaller wooden boxes were removed and these were bound with rough ropes which where then tied to long poles. Whilst the men worked half a dozen more men emerged from the jungle and joined in helping to lash the smaller boxes with ropes. One of the men stood out from the others: he wore khaki trousers tucked into high leather boots and a kaki safari jacket and slung around his chest was a bandolier of bullets and he had a rifle slung over one shoulder and a pistol in a holster strapped to his waist. Tanya guessed that he must be the leader of the men and she was not surprised when he left the others to do the physical work and he came to the boat to inspect his unexpected acquisition.

'What were you doing on the container ship?' he asked, regarding her from the jetty where he stood.

'You speak English?' Tanya said, forcing a smile and now for the first time feeling conscious of her nakedness.

'Answer my question.'

'I was kidnapped.'

'You're lying,' the man spat a cheroot he was toying with aside and removed his sunglasses.

'No, really, I was abducted when I was on holiday and…'

'Your name is Tanya Hutchinson; you were on Sturmberger's payroll.'

'How do you know?' Tanya blurted.

'My men questioned the ship's Captain; he told them; you were pay-rolled as "crew entertainment". My men brought some interesting items from the room where you worked. Very interesting…'

'Please… I didn't know what was expected of me… I thought I was only…'

'Be quiet, I've listened to enough of your lies. We're ready to move out. Since you haven't any footwear or clothes you can't walk so I've arranged for my men to transport you. Stay there until they come for you, don't even try to climb out of the boat without their help; if you fall in the water you're dead meat,' the man warned then turned and strode away.

'What are puraque?' Tanya called after him, glancing down at the murky water.

'Electric eels; their shock is enough kill if you're lucky; if you're unlucky you'll just be stunned and then you simply drown. That's if the piranhas don't get to you first.'

'Thanks for the information,' said Tanya, backing away from the edge of the boat.

Tanya was transported in identical fashion to the wooden crates; that is to say; her ankles were roped together and then a long wooden pole was drawn between the ropes that bound her ankles and wrists. With the pole lifted onto the shoulders of two men, one at each end, Tanya was left dangling upside, suspended by her ankles and wrists, her bare rump swinging just a few feet clear of the ground. The party made off up a narrow track marked by machete-hacked undergrowth which climbed steeply uphill. The heat and humidity were intolerable and Tanya, having drunk only a mug of coffee since her abduction, felt weak with dehydration. After an hour or so despite the discomfort of being carried like some slain big cat trophy, Tanya drifted asleep, all but overcome by the unbearable heat.

CHAPTER FOURTEEN

'I think she's had enough, perhaps we should call it a day?' Miles suggested.

'Quite so,' agreed Sturmberger.

'Shall we untie her?' Miles suggested.

The Australian girl looked hopefully at the two men regarding her. Her slender but well toned arms and legs were all immobilised by belted canvas straps that secured her to a gynaecologist's chair that Sturmberger had installed in a basement room he had converted for his own amusement and the suffering of any girl unlucky enough to be lured into his pay. After subjecting Becky to a merciless shafting and then softening up her thighs with ten minutes on the receiving end of a horsewhip, the men had dragged the girl from the gym and down to the basement.

Now Becky was strapped into the large black leather chair, canvas straps tight about her thighs and arms as well as two that held her immobile, one snug across her stomach and fastened at the back of the chair and the other tight across her chest just above her breasts but under her arms. As well as the straps, she wore wrist and ankle cuffs of black PVC that were fastened by clips to hooks on the chair, added for the purpose. The hood had been removed from her head, as had the ball-gag from her mouth. The basement had been deliberately and comprehensively soundproofed by Sturmberger and for the last hour or so the Becky's screams and cries had added to the men's amusement.

'Shall we untie her then?' Miles repeated.

The girl looked quite exhausted and he felt a pang of sympathy for her. Strapped into the chair Becky had endured enough to satisfy Miles and having enjoyed her deliciously tight young pussy and then enjoyed watching her lithe young body writhing feverishly as she was tormented, Miles was ready to leave his business associate's house and to go home.

'I'll give her ten minutes to calm down,' said Sturmberger,

gesturing to the basement exit.

Leaving Becky bound to the chair the men left the room. A few moments later and Miles was walking home through an early evening mist and drizzle and Sturmberger had returned to the basement.

'Are you going to untie me then?' Becky demanded impatiently as soon as she saw him enter the room.

'Not just yet,' Sturmberger answered.

Becky looked apprehensively at the man as he stood at the end of the chair and effortlessly pushed the two legs of the chair wide apart. With her feet trapped in the stirrup cups by the ankle cuffs that were clipped to the frame and her thighs strapped down, Becky could do nothing but sigh despairingly as Sturmberger effortlessly spread wide her legs.

'Haven't you done with torturing me for today?' Becky complained as she was forced to watch helplessly as Sturmberger calmly stroked her exposed sex.

'No please, too tender…no…uhh…' she bit down on her lip as the man fingered her achingly tender pussy.

The men had earlier fastened chains hung with weights to her labia and had watched her writhing against the straps as her sex lips had been distended. The whole situation of being on the other side of the globe to her home and familiar surroundings, held prisoner in a soundproofed basement whilst two men she didn't know calmly and systematically tortured her was, she had to admit, exquisitely exciting and deliciously arousing. As much as she may have struggled, the sensation of having her labia weighted had served to bring her to orgasm and this had convinced Sturmberger, quite rightly, that she was game for more suffering.

'Calm down my dear, I am not going to do anything to you that doesn't give you pleasure.'

Becky knew that the German had judiciously subjected her to harsher and more demanding sessions as his submissive each day she'd been in his employment but as yet, though she had been given the chance each day, she had never walked out.

'Uhhh… please…so sensitive…stop it…'

She tossed her head from side her, sighing plaintively as Sturmberger fingered her labia, teasing the swollen lips of delicate flesh. She was very wet and hot to his touch and with her legs widely spread by the chair, he was afforded a pleasing view of her young sex.

'Now I have a nice treat for you, so you can just lie back and enjoy my new toy.'

'You bastard! Let me out of here, damn you!' she swore, knowing that what he wanted to hear was her complaining and struggling to resist what he was subjecting her to. It wasn't hard to struggle, the pain had been real enough but then it had been deeply satisfying for her as well as for the men and she was grateful to have found such a mercilessly hard and imaginative master.

Ignoring her demands Sturmberger drew the little portable trolley closer to where he was standing. Having seen what was on it, Becky was now having quite a temper tantrum and he was given the satisfaction of watching her strain against the straps that held her down whilst he calmly took a peg from the tray and fastened it to one of her outer labia. He then cut a small length of sticky tape and stuck it across one shaft of the peg and then holding the peg against her thigh he smoothed the tape across her skin.

'Not fair…please, I want to stop!'

'Dear girl, stop whining or I'll gag you.'

Sturmberger fastened a second peg to her labium and then another two pegs to her other sex lip, leaving Becky to gaze down in growing despair as she saw that her labia had now been pegged widely open to fully reveal the delicate pinkness of her sex. She watched the man pick up the electric wand, she'd seen one once before and had heard from another girl that judiciously used the device would make a girl orgasm repeatedly and intensely as the wand delivered an electric shock that was not quite enough to be harmful but more than enough to be as painful as it might be stimulating.

To test the effectiveness of the wand Sturmberger first applied it to one of Becky's tits and her anguished cry and subsequent swearing and cursing was vociferous enough to convince him that the device was as good as its reputation suggested. Becky was trembling with apprehension as he placed the slender tip of the wand against her exposed sex and flicked the switch.

'Uhhh!'

Her cry was so intense that he instinctively withdrew the device from contact with her and the girl was left trembling and sobbing, her arms and legs twisting under the straps. Her gaze was abruptly no longer one of defiant anger. She was panting hard, her eyes wide with fear and wet with tears and her lips trembled, she shook her head urgently as she begged him to not repeat what he'd just subjected her to.

'Please don't do it again, it's too much, please...'

Sturmberger smiled an insincere apology and touched her exposed sex once more with the tip of the wand then he flicked it on. Becky's body convulsed against the straps, she bit down hard on her lip then her mouth was torn open as she cried out. Her thighs strained against the straps, her arms dragged ineffectually to free themselves. Her cry turned to a fevered whimper, her head tossing from side to side, her breathing increased then became ragged as she climaxed. Sturmberger switched off the wand, slid the tip a little way into her sex then flicked it back on again and even before her climax had subsided she was forced to orgasm again as the electric shock stimulated her sex more than she imagined possible and more than she was certain she could bear for much longer.

'Stop...please...enough!' she gasped breathlessly.

The tip of the wand was withdrawn from her sex but the

next second she felt it prod against her anus and then penetrate her there. When the shock was delivered into her anus she cried out again, writhing desperately and panting breathlessly.

'Uhhh… stop…no… more…please…'

The sight of the young girl, helpless as she strained against the straps and cuffs, her slender body heaving for breath as he withdrew the wand from her rear, was enough to make Sturmberger's already heavily engorged cock strain against the fabric of his pants which was damp from his arousal. Becky was panting so hard after her multiple orgasms that an idea struck him and he grinned maliciously.

Dazed after what had just happened to her, Becky was still trying to recover her breath when fingers abruptly coaxed her jaws open and a small soft ball was forced into her mouth. She shook her head vigorously as straps were pulled taut against her cheeks and at her nape the Velcro ends were secured together. The ball in her mouth was too small to silence her until with dismay she watched Sturmberger blow into the exposed valve.

'Nuuhh…'

With each breath the man applied to the valve the soft rubber ball grew gradually larger until she felt it filling her mouth. The sensation was potently arousing as she felt her helpless increased.

'Now let's resume where we left off.'

Becky shook her head, looking with wide-eyed alarm at the wand. As her nervousness increased she panted harder but now she could scarcely breathe through her mouth thanks to the ball-gag and when the tip of the wand was placed against her exposed sex again and switched on, the sensation was not only intense enough to bring her to another climax but this time she was left all but breathless and panting madly through her nose as her body struggled frantically against the straps as the wand was drawn slowly across the moistness of her delicate inner labia until its vicious sting was delivered to her clit. A fresh wave of orgasm washed over her and she was left so breathless now she imagined she would faint.

She would have been grateful if Sturmberger had concluded the session there, she'd climaxed more times than she could count, her body felt satiated with sexual satisfaction and also ached excruciatingly from her relentless struggling against the straps that held her in the chair. The young German however was far from finished. Dazedly and deliriously starved of breath after her repeated climaxes, Becky watched as the wand was brushed against her clitoris, flicked on and a jolt of electricity lanced into her sex making her cry out then as she was gasping what air she could through the gag, the wand was pushed again into her anus and switched on.

'Nuuhh…'

Becky tossed her head from side to side, all but delirious now as the wand remained buried inside her arse until, writhing madly against the straps that were taut across her naked young body, and she was brought to another breathless climax.

The sight of her condition was enough to make Sturmberger feel himself about to come and he quickly withdrew the wand from the girl's arse and dropping his trousers and pants he pressed a button on the chair until it was lowered to just the right height for him to spear his throbbing cock into her sex. He smiled appreciatively at her young pussy, her outer labia pegged open like a butterfly in a trophy box, her clit swollen with arousal and doubtless throbbing from the shocks to which he'd subjected her. Becky gave a gag muffled groan as his cock sank into her and the tight slickness of her sex was enough to trigger his ejaculation.

CHAPTER FIFTEEN

When Tanya woke she had no idea how long they had been travelling but they had reached a hillside plateau where a large villa stood, flanked by lawns and encircled by the jungle. There was evidently a road or track leading to the villa since several gleaming new 4X4 vehicles were parked outside and under a thatched lean-to a little way from the house were an old army truck and a jeep. There was a small outdoor swimming pool that was sunk into the hill abutting a cliff face over which tumbled creepers and wild flowers as well as the surplus water from the pool, which was in turn fed from a stream that ran down from a waterfall that tumbled down a rocky gully.

On the veranda of the villa the crates had been deposited and were now being opened up, their contents laid out for inspection. It was when Tanya had been lowered to the ground that she'd woken and now the first thing she saw was rows of guns laid out on the wooden decking. When the man in charge saw she was awake he walked over to her, one of the new guns in his hand. Whilst Tanya knew next to nothing of guns, she recognised that it was a machine-gun and it looked to be brand new.

'Just like you;' said the man, ' very pretty, nicely shaped and pleasing to hold.'

He stroked the barrel of the gun affectionately and then held the weapon at arm's length, holding it one handed and regarding it critically. Evidently satisfied with it he tossed the gun to one of his men to catch and he turned back to Tanya.

'Sixty brand new Ak.74 assault rifles, five thousand rounds of ammunition and ten rocket propelled grenade launchers. Sturmberger shipping has certainly diversified since they started importing machine tools and televisions and exporting hardwood and bananas. I wonder if they'll be making an insurance claim for the loss of this little consignment? Somehow I doubt it!'

'I can guess why you'd want to steal them but what do you want me for? What good am I going to be to you?' Tanya asked.

The man looked down at her smiling and gestured for her to stand up which she did. He regarded her critically from head to toe and his gaze lingered on her generous but firm breasts. Tanya swallowed a nervous lump in her throat and glanced down unable to meet the man's stern gaze and she saw a tell tale bulge in the fabric of his trousers.

'Why do you think?' asked the man. 'For my pleasure, for our amusement. This villa is so secret that none of my men that who of it are allowed to breathe a word to anyone. I have several homes and many camps and I am always on the move since the government is always hunting me. I have hundreds of men at my call and we control hundreds of square miles of the countryside but it is best to always have one place that is kept so secret that I can be assured of complete safety. This villa is that place, so only my personal bodyguards know of its existence and whereabouts. Of course these men are paid very well and very carefully picked but I like to try to give them other rewards.'

'So you're going to give me to them?' Tanya suggested.

'Certainly. The men are sometimes stuck here for weeks at a time and that can be very frustrating for them, especially when they have to watch my daughters wandering around the place if they are staying here with me. I see their eyes. They wouldn't dare touch them but it is hard for them, such a visible reminder of what they are missing out on. So from now on you will keep them amused.'

'For how long will I be kept a prisoner here?' Tanya asked.

'Until they tire of you I suppose, then...'

'Then you'll let me go?' Tanya asked, hardly daring to hope that the man would say yes.

'Then we shall have to see.'

'Meaning you'll kill me?'

The man gave her a reproachful stare.

'I may be an outlaw in the eyes of those scum that run our country but I am have no interest in any unnecessary killing. Besides, a pretty white girl like you, and one so young, you'll fetch a good price on the slave market.'

'The slave market, don't tell me there's really such a thing, not in this day and age?' Tanya answered.

'It might not be quite what you imagine but it exists and for a very modern purpose: the wealthy and corrupt men who run the big businesses of this country have learnt that they can buy anything that they wish; everything has a price, even people. A few years ago it was for mestizo girls. Now the fashion is for white girls.'

'Mestizo?'

'Girls of mixed blood, half European half Indian. But they are no longer in fashion.'

'Fashion? What do you mean? What do they want the girls for?'

'For sex slaves: they are locked up in their big country mansions away from prying eyes, they are usually kept drugged at first, they are held prisoner for the men's amusement and satisfaction.'

'So you're telling me that when you've finished with me I'll be sold on and still kept as a sex slave?'

'What else can you expect? Are you worth a ransom? Is someone going to bother to search for you and rescue you? It seems to me that you were a sex slave on board Sturmberger's ship, is that not the case?'

'But that was of my own choosing!'

'Well, too bad, you have to learn that in this country you have no choice; from now on you can forget who you were back in England.'

'You don't seriously think you can get away with this?'

'My dear girl, I know that I can get away with it. You are my prisoner and however hard it may be for you to accept; your fate is now entirely in my hands.'

Tanya was about to answer the man but their attention was diverted. Two girls had just emerged from the entrance of the villa and for fraction of a second all the men stopped working then swiftly they resumed their tasks turning their eyes reluctantly from the girls who were evidently twin sisters and of quite stunning appearance.

Tanya reckoned that they couldn't be much older than she was; they were tall though and very slim; with long dark hair that fell over their shoulders and with dark, smouldering eyes and beautiful yet stern faces. When they saw that their father, the man who was addressing Tanya, had seen them, they both smiled and their faces were transformed into those of angels, their eyes warm and full of delight, their sensual mouths transformed by broad smiles of almost childish pleasure. One of the girls was wearing a simple black one-piece halter swimsuit that was cut high at the hips and scarcely covered her breasts whose outline could be seen clearly pressing against the tight fabric. The other girl wore olive green shorts and a white crop top that left her taut stomach exposed as well as her slender arms and like her sister the fabric of the top tightly hugged her breasts, emphasising her generous cleavage and allowing her dark areoles and nipples to be seen visibly pressing against the white cotton.

'Who's this, daddy?'

The girl wearing the swimsuit looked appraisingly at Tanya and smiled as she saw the rope bound repeatedly around her wrists.

'She was on the ship; she was providing on-board entertainment for the crew; go and have a look at what's in the last crate.'

Tanya watched as the two sisters strutted across to the last crate which the men had yet to open and all too aware of how their bodies drew the men's gaze stood over them and ordered them to open up the crate immediately. All Tanya could do was stand and watch whilst to her dismay the men lifted out from the crate the mechanical phallus and alongside it they produced the nasty little black box with its trailing wires that Tanya knew all too well and as if that wasn't enough they'd even snatched some of the leather cuffs and gags and other accessories that had furnished the ship's games room.

The girl in the shorts and crop top spun around on her heel, some weights dangling from silver chains in her hand.

'At least now we've got some toys to play with to relieve the monotony of being stuck here!' she laughed then she tossed the weights to her sister and promptly picked up a rubber face gag and said something in Spanish to her sister.

Tanya stood watching whilst the girl in the swimsuit discarded the weights and stood obligingly still whilst her sister stood behind and made her try on the gag. It was like half a mask, which fitted across the recipient's face and snugly under their chin. The black rubber once pulled tight by means of elastic straps covered not only the mouth but also a broad strip was drawn across the wearer's eyes, effectively blindfolding them. On the inside of the gag where it covered the mouth was a short but thick rubber phallus which the person wearing the mask was obliged to take into their mouth.

With the gag now buckled snugly around her sister's face the girl in the shorts stepped back, laughing to see what her sister would do next. The girl wearing the mask made some incoherent noises; whatever she was trying to say the gag effectively muffled her words. Holding her arms up before her, clearly unable to see where she was going the girl in the swimsuit took a few tentative steps. Laughing at her sister's helplessness the other girl caught hold of her by the shoulders and spun her around several times. She then took her by the wrist and led her purposefully towards the swimming pool.

Tanya and the man and indeed all the other men, stood in spellbound silence whilst the two girls approached the pool but at the last minute the girl leading her masked sister halted and made her stop right at the edge of the pool. She then made her sister turn around so that she wasfacing the pool and then she unbuckled the mask. As she eased apart the two elastic straps she then stepped back a pace. The girl wearing the mask instinctively reached up with both hands to finish removing the rubber mask but even as she drew it from her face her sister turned sideways, lifted one legs and planting her bare foot against her sister's back extended her leg, pushing the girl in the swimsuit into the pool before she knew what was happening.

Both girls thought this was highly amusing and Tanya was left watching one happily swimming around the pool whilst the other sat on the edge, her feet dangling in the water. The men resumed their work, collecting up the guns and moving them into the villa, whilst their leader ignoring Tanya, went into the villa. With nothing else to do she sat down on the grass and looked resignedly at the rope that repeatedly bound her wrists. Her skin under the ropes felt hot and sore but there was no way she could extricate her hands, so tightly and effectively bound was the rope. In films, the heroine, when she was tied up had the rope bound around the outside of the circle formed by her two wrists being placed together and with some effort she invariably managed to squeeze one hand out from under the rope or else she was afforded the chance to pick loose the single knot that held the rope tight. Whoever had tied Tanya's wrists though clearly knew just what he was doing. The rope was bound tightly in a figure of eight around her wrists and knotted repeatedly, she would never be able to get her hands free, she decided.

In the time she had been at the villa the morning sun had risen to its zenith and now the villa and its encircling lawns were bathed in bright sunshine and the temperature leapt even higher. Tanya, sitting on the grass watched the perspiration form in droplets on the bare skin of her shoulders and run down onto her collar bone from where it trickled down to her breastbone and then the glistening droplets trickled between her breasts. It was too hot to do anything now and the men having finished their work of moving the guns had retreated into the shade leaving Tanya alone with just the two raven haired sisters for company.

The sister wearing the shorts had discarded them. Underneath she was wearing only a black thong and Tanya gazed at her whilst the girl had her back turned. She had a firm young arse, the deeply tanned skin was flawlessly smooth and her buttocks were enviously generous yet taut. Discarding her crop top, she turned to look at Tanya and for a moment the two girls gazed at each other. The Latin American girl's breasts were smaller than Tanya's but perfectly formed and her dark areolas were large with pert nipples that she now shamelessly displayed doubtless all too aware that from their shady viewing places her father's men could feast their eyes hungrily on the forbidden fruit she could teasingly show them but which remained beyond their reach.

There was a loud splash as the girl dived into the pool. Some parrots, startled, took flight from some nearby trees and a monkey, invisible to the eye gave a screech of alarm. The girl began to breaststroke from one end of the pool to the other and a silence descended once more. Her sister eased herself from the pool and stood on the lawn, sparkling droplets of water falling from her slim tanned body as she combed her long hair clear of her face with her fingers and then walked around the edge of the pool and across to where the items looted from the ship's games room lay on the lawn. Picking up the rubber mask that she had earlier been made to wear she walked across to where Tanya was sat.

'Keep still, English girl,' she ordered, crouching behind Tanya, who knew that to try to resist would be futile.

The rubber mask was pressed against Tanya's face and abruptly everything went black as the rubber covered her eyes. She swallowed and flexed her jaws as the hard rubber phallus was coaxed into her mouth. The feeling of the cock shaped gag filling her mouth was powerfully erotic and as her tongue was kept pressed down by the device she felt a sudden stirring in her loins as the girl kneeling behind her fastened the masks straps.

The girl called in Spanish across to her sister and then Tanya was being encouraged to stand up.

'Okay English girl, come here.'

Held by her arm Tanya was guided and though unable to see where she was being led she followed, again knowing all too well that to resist was pointless.

'Now, stand still, there's a good girl.'

Tanya did as she was instructed. She could hear the other girl splashing in the pool and then the sounds, she guessed, of her getting out. Tanya guessed that she was now standing close to the water and it was a fair bet to expect that the sisters would delight in plunging her blindfolded and gagged into the water where she'd be even more at their mercy. It was too late to shout for help and what help could she expect anyway? Their father would doubtless be amused to see what they were up to and anyway Tanya was sure that once she was taken into the villa she could expect easily as much sexual torment as she'd been subjected to on the sea journey.

'So you like to do this for money yes? You sell your body to men, yes?'

Of course Tanya couldn't answer this question thanks to the gag and as she was forced to feel the rubber phallus thrust inside her mouth provocatively and the broad rubber of the mask snug against her mouth and eyes she could do nothing but reflect on the question. Yes, she realised, she had sold her body for pleasure, but not just for the men who paid; but for her own; she had signed up to do the film work in Scotland and had signed up to Sturmberger because it offered her the chance to act out her own sexual fantasies. Only now, lost in the jungle of South America and at the mercy of two beautiful, sultry girls probably not much older than she was, Tanya found it hard to believe where her adventure into fulfilling her desires had led her.

As she stood passively awaiting her fate at the hands of the sisters, Tanya felt the soft brush of hair against the backs of her legs, and then a pair of gentle hands was carefully wrapping something around her right ankle. When the material was drawn tight, she recognised the sensation; a leather ankle cuff had been fastened snugly upon her and sure enough a moment later her left ankle was given the same treatment. Tanya's heart was beating quicker now and she nervously twisted her hands against the rope that bound her wrists even though she knew she could never extricate them.

'Okay English girl, let's see how good you swim.'

Soft hands rested palm down against her back and then she was pushed backwards.

The warm water closed over her and immediately the memory of the treatment in the bath that Miles had subjected her to came back to her. This time though she was submerged under more than a few inches of water and now there were now hands to help haul her back to the surface. The rubber gagging and blindfolding her Tanya still cried out and tried to see where she was but she remained enveloped not just in water but in impenetrable darkness. Urgently she twisted onto her belly and then tried to kick out with her legs only to find that the ankle cuffs had been tied together and all she could manage was to flail her legs a few feet. With her wrists bound together she could do nothing with her hands other than thrust her arms out in front of her as she desperately kicked out with her hobbled legs. She felt her long hair swirling around her face and the warm water was still enveloping her and she had no idea how deep she was and whether she was actually making any progress towards reaching the surface of the pool.

The next instant she felt fresh air against her face and

gratefully she inhaled through her nose before her head momentarily bobbed back under the surface.

'Are you enjoying your swim, English girl?'

Tanya swung her body towards the sound of the voice and kicked out urgently with her legs as best she could. A moment later and her hands struck the side of the pool and she had her forearms balanced on the pool's edge whilst she trod water and recovered her breath.

'You're not a very good swimmer are you?'

This time the taunting voice came from behind Tanya and she suddenly realised that one of the girls must have swum up behind her. Female hands, soft but determined settled at her waist and then abruptly pulled her down. Before Tanya could react the girl had her hands on Tanya's shoulders and pushed her down below the surface. Tanya kicked out desperately and she recovered the surface but had only a few seconds to pant some air through her nose before she was dragged back under again.

Quite how long the sisters amused themselves in this way with Tanya struggling against them in the pool, she had no idea but before long she was utterly exhausted and when finally she was dragged from the pool, she was too tired at first to care what happened next to her or to try to offer any resistance.

* * *

Ricardo di Contas, drew on his cigar and allowed himself an indulgent smile as he watched four of his men carry the English girl from the poolside to the room in the villa he had prepared. The girl appeared unconscious at a distance but as she was carried into the villa he could see that she was still conscious despite the amount of time his daughters had kept her submerged in the pool. Julietta and Catherina deserved some pleasure and amusement he reminded himself.

Since they had lost their mother when her car was

ambushed and she was gunned down by Government troops who had hoped to ambush Ricardo, he had been forced to bring them up as best he was able. As a revolutionary-turned-bandit who still held control of hundreds of miles of remote jungle he had some freedoms but for now sadly he could not risk letting his daughters travel to the cities of the coast. So it was that from the ages of fourteen and sixteen their education had been completed by a Jesuit priest and by a drunk old Englishman who Ricardo had liberated from slavery in a remote rubber plantation and had made him the girls' private tutor.

Patrick Hamilton had claimed he was an explorer and had been lost for years in the jungle before he was captured first by Tapuya Indians and then by ruthless rubber plantation owners who had made a slave of him just like so many other hapless innocents who were caught by them. Ricardo guessed Hamilton to be in his sixties or seventies; he had forcefully dried out the old soak during the first year he'd taken him under his wing and for the next four years he had acted as tutor to Ricardo's daughters. Now as the half drowned English girl was carried through the villa's hall by four of Ricardo's men, each holding one of her slender limbs, Hamilton stood at the foot of stairs watching disapprovingly but saying not a word. He exchanged glances with Ricardo who shrugged apologetically as they watched the girl being carried past them and into another room.

Julietta and Catherina followed, the younger, Julietta, just two days past her nineteenth birthday was grinning widely at the prospect of what would happen next. Catherina, twenty-one, was altogether cooler and only her eyes betrayed her excitement. Ricardo regarded the old Englishman as he watched the two sisters walk past him. Julietta in her skimpy black swimsuit, high cut at the hips with her teenager's long legs looked colt-like and she almost skipped after the men carrying their new plaything. Catherina followed unhurriedly, her head held haughtily high, her shoulders drawn back a little self consciously as she flaunted her achingly desirable cleavage, her firm young breasts still soaking wet and clearly visible under the now damp crop-top that she had pulled back on. Her shorts she had not bothered with and Ricardo might have rebuked her for such a display in front of his men were it not for the English girl. He knew that his men's attention would be focused on their prisoner and he would let his men enjoy her and thereby distract them from his older daughter's equally desirable young body.

Depositing the English girl on the wooden floor his men stood back to await his orders. If their eyes strayed from the naked English girl, lying groaning into her gag it was only to glance at the machine they had taken from the ship. None of Ricardo's men would dare to openly gaze lasciviously at either of his daughters. They had too much respect for their leader and they were too fond of his daughters. Besides which one man once had been stupid enough to try to seduce Catherina and when he had refused to take no for an answer she had calmly pulled a small knife from her boot and had rammed it to the hilt into the man's buttock. When Ricardo had discovered the explanation for his screams he had offered to execute the man if Catherina so wished. The girl had said to spare the man his life but everyone knew Ricardo never made idle threats and the warning was enough to the other men to keep their hands off the sisters.

'Take the gag off her,' Ricardo ordered.

Immediately the order was carried out, the rubber mask was unbuckled and the blonde girl was gazing up at him as he stood over her, her eyes blinking and her pretty mouth hanging open as she gasped breath gratefully through her mouth once more. She had sensual bow-shaped lips and perfect white teeth. Her lightly tanned skin was slightly freckled about her cheeks and she had high cheekbones and attractive light blue eyes that now looked pathetically at him as she realised all too well that in his hands hung her fate.

'Tie her down over the bench.'

His men carried out the order. Keeping the girl's wrists bound together they tied another rope around the one already in place, pulled it taut and so drew Tanya's arms out in front of her and along the bench to which she had been forced to lie face down. There was a rope, badly tied, maybe fifty centimetres in length, between the girl's ankles - Catherina's handiwork - and now this was removed, the English girl's legs were spread and then tied to either side of the bench by binding leather cords through the steel rings that were sewn to the ankle cuffs she wore and then the cords were pulled tight around the legs of the bench and tied fast. The blonde girl's pale white arse, firm and begging for attention was left thrust high and well exposed. Her generous breasts were pressed under her against the bench and though she tried experimentally to move her arms and legs, she could achieve little and would certainly never be able to extricate herself from where she was now tied down.

Catherina and Julietta circled their victim. Their father would turn the English girl over to his men come nightfall but for what remained of the afternoon, he had agreed to allow them to indulge themselves by subjecting the girl to whatever pleased them. Julietta was eager to try out the machine but first Catherina wished to see how the English girl could take a whipping. Catherina also had other ideas as well and she was impatient to begin though anxious not to seem so.

'Let me give her a taste of the whip, papa,' she asked, picking up a slender, long whip of plaited leather and looking endearingly at Ricardo, who nodded his agreement. Settling himself into a high backed carved chair he placed the heels of his booted feet crossed at length on the end of the bench to which the English girl was tied down. From where he was sat he had a good view of her face and he watch her eyes to gauge when she'd suffered enough. He had no qualms about allowing his prisoner to suffer for his daughters and his men's amusement and pleasure but he knew that although she might be a willing sexual submissive given that she was payrolled by Sturmberger shipping for such a role, she'd have a limit to her endurance.

Thwack!

'Uhh!'

Without any preamble or hesitation Catherina had brought the whip down upon the girl's back. The English girl was trembling now and a faint red line appeared running from her left shoulder diagonally across her back to her slender young waist.

Thwack!

'UUHH!'

The second blow was harder and Ricardo watched as the English girl jerked urgently with her arms against the ropes that held them helplessly outstretched. She looked up at her, her mouth trembling and her blue eyes moist with tears that were ready to fall but for the moment she just managed to hold in check.

'Slowly Catherina, she's a girl like you. Not some dumb pack animal you are trying to hurry along,' Ricardo cautioned.

'She's trembling,' Catherina laughed.

'What's her name father?' Julietta asked, circling the bench and gazing with fascination at Tanya's helpless condition.

'Tanya,' Ricardo answered.

Julietta knelt beside the bench and taking a hold of Tanya's tousled blonde hair made her turn her head to meet her gaze.

'How does it feel? Does it excite you? Do you want Catherina to stop? Would you like it if we were more gentle with you?'

'Stop teasing her,' admonished Catherina, ' and get out of the way in case I catch you with the whip.'

Julietta stepped back and Ricardo watched his older daughter bring the whip down again. She was well practised, he mused, as good with a whip as she was with a knife or gun. At twenty-one Catherina already knew how to look after herself and he was well pleased that she had her mother's feisty nature and his own instincts for self preservation.

Thwack!

'Uhh…'

This time the whip cut across Tanya's exposed buttocks and the force with which the blow was delivered was far more restrained.

'How did that feel?' Catherina teased, moving close to behind Tanya's tied legs and allowing her hand to caress between the girl's spread thighs.

'Hasn't she got a small arse?' Catherina laughed, 'Even smaller than young Julietta's!'

'Good tits though wouldn't you agree sis'?' replied Julietta, ' compared with yours that is.'

Ricardo grinned as his daughters exchanged snipes. Tanya gazed at him, a resigned expression on her pretty young face and for a brief moment he felt a little sympathy for her. He then reminded himself that she had obviously entered into her duties on board Sturmberger's ship well aware of what was expected of her and she was therefore the ideal person for his men's satisfaction and his daughters' amusement.

Thwack!

'Uhh!'

'Let's feel how you like that?' Catherina once more caressed between Tanya's forcibly spread thighs and this time she smiled triumphantly.

'You know what? She's getting wet; I do believe the little slut is getting turned on by being treated like this, I think it's time she suffered a little more vigorously!'

Taking hold of the hardened leather handle of the whip at

the other end, Catherina smacked the whip's stiff handle down against Tanya's rump, making her grunt in anguish.

Smack! Smack!

'Oww! Please, stop it!'

Smack! Smack!

'Uhh!'

Twice on each taut young buttock the handle of the whip was cruelly brought down with rapid speed.

'You see, Tanya, there are lots of ways to use a whip,' warned Catherina

Tanya could only squirm and gasp as she next felt the bulbous end of the whip handle being rubbed between her spread thighs and the hard leather, warm from the other girl's grasp, was stroked against the lips of her sex making her gasp and then sigh with sudden and unexpected pleasure.

'Does that feel nice, Tanya? I bet you're desperate for the feel of your pussy being filled up, aren't you?'

'Uhhh... please...no...'

It was evident from Tanya's breathless tone and her uncontrolled writhing that she was as eager for satisfaction as Catherina was suggesting as she now rubbed the end of the whip handle more firmly against Tanya's vulva.

'Why don't you beg? Tell us how much you want it, go on,' coaxed Catherina, now warming to her role.

'Uhh! Stop... hurts... please...'

Ricardo watched Tanya struggling now against the ropes as his daughter lightly tapped the tethered girl's exposed sex with the end of the whip. Looking at him with wide, begging eyes, Tanya shook her head, biting down on her lower lip and her pretty blue eyes, full of anguish now rolling upwards in pain as the plaited leather handle of the whip was repeatedly and mercilessly struck against her clitoris with more than enough vigour to cruelly stimulate her and just enough hardness to make the pain a little more intense than the pleasure.

'Is that too much for you? Would you prefer it if I just

stroked you here, like this?'

Tanya could only sigh and writhe helplessly as she felt the handle of the whip being used to tease her pussy. Soon enough she was slick with arousal and Catherina seeing her condition adjusted her grip on the whip handle and calmly drove the end into Tanya's sex, drawing a gasp of surprise from her then an uncontrolled sigh of pleasure.

'How deep do you like to feel it, Tanya? A little more perhaps?'

'Stop... enough... please...'

Tanya tossed her head from side to side, dragging her legs against the tethers that held them spread as she felt more and more of the whip handle being slowly pushed into her pussy.

'Please...uhh... no more...' she begged, looking up expectantly at Ricardo clearly willing him to make his daughter halt. If Tanya though had hoped that Ricardo might provide some degree of a restraining influence on his daughter's sadist nature, she was sadly misguided.

'Why don't you try the machine out on her: there are some attachments for it that look far more challenging than the handle of your whip, Catherina?' Ricardo suggested, a broad smile on his face as his gaze met Tanya's. Her eyes wide with fear, she shook her head urgently, her arms dragging ineffectually against the rope that held them outstretched. Ricardo watched her struggling intensify as his daughters moved the machine to directly behind Tanya's spread and tethered legs.

'Just remember that tonight she'll be servicing all the men so don't tire her out too much,' cautioned Ricardo.

He glanced at Tanya and gave her a brief and half-hearted apologetic smile before walking out of the room and gesturing for his men to follow him.

'Leave my daughters to their fun and games, our presence will only inhibit them and besides there is work to be done.'

Ordering his men out of the room ahead of him, Ricardo

lingered a moment in the doorway. When Catherina selected the largest of the dildo heads to screw onto the machine he grinned to himself. The poor English girl was in for a hard time that was for certain, he decided. Whilst his men would no doubt fuck her senseless tonight, long before then he reckoned that his daughters would have her begging for a respite from the merciless treatment they had planned for her tender young body.

CHAPTER SIXTEEN

'Please, no....uhhh...uhhh!'

Tanya shook her head, writhing urgently against the ropes that held her down over the bench. The rubber phallus that was now fixed to the piston of the machine was sinking relentlessly into her pussy, stretching her sex wider than she'd ever experienced soon filling her and ploughing deeper into her than she imagined she could bear. Just as she was certain she couldn't take any more the enormous rubber dildo withdrew almost completely. Before Tanya could heave a sigh of relief though she felt it slowly penetrating her once more.

'That looks perfect, now let's set a decent speed,' announced Catherina.

'No... too hard... please stop...please!'

Tanya writhed and twisted helplessly as the phallus began to rhythmically assault her sex, the piston working easily as fast as any shafting she'd experienced but the phallus itself far larger than any cock she'd ever welcomed into her pussy in pursuit of sexual gratification. Even Miles, with his monster cock, filled her less than this machine, she thought dreamily as her pussy quickly learnt to accept the broad girth of the dildo that was being rammed repeatedly in and out of it.

Soon enough the relentless mechanical shafting to which she was being subjected brought Tanya to a piquantly exquisite orgasm but the machine did not stop or even slacken in sympathy to the fact that Tanya now felt sexually satiated. On and on the machine pounded her young body, Tanya struggling desperately against the restraints until she was forced to accept that escape was impossible and that the two cruel sisters had no intention whatsoever of showing her any respite.

'Have you had enough for one day?' asked Julietta, circling the bench so she could feast her eyes on every inch of Tanya's helpless body as she writhed and squirmed, the sweat pouring off her smooth skin and her blonde hair tousled about her face that showed her anguish at what she was being forced to endure. If at first Tanya had revelled in the sensation, she was now bitterly wishing that she could escape from being on the receiving end of the machine. The relentless deep penetration from the phallus was too extreme even for Tanya. Her poor pussy throbbed from the continual shafting to which she was being subjected.

'Please stop… can't take…any more…' Tanya begged, as the sensation of the rubber phallus pumping into her sex became all but unbearable.

'Surely you haven't had enough yet?' laughed Catherina.

'I thought one could never get too much of a good thing,' taunted Julietta as she stood at the end of the bench directly facing Tanya and watching the expression of resigned suffering on her pretty face.

'Please…make… it…stop…' Tanya begged, a ragged gasp being forced from her mouth with each thump of the machine's piston.

'Shall we make it go faster Catherina?' Julietta suggested, deciding that she thoroughly enjoyed seeing the English girl's distress and finding that she was getting really quite turned on by watching the naked girl writhing against the ropes and cuffs that held her down whilst the machine pistoned the phallus into her sex unceasingly. In truth, Julietta was imagining what it must feel like being in the English girl's position and there was something potently exciting about seeing her suffering.

'Or what if we make it go deeper?' suggested Catherina.

'NO! Let me go!' cried Tanya, the thought of worse than what she was already being subjected to galvanising her into a vociferous protest as well as a determinedly energetic one.

The two sisters laughed as they watched Tanya struggle desperately to drag her legs and arms free but her efforts however vigorous were hopeless. Worse, in response to her increasingly loud pleading for them to stop, Tanya leant too late that the young girls had no inclination to listen to her screaming. Whilst Julietta held Tanya's thrashing head still, her older sister calmly applied a dental gag to Tanya and when the girls stepped back to regard their handiwork, she was left with her jaws forced and held wide by the slender tubes of rolled steel that were sprung like an animal trap in reverse. Tanya's sensual mouth was now forced wide so that her loud cries were reduced to a semi-coherent gurgling protest, as she was deprived of the ability to enunciate. Whilst she could still wag her tongue her plaintive protest was now reduced to an incoherent and muted noise.

'Something the matter Tanya?' teased Julietta.

Tanya groaned and gurgled as best the gag allowed, saliva trickling over her lips and Julietta laughed delightedly with the effectiveness of the gag.

'I think she's asking for deeper penetration, she likes it so much,' suggested Julietta.

'Well, we must look after our guest and give her what she wants,' Catherina replied and promptly she gave one of the dials on the machine a small twist and Tanya felt the phallus immediately sink even deeper into her aching sex.

'Nnnnhhh…'

'You're enjoying that, aren't you?' Julietta crouched for a moment before Tanya's anguished face and smiled sweetly at her before carefully wiping away fresh tears that welled from her wide blue eyes. Glancing up at her sister, Julietta smiled.

'A little deeper, I think,' she suggested.

'Nnnhh!'

Tanya shook her head vigorously, gazing imploringly at the girl her own age crouched before her, her pretty face transformed by a cruel smile, her dark eyes sparkling with amusement at Tanya's suffering.

The machine thumped the phallus back into Tanya's

throbbing pussy now so deeply that Tanya imagined she was going to faint. She twisted her arms urgently but the rope was bound too skilfully, too tightly for her to extricate her wrists. She pulled with her legs but the thin leather cords held stubbornly firm and the leather cuffs around her ankles twisted a little against her skin but that was all.

Thump! Thump! Thump!

The phallus kept on shafting her tender sex and if ever Tanya wished that something would stop it was the terrible machine to which she was so irrevocably attached. The two Latin American girls stood over her, watching her suffering and with utter dismay Tanya realised that they had no intention of stopping the machine and indeed when they decided that Tanya was surviving the ordeal thus far another dial on the machine was adjusted and the speed of the assault on her aching body was increased. For what felt like an eternity Tanya was left to writhe and endure the machine until the sensation of the relentless assault was too much and she fainted.

'Wake up Tanya, we've not finished with you yet.'

Tanya groaned through the gag, blinking then focusing on the smiling face close before her. She had no idea for how long she'd passed out but Julietta was again crouched before her and was lightly slapping her cheeks until Tanya was revived.

The shafting of her poor pussy was concluded but the sisters' games were far from over. Tanya remained tied down over the bench whilst the phallus glided to a halt, the machine was switched off and Tanya was left trembling as she lay tied down, her sex throbbing from the cruel treatment to which the girls had subjected her.

'Now let's see how she enjoys it another way,' grinned Catherina.

Tanya was forced to watch as the older sister took a bottle of body lotion and poured a generous amount into her palm. She then placed her hand on the small of Tanya's back and slowly stroked her palm downwards so the well-oiled palm glided over the crater of her anus and here she held her hand snugly making Tanya squirm with embarrassing pleasure at the sensation.

'Now, let's feel here...'

Tanya sighed as the other girl rubbed one fingertip slowly over her anus and then after a moment she eased the tip of her finger into the crater of the tight muscle.

'Uhhh...'

'Is that good? You like the feel of that, yes?'

Tanya could scarcely deny it and for a moment she was glad that the dental gag deprived her of speech. Yes, being tied down and treated like this by two beautiful young girls was, she had to admit, potently erotic.

'Now, let's see how soft and welcoming we can make you.'

Slick with the body lotion, Catherina's fingers coaxed Tanya's rear passage to open up and admit first one finger fully and then several.

'Now, let's see how you like the machine servicing you this way,' Catherina laughed, withdrawing her fingers and gesturing to Julietta to help her align the phallus of the machine up against Tanya's rear. Tanya was certain that in the next moment she would be suffering even worse than what had gone before but then there came a sharp knock at the door and the sisters' attention was distracted.

'Your father sent me,' Patrick Hamilton said, not having waited for a response to his knock at the door. 'Government troops have been seen at Cheuri village; six jeeps, moving fast and coming this way. You have to pack immediately.'

For a second the sisters were too stunned to speak but then Catherina quickly recovered her senses.

'Where is Papa?'

'Organising the men; they are moving the guns out by road but he and you will leave by the river.'

'But what if...' began Julietta.

'There is no time for what if's,' snapped Hamilton, ' we all have to leave and fast!'

'What about her?' Catherina pointed at Tanya.

'Your father didn't say,' Hamilton answered.

The two sisters hurried from the room without so much as a backward glance at Tanya. However the moment they had left Hamilton walked across to where Tanya lay tied down over the bench.

'I dare say Ricardo will want to take you with him; you'll need something to wear. Can you stand?'

'I can try,' answered Tanya as she lay patiently still whilst Hamilton untied the rope and cords that held her prisoner.

'Follow me,' he ordered.

Tanya hauled herself from the bench and after quickly rubbing her arms and legs to get some movement back into her limbs she followed the man from the room.

Ten minutes later they were gathered on the front lawn, Tanya wearing some sandals, a short skirt and a T-shirt borrowed from Julietta. The sisters were in stout trekking boots, shorts and short sleeve shirts; Julietta in olive green and her older sister in khaki shorts and a black shirt. Both had small backpacks and Tanya saw they both had holstered revolvers and sheathed knives hung from their waist belts. Their father's men were rushing back and forth loading up the 4X4s with the guns and in no time at all the vehicles roared away with all the men except for six. Two of these set off ahead of the rest taking the path that wound down the hill and led to the river where the speedboats were hidden. One of them took a two-way radio and another man, the young lad who had guarded Tanya on the speedboat, carried another two-way radio.

'Are the booby-traps set?' Ricardo asked.

A tall bearded giant of a man with a scar across his forehead, nodded.

Ricardo took one last look around and then nodded, satisfied that nothing else could be done except for heading off into the jungle.

'Why don't they ambush the soldiers? They've got enough guns and there are enough of them, don't they have the stomach for a fight?' Tanya asked the Englishman standing close by her. Patrick Hamilton smiled and shook his head.

'Ricardo likes to choose when and how he fights and he will never squander the lives of his men in needless battles. Besides,' said Hamilton, ' this way the government will never know whether Ricardo was here or with how many men. The vehicles with the new cache of guns will use one of the old loggers' tracks to evade being caught and we'll slip away with the boats. The soldiers may find the villa, someone must have tipped them off that Ricardo is in the area but when they arrive they'll find nothing and see no one. They'll be none the wiser unless they are foolish enough to try to poke around and then they'll learn that Ricardo was using the villa and it will cost them.'

'Booby traps?' said Tanya.

'Certainly.'

'What if they follow us?'

'We will be at the boats and away before they can catch us up.'

Their conversation was cut short as Ricardo ordered them all to set off down the track that led through the jungle the way Tanya had come that morning.

The path was only wide enough for one person and so Tanya followed behind Hamilton and doubtless by design she realised they were in the middle of the strung out party, effectively putting paid to any notion she might have entertained that she could escape by running back to the villa and the government soldiers.

'Are you his prisoner too?' Tanya asked.

Hamilton glanced back over his shoulder and shook his head.

'Hardly; Ricardo freed me from a pretty wretched time. I

have stayed with him and in return for giving me my life back I help him by trying to teach his daughters a few things more intellectual than learning how to skin and cook a snake.'

'Don't you ever think about going back to England?'

'I don't think I could cope with the change now; I've lived out here too long and I have come to appreciate the beauty of the jungle too much to turn my back on it now.'

'But you're working for a bandit!'

'Perhaps it's better than working for the government's tax collectors. I had to spend years and years working to pay off the death duties from my father's death and I had to sell off too much of the family land. I think now I bear too much of a grudge against our Government to go back to their clutches.'

'Well,' said Tanya, ' you must have been pretty rich to have had so much trouble with death duties. My parents were both killed in an accident years ago and even though my father earned pretty good money I haven't seen much of it.'

'Maybe it's held in trust for you for when you grow up?'

'Grow up? You cheeky sod, I'm nineteen!'

'Well, perhaps when you're twenty-one you'll inherit it?'

'I suppose I should know but I was too young to remember much of the details of the their will, I guess I was too upset by it. I've had a miserable Godfather look after me since and whenever I ask him questions about my parents' money he's always very vague and tells me not to worry.'

'Sounds suspicious to me, you'll have to sort him out when you get home.'

'Get home? How the hell am I going to manage that? Ricardo has told me he'll sell me as a slave when he's bored with me, I'm never going to get out of here.'

'Of course you will,' said Hamilton, ' you just have to use your feminine charm to persuade him to look after you properly and to see you right.'

'You're optimistic!'

'Of course I am; how do you think I've survived over ten years in the jungle? Trust me Tanya, you have all it takes to win Ricardo's sympathy, you just have to work at it. If the man has a soft spot it's for a pretty young girl and from what I've seen of you, you certainly fit that description.'

'Thanks for the compliment!' Tanya laughed.

Ahead of her the bearded giant turned in response to her laugh and shot her a glance to warn her to be quiet. Tanya muttered a sorry and whilst she concentrated on not losing her footing on the increasingly slippery path. She began to mull over what Hamilton had said.

CHAPTER SEVENTEEN

'Miles, it's Frederick here, if you're there pick up the phone. If you're not there then call me back on my home number when you get this message.'

The phone went dead. Miles rolled over in bed and gazed across to the window. A pale early morning light was filtering around the edges of the curtains. Throwing back the duvet cover he hauled himself from his bed and walked through to the en-suite bathroom.

'Sleep well?' he asked, looking down at the girl who was curled on his bathroom floor. The girl blinked and yawned and stretched and moved herself into a sitting position as best she could given that she was handcuffed by the right wrist to the heated chrome towel rail.

'I feel stiff! I want a drink. I hate you,' the girl answered, glaring at him.

'Stop complaining Becky, you could still be suffering at Sturmberger's hands if I hadn't acquired you from him,' said Miles good-humouredly before stepping into the shower and standing under the cascading hot water, steam billowing out into the room.

'You're just as bad as him!'

'Oh rubbish, Frederick Sturmberger is far more devious and cruel than I am: all I ask for is a decent shag!' Miles laughed, switched the shower off and took a towel from the towel rail and rubbed the excess water from his shoulders and back. He grinned at the Australian girl who a few days earlier he had won in a game of cards round at his friend's Mayfair mansion house.

'Why can't I sleep in your bed?' demanded Becky, irritably tugging against the handcuff that kept her shackled to the towel rail.

'Because you're not my girlfriend, you're my slave. Now stop complaining and run along and make me some tea and bring me some breakfast.'

Miles crouched down beside the girl and dropping the towel over her head so her view was obscured he turned the combination lock on the handcuffs until the steel sprang open and sending the girl on her way with a slap to her bare bottom he went back into his bedroom and returned Frederick Sturmberger's unsocially early telephone call.

'Sturmberger speaking!'

'It's Miles, what did you want? Don't tell me another one of your ships has been attacked by pirates again?'

'No, no, it's about the girl.'

'What,0 Becky? Do you want her back?'

'No, You keep her, I've had enough fun with her and to be honest I prefer someone a bit more submissive, or at any rate less loud. She was always complaining and swearing. Such bad manners, you know. I have a lovely little Japanese girl coming for a second interview this afternoon; she looks very promising.'

'So you weren't phoning about Becky?' said Miles, grinning as he watched Becky walk back into the bedroom a tray in her hands, her shapely young body quite naked apart from a lacy apron tied around her slim waist.

'No, it's about the girl who was on the ship; Raglan, Tanya Raglan.'

'What about her? I thought she was abducted by the pirates who stole your guns?'

'Sshh!' hissed Sturmberger, 'a bit of discretion please! They stole some crates of machine parts, how many times do I have to remind you?'

'Yeah, okay, machine parts, Freddy, just whatever you say. Now, tell me about Tanya.'

Whilst he was speaking, Becky put the tray on a wooden trunk that was in the window where she drew the curtains back and then after gazing down from the penthouse window at the early morning mist-shrouded London cityscape, she poured Miles a cup of tea and handed it to him. Propping himself back against some pillows, Miles took a sip of tea and handed the cup back to Becky.

'I have received a report about her from the government of the country that the ship was sailing to.'

'Saying what?' asked Miles, spreading his legs across the bed a little to allow Becky to kneel between them.

'She's being held prisoner by a bandit up in the remote northwest jungles. The military are trying to capture the bandit, someone called Ricardo Rueda; he was once a supporter of the failed popular revolution the military put down a few years ago. Anyway, apparently...'

'Good girl.'

'What did you say?'

'Nothing Frederick, sorry, carry on, I'm listening,' said Miles, ruffling Becky's hair with one hand whilst holding the phone with the other. Becky, crouched between his legs gave his cock another leisurely lick, her tongue working its way slowly from base to tip, where she lingered, teasing the cock's tumescent head with her tongue until Miles was unable to stifle a groan of pleasure.

'Well anyway, one of this bandit's men informed about his location and the military launched a raid to capture him. He managed to get away but they have been informed that Tanya Raglan is being held as his prisoner.'

'That's good,' sighed Miles.

'Good? What do you mean, good?' Sturmberger snapped.

Miles glanced down as Becky lifted her head back and grinned at him. With one hand she was fondling his testicles and with the other she now stroked with one fingernail his heavily engorged shaft, which twitched under her touch.

'I mean interesting,' Miles corrected. ' Very interesting.'

He watched Becky reach for the cup of tea he had placed on the bedside table. Taking a mouthful, she put aside the cup and then bent over him again. This time when she slipped her mouth around his cock, her mouth was still full of tea and the hot liquid against his erect cock dragged a gasp of pleasure from him.

'Miles, what are you doing? Am I interrupting something?' Sturmberger asked tersely.

'No, no, just having a spot of breakfast, that's all,' Miles answered.

Becky leaned back, grinning at him before she caressed his scrotum with both hands and with his balls caressed between her palms she proceeded to rub the testicles against each other.

'This is serious Miles, if the military capture him and they find out about the guns I sold him Sturmberger Shipping could be in deep water!'

'I would have thought that with the size of your ships you felt most comfortable when they were in deep water?' Miles laughed.

'This isn't funny, Miles!'

'I know... it's very...' Miles gazed down at were Becky was ministering to him; she was successfully distracting him from his telephone conversation and he was now more interested in what she was doing than in what Sturmberger was talking about.

'Very what?' snapped Sturmberger.

'It's very...' Miles gazed down at his heavily engorged cock. Becky was rubbing her palms together as if to keep her hands warm but his balls were trapped between her palms and they now felt so hot that they ached pleasingly and he was sure that this alone if continued for a few more moments would be enough to make him ejaculate.

'It's very hard...very hard...' he sighed.

'Yes,' muttered Sturmberger, oblivious to the fact that Miles was referring more to the state of his engorged cock than his South American problem.

'It's all right for you Miles, you won't be implicated in the illegal sale of the guns, you haven't got anything to worry about, but this could sink Sturmberger shipping!' complained Frederick Sturmberger.

'If there's anything I can do, let me know Freddy; look

I'll have to go.'

'Is something wrong?' Sturmberger asked.

Miles now had his hands folded behind his head, which rested back against his propped up pillows so he could watch Becky. She had now stopped fondling his balls and was instead rubbing the tip of one finger slowly over the tumescent head of his cock.

'No, nothing wrong,' Miles answered. 'Talk to you later.'

He hung up and sighed contentedly. As fast as droplets of sticky pre-come fluid were welling from the eye of his cock head, Becky was lightly massaging the liquid over the purple head. Miles' cock began to twitch. Becky exchanged glances with him and she smiled indulgently.

'How would sir like to come this morning?' she asked.

Miles gazed affectionately at the pert breasted naked girl sat on his bed. She smiled at him and as her mouth curved into the smile and their eyes met he imagined forcing her to take his cock in her mouth. He would hold his hands against the back of her head so she couldn't pull back and he'd ejaculate into her pretty mouth, forcing her to drink down all his come.

'Well?' Becky prompted.

She stopped stroking the tip of his cock and instead lightly furled her fingertips of both hands each around one of his balls and he felt her fingernails gently pulling against his balls. The effect was potent and Miles gasped, certain that he was now just a moment or two from having an intensely satisfying and prolonged orgasm. He imagined making her turn around and bend over. Whilst she had her face buried against the duvet and her firm and rounded young arse thrust invitingly high, he would take her from behind and sink his throbbing cock into her tight little pussy.

'Maybe you'd just like to lie there and let me look after you?' Becky suggested.

Miles groaned as he felt her pull on his balls; they ached exquisitely now they needed to come and his cock swayed and throbbed with a life of its own.

'Maybe....' he sighed.

'I think sir should just stay still and let me look after him,' suggested Becky.

'Yes...yes...' muttered Miles, certain that he was going to shoot his load anyway now, before he could do anything else.

Becky smiled triumphantly, proud and pleased to have Miles willing to let her decide. Like any man, she thought to herself, as long as he was regularly serviced, he was satisfied. Of course, she was desperate to have an orgasm herself but she knew she'd have to wait. She knew though that depending on how she made Miles come now and what she then did to him, she could lay the groundwork for getting herself shagged, which with Miles' skill and cock size would be enough to make her come, or she'd end up being punished which though it invariably took longer and hurt was just as pleasurable a way to have an orgasm. Either way, she knew she'd be satisfied; the question was what she fancied today; a nice hard shafting by Miles or some prolonged torture... it was a hard choice, Becky mused.

Miles' cock was now so hard, every vein stood out like a ridge and it was as big as Becky had ever seen it. The art of giving a man a good orgasm, she knew was to make him wait and this morning she had dragged out Miles' satisfaction for quite some time.

'Would you like it if I sucked you a little?' Becky asked, making her voice deliberately treacly sweet and innocent.

'Yes... do it...do it,' Miles sighed.

He was ready to come now and his cock ached with the urgent need so much that he was past caring how he had an orgasm. All thoughts of shafting Becky had evaporated, he had no will to move from where he lay and all he wanted was for her to finish jerking him or sucking him off.

'Miles, look at how big and shiny the head of your cock is,' said Becky, knowing that when Miles looked down he would see not only his swollen cock head, dark purple and shiny as it was now engorged as much as was possible but he would see her pretty lips inches from his organ and even as he watched she would stick out her tongue and delicately lick the tip of shaft, ever so slowly and ever so lightly, so that the touch of her wet warm tongue was not so intense as to trigger his orgasm but that it would nudge him just a little further towards the brink.

'Just suck it, Becky, there's a good girl,' Miles urged, unable to contain his excitement any longer and certain that he would come if she would just envelope his cock head with the heat of her mouth.

Becky stopped ministering to his cock tip with light licks of her tongue and she knelt back on her heels and smiled sympathetically. Miles' cock oozed more viscous fluid from its tip and the shaft swayed and twitched.

'Wouldn't you like to shove your cock up into my little pussy; you look ever so big now and I feel ever so wet. Shall we do that? Shall we?'

However much the image appealed to Miles he was certain that his cock would erupt before he could manage to sit up and Becky could turn around. As it was, just gazing at her naked body, knelt invitingly before him was, given his hopelessly aroused condition, almost enough to make him ejaculate.

'Just suck it…' he sighed.

'If that's what you want?' Becky asked, smiling.

'Yes, do it!'

Becky leant forwards once more and cradled his balls in her hands. Miles groaned uncontrollably.

'They feel so heavy… I think they've swollen, don't you?' Becky asked in her singsong voice.

'Going to come…' Miles muttered.

Becky bent her head over his cock and strands of her hair teased his cock shaft. Miles groaned. He gazed down and watched as she slowly slipped her open lips around the head of his cock. Rather than taking as much of his shaft in her mouth as she could she instead encircled the head of his cock with her lips, her teeth lightly resting against the rim of his cockhead and thereby restraining him from pulling back from her. There was a second or two's pause and then Miles felt her tongue lick over the head of his cock. At the same time he felt her fingers tighten their embrace of his aching balls.

'Uh, Becky… good girl…'

Her lips tightened around his cockhead forming a seal around the tip of his throbbing organ and then she sucked. Miles' cock erupted immediately. Becky made no attempt to swallow any of the copious amount of come that spilled into her mouth, instead she waited until he was spent and then she slowly eased her mouth back allow his come to dribble out from her parted lips and spill down over his cock shaft.

'Look at all your milky come, Miles, there's so much,' Becky cooed.

Miles gazed dreamily at down at the girl knelt between his legs. His cock was slick with come as Becky now proceeded to massage it with her hands. There was more though than Becky could easily rub into the skin of his cock so she wiped her still sticky hands over her breasts, massaging the milky fluid all over them until they glistened and her nipples stood proudly erect.

Whilst Becky massaged her breasts, rubbing Miles' milky come into her smooth skin, Miles watched her spellbound and when she glanced back down at his cock, more come was trickling from the still tumescent head.

'Did that feel good?' Becky asked, caressing him with one palm and rubbing the last of the sticky fluid into his cock as she slowly slid her hand up and down his shaft.

'Very… yes, good girl,' Miles sighed. He watched Becky as she unhurriedly pumped his cock with her palm, sperm oozing between her fingers as she tightened her grip and subtly increased her tempo.

'What would you like to do next Miles?' she asked, not for a moment slackening her grip but, even as she spoke, with her other hand she stroked with her fingertips between his thighs were she knew the skin around his anus was especially sensitive to touch.

Miles gazed at the naked girl ministering to his needs. Her achingly fit young body was a magnet to which he felt continually drawn. He feasted his eyes on her firm, perfectly rounded breasts, the skin glistening invitingly from the come that she'd rubbed all over her tits. Becky was leaning back, her pert arse resting on her heels. Her hair tumbled over her smooth shoulders and her slender arms were extended a little way beyond her slim waist as she caressed his cock with both hands. She hadn't given him a chance to lose his erection and as he gazed at his rock hard cock the urge to ram it into Becky's young body was irrepressible. There was only one other course of action that appealed as much to Miles and that was to subject Becky to an hour of torture before he shafted her and by then of course he'd be nicely ready to shoot some more spunk into her tight little sex hole.

'Right,' Miles announced decisively, 'off the bed and into the shower!'

As soon as both of them had showered, Becky diligently soaping her master from head to foot and all the time keeping his cock ramrod hard by constant caressing, they returned to the bedroom where Miles allowed Becky to rub him dry whilst she was forced to remain soaking wet. He then led her through to the kitchen and ordered her to bend from the waist over the large sink and with a roll of broad, black tape he bound her by the wrists to the taps. The tape, designed for bondage, was only sticky when it was in contact with itself, so by wrapping it repeatedly around her wrists the soft tape became as effective for binding Becky as if Miles had used the stickiest electrical or masking tape.

'What are you going to do to me?' Becky begged, hardly able to conceal her excitement.

'Be quiet,' Miles warned.

For a moment Becky couldn't see what he was up to without craning her head back over one shoulder or the other so she contented herself with gazing out of the penthouse kitchen window at the early morning view of the London docklands.

'Open your mouth wide, it's breakfast time,' Miles ordered.

The next she knew was happening was when a crisp, green apple was being wedged into her mouth. Trying to bite down on it and chew a mouthful out was a mistake for all Becky achieved was to leave her teeth sunk inextricably deep into the firm fruit whilst Miles deftly wrapped some more tape across the apple, around her cheeks and neck and fully overlapping it once he then cut the end and smoothed it against the tape already tight against her nape.

'Nnnhhh...' Becky shook her head experimentally and tried to bite through the apple but it was impossible. She pulled experimentally with her hands but her wrists were closely bound against the taps.

Miles ran his hands indulgently over her bare arse then slid one hand between her legs and finding her sex already warmly inviting he slid one finger into her moistness and Becky unable to control herself pushed her bottom back against his hand, sighing through the gag.

'I suppose you'd like it if I gave you a good, hard shafting?' Miles suggested.

Becky nodded affirmatively. She knew Miles' cock could fill her almost unbearably full but it was an exquisite sensation and she was now desperate to come.

'Well, I think you may just have to wait.'

Becky could do nothing but watch as best she was able whilst Miles now calmly stood directly behind her, his hands on her hips as he rubbed his engorged cock between her legs, the bulbous head brushing continually against her vulva.

'Mmmm...' Becky groaned into the apple that filled and gagged her mouth.

'Good isn't it?' Miles sighed with satisfaction.

It didn't take long before Miles knew Becky was about to come and he himself wasn't that far from having his second orgasm of the morning. Easing his cock from between Becky's legs, Miles took a wooden spoon and smacked it repeatedly against the girl's buttocks making her jerk her arms against where her wrists were bound to the taps. A little harder he smacked the spoon down against first one cheek of her arse and then the other until both glowed red. He then held the spoon by the head and dipped its long slim handle into a tall bottle of olive oil. Becky looked at him wide eyed with alarm. Miles grinned sadistically.

'Nnhh!'

Becky shook her head vigorously as she felt the oil slick spoon shaft penetrate her arse.

'Nnnnhh...'

Her protest was ignored and she was forced to feel the wooden handle being sunk into her rear. Quite how deep Miles forced it she couldn't tell but the next instant he began to wiggle the spoon and the sensation was so intense Becky, gurgling into her gag, came, a long protracted orgasm as Miles continued to lever the spoon shaft so its tip, deep inside seemed to wriggle about with a life of its own. Becky was still panting hard through her nostrils when Miles withdrew the spoon shaft from her rear and promptly drove his cock into her throbbing pussy.

CHAPTER EIGHTEEN

Wearing only flat-soled sandals it was hard for Tanya to keep up and keep her footing as the party hurried through the jungle. The path ran downhill continually and was in places, slippery in the extreme. As they drew close to the river and where the three speedboats would be waiting, Ricardo ordered them to halt and they stood as quietly still as they could whilst he and the other men strained for sounds. To Tanya's ear everything sounded quiet but then perhaps that was the problem she thought, recalling how as they had hurried through the jungle there had always been the noise of unseen wildlife a little way ahead of them and behind them. It seemed that as they approached one place the animals in hiding would fall quiet at their approach and then when they had past the creatures would resume their chatter. Now, everything was eerily quiet.

'Is something wrong, signor Ricardo?'

It was the bearded giant who broke the silence with his question and from the look that Ricardo shot him; Tanya could see that he was not happy that the man had spoken without permission.

'The men we sent ahead: they should have signalled,' said Ricardo.

'Shall I go forwards alone and see?' the bearded giant offered.

Ricardo hesitated. Tanya could feel the tension in the atmosphere. The other men, there were three; all fingered their guns nervously. The two young sisters stood quite still, straining for any noise, Julietta glancing back the way they had come. Patrick Hamilton exchanged glances with Tanya and shrugged.

'All of you wait here, Kachasa, come with me.'

Ricardo beckoned the bearded giant to follow him and the two men stealthily made their way further down the twisting track and soon were lost to view.

'Kachasa,' said Hamilton, 'is the man who tried to ravish Catherina. I am surprised that Ricardo has continued to keep him as one of his bodyguards. Whilst the man seems now loyal to a fault there's something about him that I just don't trust.'

'He must have been pretty stupid to have tried it on with his boss's daughter?' Tanya suggested.

'He was drunk at the time: Kachasa is the name given to cane alcohol that they distil. He was so fond of it that the others made it his nickname. He was lucky he got away with a knife in the buttocks and nothing worse.'

Tanya glanced at the other men and the two young girls. No one spoke, no one moved, the jungle was still all around them and as the minutes slid past the tension grew even more palpable. After maybe half of an hour, it was Catherina who broke the silence.

'The river is less than ten minutes from here; they should have sent someone back by now if it was safe to go on.'

'What do you want to do, Catherina?' asked Hamilton.

'We have little choice,' answered Catherina, 'we go forwards but be ready to fight.'

Tanya watched as both sisters drew their revolvers from their holsters and with Catherina taking the lead, the party edged cautiously forwards.

The last few hundred yards of the track were the steepest and narrowest as it plunged down the hillside to the little stretch of mangrove where there was a sand bank and the wooden jetty had been constructed. Tanya and Hamilton were now at the rear of the party except for the young lad who was carrying the two-way radio. As she slithered down the track, grasping over-hanging branches to steady herself, Tanya glimpsed through the foliage the dark green water of the river and the sliver of dull yellow sandbank. She could just see the jetty and the speedboats but there was no sign of Ricardo or the others.

Tanya and Hamilton were still on the jungle track and,

leading the party, Catherina was cautiously advancing over the sand towards the boats her revolver in hand when suddenly she raised her hand urgently to her cheek and even as she turned around, Tanya watched speechlessly as Catherina stumbled then dropped to her knees. The next second one of the men gave a cry of alarm and snatched a small dart that protruded from his shoulder.

'Back! Back!' shouted Julietta but even as she began to retreat, she too was hit by one of the darts and she only managed to stumble a few yards before she fell into the sand. Tanya needed no encouraging and with Hamilton hard at her heels they fled, brushing aside the youth burdened with the enormous two-way radio strapped to his back. There were a couple of gunshots and then in reply two or maybe three machine guns shattered the silence. From all around the undergrowth erupted as men with blackened faces and camouflaged jackets burst from their hiding places, each man armed with a machine gun. They had the path and the only line of retreat covered and Tanya lurching up the steep and slippery path came face to face with two soldiers who grinned delightedly when they saw that they had caught such a pretty girl.

Tanya and Hamilton were marched at gun-point back down to the sandbank where they found a dozen or more soldiers and two loin cloth clad natives who were holding long blow pipes. Two of Ricardo's three men lay dead and the third stood passively whilst his hands were bound behind his back. Half a dozen soldiers were clustered around the Catherina and Julietta and having stripped the girls of their weapons they were binding their hands behind their backs.

'They're not dead?' Tanya asked.

'Evidently not,' answered Hamilton, 'the blow pipes must have fired not poisoned darts as is usual but darts tipped in some drug strong enough to knock out the person on the receiving end.'

'Look, there's what's-his-name!' Tanya blurted, seeing

the bearded giant emerge from the trees, an evil grin on his face.

'Kachasa!' Hamilton spat out his name, 'I knew he couldn't be trusted. I bet he was the one who told the army of Ricardo's whereabouts. He must have been biding his time he could get his revenge.'

Tanya and Hamilton were questioned by the commander of the soldiers but he seemed convinced that both Tanya and Hamilton were actually just two more of Ricardo's followers. Despite their protesting their innocence, both were, like the sisters, subjected to having their hands bound behind their backs. They were then marched across to the speedboats where they saw Ricardo, bound hand and foot in one boat, half covered by a blanket. He was only semi-conscious and his face bore an ugly bruise across one side.

'Put the girls and the old man in the other boat,' ordered the Lieutenant commanding the soldiers.

One of the soldiers had a two way radio and with it news of the successful ambush was relayed and a few minutes later a large, olive green speedboat came roaring up the river, one soldier steering the outboard engine from a centrally mounted steering wheel and another soldier leaning on a heavy machine gun that was mounted at the prow.

'Well men, we'll be well rewarded by nightfall,' announced the Lieutenant, 'there is a heavy bounty on Ricardo Rueda's head and you'll all get your share. What's more, by nightfall we can be back at base and we've got his daughters for company!'

There was a rush of laughter from the men. Tanya was prodded at gunpoint onto the military speedboat and behind her Hamilton followed, grumbling under his breath at the way they were being treated.

'Sergeant, take three men in one of the bandit's boats and take responsibility for Rueda. We'll keep him separate from his daughters.'

The Lieutenant then walked onto the jetty and looked down at where Ricardo lay in one of his boats, bound and bruised.

'If you try to escape, one of your daughters dies, understood?' he warned.

Ricardo nodded grudgingly. The Lieutenant then turned to the two sisters who, having regained consciousness, were being led onto the jetty.

'If either of you tries to escape, your father will be executed, understood?'

Both girls nodded sullenly. Tanya watched as the evil bearded Kachasa strolled onto the jetty and staring lecherously at Catherina, made his way to the end of the jetty where the Captain stood overlooking the boat where Ricardo was held prisoner.

'You won't forget my reward, will you?' Kachasa said, loudly enough for everyone present to hear.

'Of course not,' answered the Lieutenant, 'why don't you say goodbye to Signor Rueda, he'll not be coming back to the jungle from the capital, you can be certain of that. If he's unlucky they'll leave him to rot in prison but I shouldn't be surprised if he faces the firing squad. Pity, given my way, I'd hang him.' The Lieutenant spat contemptuously.

Tanya watched as Kachasa walked up to the end of the jetty and looked down at Ricardo and he gave an evil laugh then spoke.

'Can you guess my reward?' he taunted, 'your daughter who likes to play with fire and knives... well, tonight I'll be playing with her and this time her hands will be well tied from the start!'

'Good luck you piece of scum,' answered Ricardo, 'I should have killed you when I had the chance!'

'Too late now, such a pity; well, it's time we say goodbye and think of me tonight when you'll be well on your way to the capital and your daughter Catherina will be submitting her tender young body to whatever pleases me! Isn't that right, signor?'

Kachasa turned to the Lieutenant for confirmation but was met the soldier's fist which connecting with his bearded chin, knocked him backwards and with a resounding splash Kachasa tumbled into the river.

'Get the girls in the boats!' he ordered.

From her vantage point, Tanya saw Kachasa tread water for a moment and then he angrily began to swim around the posts of the jetty, the wooden decking being just a little too high for him to reach from where he'd been knocked over. By the time Tanya had been cajoled at gunpoint to climb onto the military boat, she saw the bearded giant wading angrily ashore. All the time the Lieutenant was watching him and he had drawn his revolver. Kachasa never made it to dry land. With a horrible scream, whilst the water was still around his thighs he lunged out and fell face first. Tanya watched him try to make a few more desperate steps. The murky green water around him was churned to foam and turned crimson. The bearded face was dragged under the water and Kachasa vanished from sight. For a few more moments the water seemed to boil but then it went eerily calm.

'Piranha fish,' announced Catherina, matter-of-factly from her seat alongside Tanya.

'What a way to go,' said Hamilton.

'No more than he deserved,' Catherina spat and she glowered around at the soldiers guarding them. Last to board the boat was the Lieutenant and once he had seated himself on one of the simple wooden benches, he ordered the boat to be cast off.

'So it seems as if Kachsa will not be sampling the delights of your tender young body tonight then after all?' he announced cheerily. 'I had planned to amuse myself with young Julietta so maybe you would like to watch?'

The Lieutenant was addressing Catherina. Tanya could see her almost visibly boiling with anger but there was of course nothing she could do.

'I dare say that would amuse you.' Catherina answered icily.

'You could offer to take her place if you wished and I would promise you that I would not touch your younger sister as long as you submitted to me. Is that not a tempting offer?'

For a moment Catherina glared at the man.

'Don't trust him!' blurted Julietta.

'My dear girls, you can trust me, I give you my word as an officer and a gentleman: if Catherina agrees to submit to my every whim, I will promise not to touch Julietta.'

'Very well,' said Catherina, 'I agree.'

'Excellent,' the Lieutenant clapped his hands in approval, ' then tonight I have your company for my pleasure and my men can have your younger sister!'

'You bastard!' swore Catherina.

The Lieutenant just laughed before turning his attention to Tanya.

'So just where do you fit into Ricardo's little following?'

'My father kidnapped her,' said Catherina quickly.

'Really? You expect me to believe that?' scoffed the soldier.

'It's true!' objected Tanya.

'I don't really care who you were; if you're someone important then after a few days I'll have to hand you over to the authorities but if not then I think I'll keep you as a servant for my household. I'm sure I can find a good use for you. Either that or I'll maybe sell you; I know some people who need girls like you,' the Lieutenant said enigmatically and with a smile that did nothing to reassure Tanya about her fate.

* * *

Her arms ached so much that Tanya began to sob plaintively. It felt like it had been hours since she had been given some water and food and the men had left. To her left, Julietta hung from her arms, bound the same way and beyond her was Catherina. Tanya gazed up forlornly; her arms were fully extended above her, her wrists bound together with rope which in turn was tied to another length of rope which hung down from one of the wooden beams that held up the old corrugated tin roof of the hut in which they girls were being held prisoners.

The journey to the military camp had taken three hours by boat and when they arrived they saw that the camp was no more than a few huts at the edge of a friendly native settlement beside the river. The soldiers had pretty much stripped the girls of their clothes; Catherina was left wearing only a her short sleeved black shirt and her briefs, the younger Julietta had been stripped of all her clothes except for her underwear, a skimpy black bra and a matching thong. Tanya had been left her T-shirt but nothing else except for the lacy, dark red briefs she'd been given for the journey by Julietta.

The hut where they were held had a small hole in the centre of the tin roof and directly below it there was an old wood-burning stove from which ran a leaking tin pipe that went out through the hole in roof. Smoke seeped from the stove-pipe but at least the hut was warm inside. It was dark now and in the late afternoon there had been a sudden downpour and the rain had continued steadily ever since and the temperature had dropped noticeably. The girls' clothes were soaked through by the time they had arrived at the camp and despite the little stove giving off some meagre heat Tanya's T-shirt still stuck damply to her skin.

Patrick Hamilton had been taken elsewhere and after the three girls were left strung up, their bare feet just brushing the bare floorboards, the soldiers had left, not even bothering to leave a guard, evidently confident that the girls could not escape. Gazing up at her hands Tanya quickly realised that with the rope bound once again in a figure of eight tightly around her wrists the soldiers' confidence was hardly misplaced. She and Ricardo's daughters were indeed as helpless as flies in a spider's web.

When the soldiers returned, there were a dozen of them and it was evident that they had not just fed but had enjoyed some drink as well. They were now in good spirits and their Sergeant, a short but stocky man in an olive green vest that left his powerfully muscled and tattooed arms exposed, circled the dangling girls, his dark eyes gleaming with satisfaction and anticipation as he feasted on their nakedness.

'Our Lieutenant says that we are not to touch you,' he announced as he stopped before Catherina. 'He will be summoning you later, when he is rested. He turned his attention to Julietta and Tanya.

'So that leaves you two for us!'

Tanya looked nervously at the man as he fingered her damp T-shirt. He then drew a short bladed knife from a sheath stitched to the side of his boot and with it he cut the T-shirt with a couple of assured strokes at the shoulders and ripped it from her trembling body. Grinning with pleasure he slipped the tip of the knife underneath the fabric of Tanya's bra between her breasts and he pulled the knife towards him. For a moment the bra stretched and then the cotton tore, exposing Tanya's generous breasts. One of the soldiers stood behind the Sergeant said something in Spanish and several of the men seemed to mutter their agreement.

'Very nice,' nodded the Sergeant, 'we shall have some fun with you.'

Tanya closed her eyes for a moment, holding her breath as the man caressed both her breasts before turning his full attention to just her right breast which he proceeded to fondle with both hands, squeezing her breasts and lifting it in his palms so he could appreciate its full weight and size.

'How old are you?' he demanded.

'Nineteen,' Tanya answered.

'English?'

'Yes, English.'

'Virgin?'

'No.'

'Pity, but no surprise; you look like the sort of girl who likes good fuck, yes?'

Tanya hesitated for a second and the Sergeant took her silence for an answer and turned and addressed one of his men.

'Her tits are like ripe melons; firmer and bigger than any of our girls. Get me a candle and some rope, I think we should give the English girl a treat.'

'Please…' Tanya began but the man turned and caught hold of her jaw with one hand encouraging her to be quiet.

'There's no need to thank me, not yet anyway,' the Sergeant grinned.

Tanya could do nothing but hang from her painfully extended arms whilst several of the soldiers, upon the Sergeants instructions, bound her breasts with a rope drawn about them in a figure of eight. The Sergeant then lit a candle and with one hand stroked one of Tanya's rope-trapped tits.

'No, please… don't…' Tanya begged.

Ignoring her plea the man held the burning candle above her bound breasts and a second later Tanya felt the first drops of hot wax splash against the bare skin of her tits.

'Oww! No…stop it! Please!' Tanya shook her head urgently. She tried to twist away but two soldiers held her by the shoulders. More wax dripped down onto her breasts, the stinging pain making her eyes smart and then as more liquid wax splashed down Tanya burst into tears.

'Had enough?' the Sergeant asked, smiling sadistically as he watched the tears run down Tanya's cheeks. Tanya nodded urgently and to her relief the man blew out the candle and tossed it aside. Tanya gazed down sorrowfully at her rope bound breasts; the cones of tender flesh that remained exposed by the ropes were spattered with wax. The Sergeant took hold of the rope that bound Tanya's right breast and used it to lift her breast then with his other hand he fingered her nipple.

'So how many you let fuck you?' he demanded.

'Not many,' Tanya lied between sobs.

The man laughed and shook his head. Tanya felt his thumb and finger trap her nipple and steadily apply more pressure until she couldn't take any more and she tried to pull free. The two soldiers holding her by the shoulders tightened their grip and all Tanya could do was writhe helplessly whilst her nipple was mercilessly squeezed, pulled and rolled between the man's finger and thumb and her poor nipple throbbed with discomfort.

'I will spend some more time with you soon enough,' the Sergeant turned from Tanya and focused his attention on Julietta.

'So, you are signor Ricardo's youngest daughter?'

'And you are the son of a monkey!' spat Julietta.

The Sergeant grinned for a moment as he digested the insult then he turned to his men and pointed to the table beside the stove in the middle of the room.

'Take the youngest of Ricardo's daughters and tie her down over the table; on her back. It's time she had her welcome drink that I know you have all been saving up for her.'

The men chorused their approval and Tanya could only watch, as Julietta was cut down then dragged across to the table. Forced down onto her back the soldiers spreadeagled her arms and legs and bound them with ropes to the corners of the table.

The Sergeant walked across to where he could stand beside the table and look down at Julietta who in turn glared contemptuously at him.

We have been planning the ambush and arrest of your father for many weeks and for many months before that my men knew they were chosen for this task and they knew that although there were risks there would be rewards: you and your older sister. In a few days' time you'll be taken to the district Governor but until then the men know that they can enjoy your company as their reward for their good work. They have all been eagerly awaiting your arrival and a couple of willing local girls have helped them to prepare a welcome drink for you.'

'What do you mean?' Julietta looked nervously around her as the men encircled the table. One of them held a plastic funnel, another a bottle and a third a jug.

'Let's just say that every evening every man has fantasised about taking your body. Can you image how exciting that prospect must be to them? Well, it was not difficult to find a couple of local girls to help the men relieve their pent up desire for you and every last drop has been saved so that you can savour its taste.'

The Sergeant laughed and so did the men and Tanya watched spellbound as one of the men now held Julietta's upturned head still whilst another forced her mouth open and a third man forced the spout of the funnel past her lips and teeth and into her mouth.

Struggle as she might Julietta could do nothing to stop the men carrying on with what they had planned for her. Tanya watched as Julietta struggled helplessly against the ropes that held her arms and legs outstretched. Several men kept her head held still and the man with the bottle moved forward.

'A little brandy to relax you,' announced the Sergeant and he nodded affirmatively to the men. A firm hand tightened around Julietta's chin to keep her still and Tanya watched a stream of amber liquid spill from the bottle into the funnel.

Julietta's young body arched and twisted but her head remained firmly held still and Tanya watched as a she was forced to swallow the brandy. After a few seconds the man with the bottle stepped aside and he was replaced by the man with the jug. When he tipped the earthenware vessel over the funnel Tanya saw a viscous milky fluid dribble into the funnel. The man upended the jar and a steady stream of the mixture poured into the funnel.

'We decided that you'd as likely bite any man who was foolhardy enough to force his cock in your pretty mouth so the men decided it would be better to save as much as the local girls could milk from them during the last few weeks and you would be given it to drink this way instead!'

Tanya could see Julietta desperately trying to escape what she was being subject to but her position was hopeless. Even when she refused to swallow, the men had only to pinch her nostrils closed and soon enough she was forced to gulp down the men's come, knowing that until she'd swallowed it all she would be starved of breath. A moment later, the jug empty and the funnel removed, the men stood back. Julietta turned her head sideways and coughed repeatedly then she was panting hard as she recovered her breath. A little milky come dribbled from the side of her mouth. She looked exhausted, shaken and bitterly humiliated.

'Now she must be nicely refreshed, I am sure she's ready and willing to service you all.'

'You bastards, you're never going to get away with this!' Catherina shouted from where she hung tethered to the roof beam.

'Be quiet or else you'll regret it,' the Sergeant warned.

'You're going to rot in hell for this, when my father gets free he's going to hunt down every last one of you who touched either of us!'

'Someone silence the bitch and teach her some manners,' ordered the Sergeant.

Tanya watched silently as two of the soldiers strode across to where Catherina was dangling from her outstretched arms. One of the men forced a rag into Catherina's protesting mouth and the other man drew a scarf across her mouth and tied it tight at her nape. The men then took two long canes and took it in turns to deliver stinging blows against Catherina's thighs and buttocks. At first the defiant girl tried to kick the men as they stepped forward to deliver the punishment but the men simply kept to opposite sides of her and one would feint, drawing Julietta's attention and the other would then step in, deliver a blow and step back before the feisty girl could try to deliver a kick. After a dozen blows, her thighs were criss-crossed with red lines and Catherina was no longer trying to defend herself. She was gazing despairingly at the scene before her, her eyes moist with tears and each time a fresh blow was delivered she gave a gag muffled cry of anguish.

'That will do, she'll not be any more trouble now.'

The caning stopped and the men all turned their attention back to Julietta who was untied from the bench and rolled over onto her belly. The men then pulled her by her thrashing legs down the table until the edge of the bench was against her slim waist. Once more her arms were drawn to full stretch and the ropes around her wrists pulled tight and the other ends fastened again to the table legs at the far end.

Tanya looked at the plight the young girl was in and knew that she was in for a merciless couple of hours at the hands of the dozen men that filled the hut. It occurred to her that if all twelve men took it in turns with her, it would probably be more than Julietta could cope with and coupled with this Tanya realised that she actually envied Julietta for what she was about to experience. Tanya had experienced Miles and his two colleagues mercilessly subjecting her to an anal shafting that had lasted an hour or more. She felt certain she could take anything these men could subject her to and if she could persuade them to use her body as well as Julietta's it might save the young girl from such a protracted suffering. At the back of Tanya's mind too was that if she could be seen to be trying to help the girls then if they did ever get rescued by Ricardo or his men, she might be rewarded in some way.

'Wait!' Tanya called out. 'That table's long enough for you to tie down two girls at a time, why don't you tie me down as well?'

The men were stunned by her suggestion. It was a moment before the Sergeant spoke.

'You little slut, you want to get shafted too, don't you? Is that what you want?'

'She'll not last if you all try to take a turn with her and what fun will it be if she faints half way through?' Tanya asked.

'The English girl has a point. Untie her and get her over here. If she wants to suffer alongside the Rueda girl, then let her!'

A handful of the soldiers untied Tanya and dragged her across to the table and taking to her the opposite end to where Julietta was tied down they forced Tanya to bend from the waist over the table. Tanya's arms were jerked out in front of her and she found she was facing Julietta, only a few feet of the long table separating them and their arms in fact drawn parallel to each others'.

'Tie their arms together as well,' ordered the Sergeant. 'They obviously want to be as close to each other as possible, let each of them feel the other struggling as we use them.'

More ropes were wound around the girls' arms drawing them together and then the ropes were pulled tight and knotted so that Tanya's own hands were almost against Julietta's shoulders and Tanya could feel Julietta's fingertips brushing her own biceps.

The red briefs that Tanya wore were torn from her and she felt someone run their hands appreciatively down her bare thighs. Looking ahead past Julietta's nervous face she could see one of the soldiers move behind the girl and dropping his combat fatigues without any preamble he drove his cock into Julietta's trembling body making her jerk and writhe against the ropes that held her down. A moment later and Tanya felt her own legs forcibly spread and a cock was speared into her sex.

'It'll be interesting to see which of them begs for us to stop first; though I think we all know which it'll be,' the Sergeant smiled cruelly at Julietta. The young girl was already struggling as the first man to take her was deliberately shafting her with as much force as he could, his hands firmly on the girl's waist as she writhed helplessly under him. Two of the other soldiers held the girl's thighs apart and pressed against the edge of the table and they had each of Julietta's slender legs trapped between their own so her struggling amount to nothing.

By the time the girls had each been fucked by three men they were both desperate to be given a respite. The soldiers were cruelly ruthless and delighted in seeing the girls struggle as they assaulted their defenceless bodies. They gave them no pause between each man taking his turn and when Julietta begged the men not to be so hard on her they only laughed with relish at her sobbing and pleading. As she struggled more desperately as a fourth man took his turn with her, her reward was to have a stout wooden stick forced lengthways between her jaws. Lengths of slender rope were bound around each end and these were pulled behind her head and wound together. The man who had just started to fuck her took hold of the rope as if it were the rein of a horse and with it he forced Julietta's head back, dragging a groan from her. Julietta looked pitifully at Tanya but there was nothing either girl could do now to help the other.

After each girl had been forced to submit to six soldiers there only remained the Sergeant and he chose to use Julietta's exhausted and aching body to slake his sexual appetites. Tanya was forced to watch whilst once again Julietta was subjected to a cruelly hard shafting. This completed, the girls were then untied and dragged back across the room to below the beam from which they had been earlier strung up. Tanya's poor breasts throbbed painfully because they had not untied the ropes that constricted them and so when she was forced down against the bench, her already aching tits were painfully trapped and squashed underneath her. By the time the ordeal was at an end her breasts ached more than her pussy but worse was yet to come.

'Crotch rope the Rueda girl but run the rope ends over the beam and tie them off nice and tight to the ropes binding the English girl's tits,' the Sergeant ordered. 'Bind the English girl's hair with a cord and pull it over the beam and tie it around the other girl's tits. Lets see which of them gives in first!'

Five minutes later and Tanya was tethered, her back against Julietta's, each girl's arms outstretched above them and roped to the beam. Worse though were the Sergeant's instructions, which had been executed with cruel pleasure by his men.

Tanya's long blonde hair had been gathered into a ponytail and separated into two lengths. Plaited together the men had woven a cord into her hair and tossed the cord over the beam. The other end was drawn painfully tight around first one of Julietta's breasts and then the other. Where the rope sank into her crotch the men had tied it into knots and one of these was sunk against her vulva making her squirm feverishly. The rope that pulled tightly up under her legs was, as the Sergeant instructed, pulled over the beam then each end was knotted to the rope that bound Tanya's breasts. Both girls' feet barely touched the floorboards. Desperate to relieve the acute pain of the cord pulling her hair and the rope pulling her breasts, Tanya struggled desperately against the ropes but the more she eased the pain she was in the more Julietta was made to suffer and the more pain she was subjected to the more urgently she struggled and in turn subjected Tanya to more distress. Eventually Julietta's strength proved greater and Tanya, exhausted from the whole ordeal, was subjected to the relentless pull of the rope against her throbbing breasts and the equally painful sensation of having her hair pulled upwards.

After perhaps half an hour of such torment, the soldiers cut the girls ropes and both tumbled exhausted to the floor where they lay dazed and tearful.

'Get me some palm oil and get the Rueda girl back over the bench,' the Sergeant ordered.

From where Tanya lay she watched as two men caught hold of Julietta's slender arms and dragged her across to the table. Once more she was forced up against the edge of it and made to lie face down against the bare wood. Two men held her arms outstretched and a third pulled a sack over her head. With the belt from his combat fatigues the man drew the sackcloth snug around the girls head and he buckled the belt close around her neck. Tanya looked on horrified, hoping that the material was loosely woven enough to allow Julietta to breathe once she'd used up what air was trapped inside the hood that completely enveloped her now thrashing head.

Standing behind Julietta, the Sergeant poured some palm oil over the base of the struggling girl's back and watched it trickle down between the firm globes of her buttocks. He then used his hands to draw them apart and, rubbing his cock against the oil slick skin, he then drove his shaft into Julietta's anus. Tanya heard Julietta give a cry and her whole body convulsed and writhed. The Sergeant grasped her narrow waist, eased his cock almost completely from her rear passage than rammed it back home. Tanya watched from where she lay on the floor whilst the man calmly sodomised the defenceless girl who soon seemed to stop struggling. When it was over and the man pulled his spent cock from her body the belt that was around Julietta's neck was loosened and the sack pulled from around her head. Julietta was unconscious but when the men let go of her arms and she dropped to the floor, Tanya was relieved to see the girl still had life in her body as she struggled weakly to move. Not wanting to risk suffocating the girl the Sergeant had previously cut a few small holes in the sack.

'Take the older sister to the Lieutenant, he'll be ready for her now,' the Sergeant ordered, 'the younger one can be tied up and left to rest. As for the English girl, she can be treated to whatever torture amuses any of you, but she's not expendable so make sure you don't get too carried away.'

Tanya watched the Sergeant turn and walk out of the hut. Once he was gone a couple of the soldiers came and stood over her. One of them crouched down and fingered the rope that was still bound in a figure of eight around Tanya's painfully swollen and now purple breasts.

'Please...untie the rope...hurts so much,' Tanya looked sorrowfully wide-eyed, begging the soldier who smiled sympathetically at her before turning to one of the other men and saying something which Tanya couldn't of course understand.

'Please... what are you going to do to me?' Tanya asked nervously as two of the soldiers lifted her by the arms and marched her across to one wall. Binding each of her wrists with slender cords that dug painfully tight into her skin the men fed the loose ends of the cords through old iron hooks that hung from the wall and pulling on the cords they forced Tanya's arms a little above her head and spread-eagled with her back pressed up against the wall. The cords were knotted securely fast, leaving Tanya with her arms dragged almost to full stretch out to each side of her. Meanwhile some of the soldiers had cut down Catherina from where she had been tied throughout the other girls' ordeals and they marched her out of the hut. Julietta had her arms bound behind her back and her ankles tied together and she was left on a pile of stale straw in one corner of the hut.

The majority of the soldiers now gathered before where Tanya was tied up against the wall. She gazed down dispiritedly at her poor breasts bound by the cruelly tight rope and then she looked up at the men stood before her.

Whilst she'd learnt to enjoy playing the sexual submissive since she'd first gone to work at Scawder Lodge, she was now feeling pushed beyond what she imagined she could normally endure and secretly enjoy. This was no game these men were indulging in with her and now as she realised that despite the pain she was in from the rope that had remained tightly binding her breasts for too long now, she knew that the men had no intention of relieving her of her suffering but were in fact about to torment her still further.

CHAPTER NINETEEN

Miles looked with satisfaction at Becky as she lay spread-eagle on his bed. She was wearing short white socks and a lacy white bra and matching briefs. Her tanned arms were extended above her head and drawn to the top corners of his double bed. Her slim wrists were bound with leather cuffs and these were tied to the tubular metal frame of the bed head. The young girl's legs were also drawn to the bottom corners of the bed and secured with similar leather cuffs. The symmetry of her slender limbs reminded Miles of a starfish. Becky lifted her head a little, straining to work out where he was. As well as having tied her down, Miles had blindfolded her.

'What are you going to do to me?' she asked, her tone, rather than sounding anxious, betrayed her eagerness.

'I can't tell you that, it would spoil then fun,' Miles answered.

Becky wiggled her bottom against the crisp cotton of the sheet expectantly. Miles stood for a moment just savouring the sight of the now helpless young girl and reflecting on how fortunate he had been to win her and how eager she had been to surrender herself so completely to him. Just like Tanya before her, Becky was a natural submissive and he marvelled at how she could actually seemingly savour such pain as he meted out to her.

He recalled the time he and Sturmberger had her in his friend's basement; strapped into Frederick's gynaecologist's chair she had been utterly at their mercy and isolated from any possible help in the soundproof basement, the men could have done anything to her. As it was having softened her up with a whipping to her thighs and giving her a good shafting, Becky had been subjected only to some measured pussy torture. Miles had been content at this point simply to watch his friend at work. Sturmberger had a penchant for such things and had refined the sexual torture of young women down to quite an art form. Miles had watched Becky, strapped firmly down in the big leather chair, writhe as best she could as she was made to suffer. Sturmberger had fastened metal clasps to the labia and from fine metal chains attached to the clasps he had hung some weights. He had allowed Miles to test the weight of the little metal spheres before telling him to let go of them. With the weights dangling freely, the chains had snapped taut and the men watched as the clasps pulled the girls' labia, making her cry out in distress.

Sturmberger had then taken a pair of long handled tweezers and trapped the girl's clitoris between their jaws. Becky had tossed her head from side to side, gasping and crying as her clitoris had been pulled and teased at the same time as her labia were distended by the dangling weights. All too soon the girl was so aroused that Miles could see she was on the edge of having an orgasm. Sturmberger, delighted by her condition had discarded the tweezers and now simply flicked his fingertip repeatedly against the girl's swollen sex, triggering her orgasm. Without giving her pause to even recover her breath he had then produced a small jar of ointment and applied a little with his finger to the exposed soft pinkness of the girls inner labia. A few seconds later and Becky was gasping then crying out as another orgasm rocked her tethered body.

Sturmberger had given Miles a jar of the ointment as a present and now as Becky lay tied spread-eagle across his bed and blindfolded he had decided it was time to give her a taste of some once again. Quite what was in the ointment he had no idea, the writing on the little jar was all in Chinese but Sturmberger had cautioned him that only a little was needed. Becky had told Miles that after he had left his friend's house, the merciless Sturmbeger had returned to the basement and had not released her from the gynaecologist's chair but had proceeded to torture her some more, using an electric rod to shock her repeatedly. Becky had given Miles a graphic account of what she had been subjected to, describing how it had felt for her as the German had shocked her already aching pussy and then her anus and then once more her poor pussy. She told Miles how he had forced her to endure one agonising orgasm after another and how he had kept her gagged and taped her nostrils so that she was so breathless that each time she climaxed she practically fainted.

The effect of Becky's wide-eyed story telling had given Miles a bone hard erection and glancing down at the bulge in his trousers, Becky had apologised if she had over excited him and without Miles needing to suggest what she should do to rectify the situation, she promptly gave him an enthusiastic blow-job and a couple of minutes later Miles was able to enjoy the delicious sensation which accompanied having his cock erupt into the mouth of a girl who was happy to suck him dry and leave his cock throbbing deliciously with the pleasurable ache that followed an intense orgasm.

Miles had been struck by the way Becky had recounted what she'd been subjected to and he could tell that she had, deep down, enjoyed the experience that Sturmberger had treated her to, secretly revelling in the skilfully administered judicious blend of pain and pleasure. Miles had decided therefore that he would be doing Becky a favour if he spiced up her days of living with him with some decent, hard sessions of sexual submission and torture.

Now Becky lay invitingly helpless, her limbs effectively restrained by the leather cuffs that held her bound to the corners of the bed. Her eyes were covered not by the delicate sort of softly padded black eye-cover that one would buy in airport kiosks for long-haul journeys, but by a broad black PVC blindfold that Miles had bought specifically for such occasions. The blindfold covered Becky's eyes and upper face and had a hole for the nose to protrude since it went well down the recipient's cheeks. At the back of the head the PVC tapered to two broad ends that each ended in long elastic straps. One end of the PVC had a hole in it and the strap from the other side was drawn through this and the two elastic straps were then pulled back around the recipient's head to be fastened with Velcro over the padding that already covered the wearer's eyes. Becky was now in a world of utter and impenetrable blackness.

Miles opened the small jar of ointment and placed it on the bedside table. He then recovered from a drawer in his wardrobe an inflatable butt plug and a small box containing some nipple clamps, chains, weights and some other items he knew he would want. He did not intend these for Becky's pert tits however but rather for somewhere even more sensitive.

'What are you doing?' Becky asked, turning her head to follow the noises Miles made as he moved around the room.

'You'll find out soon enough.'

Miles glanced down at her and smiled. Obligingly Becky was squirming, making a show of how helpless she was thanks to the leather cuffs that bound her wrists and ankles. She was breathing quite quickly now, her taut stomach rising and falling, her breasts under the pretty little bra heaving as she pulled experimentally with her arms against the restraining cuffs and ties.

Sitting on the edge of the bed Miles stroked his hand up the inside of her bare thigh and Becky's slender legs slithered a little over the crisp cotton sheet. He traced the edge of her lacy briefs with one finger and watched her lips part fractionally, her head tilting back a little as she emitted a faint sigh of pleasure. He eased the fingers of one hand under the waistband of her briefs at its narrowest point, her hip, then with a pair of large scissors he calmly cut the material. Repeating the process on her other leg he flicked the gossamer fabric aside, revealing her sex. The loudest sound in the room now was Becky's breathing. Miles left the bedroom and went into the bathroom, returning a moment later with his razor, a canister of shaving gel and a damp flannel. Applying the gel to the thatch of soft, gently curling hair that was between Becky's legs, he calmly set about shaving her. Becky remained silent and still, sensing that this was not the time to be complaining or struggling. Once Miles had shaved off all her pubic hair he wiped over the now bare skin with the flannel, returned his shaving kit to the bathroom and returned with a bottle of moisturising oil. Dribbling some of this between her legs, he leisurely rubbed it into the freshly exposed skin. Becky now started to wriggle a little and sighed appreciatively. Miles put aside the bottle of oil and regarded her exposed sex lips. Now the fun could start, he mused.

Stroking his victim for a few minutes around her sex, he grinned as Becky sighed, her head tossing from side to side and her back arching a little.

'Is that nice?'

'Mmmm…'

'How does this feel?'

'Uhh…mmm…'

Miles caught her exposed outer labia between his fingers and thumb and he gently pulled the soft fold of flesh seeing how far it would extend. Becky seemed to like this and even seemed to enjoy the sensation of a peg closing over the soft lip of flesh. Miles already had a strip of electrical tape dangling from one of the peg shafts and he smoothed it down against her skin. Copying what Sturmberger had done to the girl in his basement, Miles pegged open Becky's outer labia, drawing the lips of flesh well back and pinning them not with just two pegs each but with three. Becky was now starting to pant. Eager or nervous, it didn't matter to Miles, he knew that before long she'd be panting helplessly as he forced her to climax after climax and he had determined only to stop once the girl had been thoroughly exhausted and he had the satisfaction of hearing her begging him to stop.

The nipple clamps were of a design that meant the more pressure that was applied to them the tighter they became to ensure that they did not slip loose. When Miles fastened the first to one of Becky's delicate little inner labia the girl gave a cry of discomfort and then as she grew accustomed to the sensation she just lay passively, making faint whimpering noises. Miles attached the second to her other little fold of flesh and he pulled experimentally on the chains already attached to the clamps.

'Uhhh….stop…please…stop…' Becky gasped, her legs and arms twisting urgently and her head shook from side to side in protest.

Satisfied that the clamps worked nicely, Miles attached weights to both fine chains. He drew out the chains until the weights hung over the end of the bed and he then gradually lowered them until the chains were fully extended. When he then let go completely of the chains Becky gave a choked cry of anguish and Miles stood back and watched her spread-eagled legs slithering urgently across the bed as she was forced to endure the sensation of her delicate inner labia being painfully stretched by the dangling weights.

'Stop it… please… enough…' Becky gasped, tossing her blindfolded head from side to side, her arms twisting and pulling urgently but helplessly against the wristcuffs and cords that held her pinned down.

After maybe five minutes Becky gave up struggling, resigned to the continuing, agonising pain, she lay whimpering and Miles stood watching her, his cock achingly hard now and pressing against his pants.

'How are you feeling, Becky?' he asked, smiling as she lay panting hard and biting down hard on her lower lip to stifle the need to cry out.

'Maybe I can find another way of giving you some vigorous stimulation?'

'No… please… no more…' Becky gasped.

Miles took the inflatable butt plug and dipped the end

into the jar of ointment that Frederick Sturmberger had given him. He then smeared the head of the butt-plug with moisturising oil and without giving Becky any warning of what was about to happen he shoved it into her anus. With the rubber shaft embedded in Becky's rear and the flared base snug against her rectum, Miles squeezed the pump that was connected to the device by a short length of rubber hose.

'No! Not fair... stop, please...'

Miles grinned at Becky's increased struggling and he gave the pump a couple more squeezes to ensure that there was no way that she could expel the now inflated plug by exerting pressure with her anal muscles. He then had only a few moments to wait before the effect of the ointment became evident.

At first Becky's vociferous objection was amusing but soon her screams for him to let her go became disconcertingly loud and Miles became anxious that the people in the neighbouring flats might just hear the girl's screams. Quickly snatching a ball gag from a bag in his wardrobe he jammed the rubber sphere into her mouth, effectively muffling her cries and he then fastened the gag's straps at her nape.

After five or ten minutes Becky's agony seemed to ease and she stopped crying into the gag and writhing so fiercely. Miles pulled on a pair of fine latex gloves and dipped one fingertip into the jar of ointment. He then drew his finger across the exposed pinkness of the helpless girl's sex, leaving glistening smears of the sticky mixture on her distended labia. It was only a matter of seconds before Becky was gurgling into the gag and shaking her head vigorously. Miles watched her young body straining to free itself and moments later she was arching her back and panting breathlessly as she was made to climax.

'Feels good does it?' asked Miles sarcastically.

Becky gave up struggling for a moment but lay, her chest

heaving and her thighs trying futilely to close against each other as if this might ease the evidently potent sensation that the ointment had delivered to her sex.

'Fancy another orgasm, Becky?'

Becky shook her head urgently but ignoring her Miles once again dipped his fingertip into the jar and smeared some more ointment between the distended lips of her inner labia.

'You like that don't you?' Miles taunted as Becky was swiftly brought to another excruciatingly intense climax. Recalling what the girl had told of him Sturmberger's treatment of her after he'd left the basement, he remembered the reference Becky made to how Sturmberger had taped her nostrils closed, heightening her sense of breathlessness. Miles looked down at the helpless young girl writhing on his bed, her hips bucking as she was brought to her second climax in the space of five minutes. Whatever was in the ointment, it was ruthlessly effective, he mused.

A moment later and Miles was back at the bedside having gone to his bathroom. He had two small wads of moist cotton wool in his palm and bending over the blindfolded Becky he pushed one up each of her nostrils.

'Nnhhh…nnhhh…'

Becky thrashed her head from side to side and one of the twists of cotton wool plopped out of her nostril, rolled over her cheek and fell on the bed. Miles could hear her making snorting noises and a second later the other piece of cotton wool was expelled. Miles smiled at the girl's efforts then he cut a thin strip of electrical tape, forced the cotton wool wads once more up Becky's nostrils and applied the tape down one side of her nose across her nostrils and back up the other side of her nose. The tape did not by any means completely block her nostrils but it served to make it impossible for Becky to now rid herself of the moist plugs of cotton wool that made breathing through her nose so difficult.

Miles watched her closely and satisfied that she wasn't going to come to any harm he dipped his finger back in the ointment jar and smeared some over Becky's clitoris.

The effect was practically instantaneous. Becky, writhing and struggling frantically as she was propelled towards another climax was left desperately gasping. Miles watched her closely all the time and as it turned out he had judged things just right and Becky though starved of air remained conscious as her body was convulsed by another shuddering orgasm. As it subsided Becky weakly shook her head from side to side and Miles could hear her muffled gasping as her lungs heaved for what air they could find.

'Would you like it if I gave you another orgasm?' Miles stroked between the girl's spread legs. Becky urgently shook her head. Miles smiled with satisfaction; so even the sexually ravenous Becky had had enough, he mused.

'Would you like me to stop?'

Becky nodded. Miles grinned and reaching down he lifted the two dangling weights in his palm, Becky visibly relaxed as he did so and the terrible relentless ache of the weights pulling her labia was eased at last. Miles let the weights slip from his palm and allowed the fine chains to run out through his fingers. As soon as they snapped taut Becky gave a gag muffled cry and her slim, long legs twisted frantically. Miles tapped the weights encouraging them to pendulum and whilst they were still in motion he smeared a little more ointment against Becky's pegged outer labia.

'Is that nice? Is that giving you enough pleasure, Becky? I can treat you to some more if you'd like?'

Becky tried to shake her head but she was too exhausted now and too weak. Satisfied that she'd endured enough Miles peeled loose the tape from her nose then withdrew the cotton wool from her nostrils. He was achingly hard and now wanted only to satisfy his own needs. Becky's sex though pegged invitingly open glistened from the repeated applications of ointment and Miles decided that he wouldn't risk getting any on his cock just in case…

Without bothering to ungag her, Miles removed the two little clamps from her sex and unfastening the cuffs that bound her ankles and wrists he forced Becky to get onto all fours so that he could take her from behind. She was too exhausted to protest and Miles soon had the pleasure of puncturing her tight little arse with his heavily engorged cock. Becky whimpered through the ball gag but made no effort to resist. Thoroughly aroused from watching and enjoying her torment, it didn't take Miles many minutes of shafting her rear before his cock erupted inside her.

Easing himself from her body and gazing down at her pert arse, he remembered Tanya and the merciless anal session he had subjected her to with his colleagues in the bathroom at Scawder Lodge up in the Scottish Highlands. As Becky slumped exhausted on his bed, Miles found himself wondering what had happened to the unfortunate Tanya. As if a couple of weeks on Sturmberger's container ship, captive in the purpose-designed room down in the ship's lower decks where she'd played sex slave to the crew for the duration of the journey, hadn't been enough for her to endure, she had ended up being captured by some pirates and was last heard of a prisoner of some brigands in the remotest reaches of the rain forest.

Miles knew that the military and the police of the country that Sturmberger dealt with were corrupt in the extreme and had a penchant for holding prisoner young girls who had the sort of tender young bodies that would guarantee the men sexual satisfaction. If Tanya was "liberated" by them her fate would be just as bad if not worse. Very often, he'd heard, after weeks of being held in prison cells or military barracks and used constantly and cruelly by the men, the poor girls would be sold to one of the firms that made hard core porn for the internet which were known to work from the country. Either that of the girl might end up the plaything of one of the rich and also corrupt local governors or bosses of some of big businesses that practically ran the country. Deciding that whatever Tanya's fate might be it was now out of his hands, Miles went through to his bathroom, leaving the exhausted Becky slumped on his bed. He was just about to switch on the shower when the phone rang and on an impulse he decided not to let the answerphone cut in but that he would take the call.

'Miles here.'

'Miles, it's Frederick.'

'How are you doing?'

'Fine, just fine. Listen my friend: I have some news; some good and some bad. I haven't called at an inopportune time, have I?'

Miles grinned as he remembered what Becky had been up to last time his business associate had rung.

'No, just finished, go ahead,' Miles answered looking down at Becky who was now fast asleep, exhausted after her ordeal.

'Some news from South America: the boxes containing the guns have been recovered but they were empty so even if they find the guns now it will be hard for them to be linked to Sturmberger Shipping.'

'Good news; now what's the bad?' Miles asked.

'Well, I have lost the guns and not got paid.'

'Is that it?'

'Yes, I hope that's the end of it, I think maybe I'll not risk indulging in such a venture again.'

'No news about Tanya Raglan?' Miles asked, trying not to sound too concerned either way.

'Oh, ja, ja, I nearly forgot to mention that,' said Sturmberger. 'That bandit Ricardo Rueda was captured by the military along with some of his men, his daughters and that girl, Tanya what's-her-name, who was on my ship.'

'So what's happened to Tanya?' Miles asked.

'The authorities linked her with my ship because she was

pay-rolled as one of the crew and her passport was still on board. Unfortunately the military commander of the area is on holiday and none of his headquarters staff seem to know where she is or what's happening to her.'

'I can guess what's happening to her,' said Miles, recalling what he'd witnessed happen to the girl Anna when she'd ended up in the police cell at Santago del Fuenta.

'What do you suppose?' Sturmberger asked.

'What happened to that girl Anna, Frederick, the one who tried to cause you trouble and who you persuaded the police chief at Santago del Fuenta to take into his custody for a night?'

'Oh her, yes I remember her vaguely,' Sturmberger answered defensively.

'So what happened to her, she's back over here I take it?'

'I don't know, sure, I guess so.'

'Frederick give me a straight answer for once!'

'Alright, alright Miles, stop getting so hot under the collar; she's just some dumb girl who was greedy for work, remember/'

'So what happened to her?' Miles repeated, guessing now that his business associate was deliberately withholding information from him.

'She's still in South America, I believe she's doing some internet porn work out there.'

'Meaning the police sold her into slavery to one of those very dodgy organisations that uses unwilling girls to model for what is supposedly consensual stuff but what is actually nothing of the sort.'

'Oh come on Miles my friend, those stories are just nonsense, you mustn't listen to them,' protested Sturmberger. ' Anyway, what has she got to do with Tanya?'

'Well,' said Miles. ' I wouldn't mind betting that she's met the same fate.'

'Oh, I'm sure that's not the case. You know what it's like with the military; lots of camps, hundreds of miles of remote jungle and troops scattered all over the place; Tanya will be stuck in one camp just kicking her heels whilst she has to wait for a jeep to become available before they can move her. I'm sure she'll turn up in the capital safe and sound in a few days or weeks. You shouldn't worry yourself so needlessly.'

'Maybe not,' muttered Miles. ' Keep in touch, I've got to go.'

Putting the phone down Miles walked back to his bathroom, glancing at the sleeping Becky as he did so. Whilst showering he pondered what to do about Tanya and as soon as he had finished he sat on the end of the bed, leafed through his Filofax, found a number and dialled it. The phone rang for a long time before it was answered and Miles had been about to hang up.

'Yes?'

'I wanted to speak to Tim,' said Miles.

'Speaking. Who's that?'

'Tim, it's Miles Fitzroy here; you worked for me briefly a few years ago when I was doing some film work out in the Middle East.'

'You were paranoid your pretty actresses would be abducted.'

'You remember. I've got another job for you if you're interested.'

'Tell me more, Miles.'

'It's abroad, South America, you'd need to start straight away and you'll need plenty of back up, I'd suggest some of your retired army chums. Interested?'

'Does it involve pretty girls?'

'Just one.'

'Will I like the pay?'

'I can double what you were paid last time and will send you a week's pay and expenses cheque straightaway.'

'You've got yourself a deal.'

'Are you still living in London?'

'Certainly am.'

'Okay, I'll leave a package with instructions and a cheque with the doorman at the Inkerman Hotel in Mayfair. The cheque will be made out for petty cash on a business chequebook for a firm called Sturmberger Shipping. You can only cash it at the Mayfair branch of the Swiss Credit International bank. Do it first thing in the morning and when they ask for the authorisation password the answer is "Munich". When you go in the bank wear a false moustache and a hat or something.'

'So I take it Sturmberger Shipping aren't aware that they're paying me?'

'They've no idea at all Tim but believe me they can afford it and they'll not be any bother to you or me from here on in.'

'Nice doing business Miles, take care.'

The line went dead. Miles walked through to his lounge, poured himself a generous malt whisky and allowed himself a smile of satisfaction.

CHAPTER TWENTY

Tanya and the Rueda sisters were held prisoner at the remote jungle camp for several days before the Lieutenant ordered that they be moved. The three girls had suffered at the dozen soldiers' hands for most of that time. They were bundled into the military speedboat and accompanied by the Sergeant and three men and taken down river for half a day until they reached a small riverside town. Here they were handed over to an army Captain who immediately separated Catherina and Julietta from Tanya and assigned them separate cells at either end of a concrete police headquarters, which was shared by the military.

Later that afternoon Tanya heard the roar of engines outside and from the sounds she imagined it must be a handful of powerful 4X4 vehicles. A few moments later and she could hear voices and then scores of booted feet marched into the back of the police building where there were a dozen tiny concrete cells, each no more than a few metres square and each with a double bunk bed. The door to one of the cells clattered open and she heard men issuing orders and then she heard Catherina answering them. Tanya lay listening to the noises, which then faded as she guessed the sisters were led away. The engines of the vehicles fired up and Tanya listened as they roared away.

Tanya looked up at the two soldiers crouched beside where she lay in her bunk. They had, just ten minutes before the convoy of police vehicles from the regional capital had arrived, bound her ankles and wrists to the four upright posts of the bunk-bed. Tanya had been forced to listen to the sisters being taken away whilst she lay helplessly just a short distance away. One of the soldiers grinned at her and fondled her breast. Finding her nipple he squeezed it hard. Tanya could only look at him, unable to move and unable to protest since her mouth was filled by a hard rubber ball gag that stretched her jaws acutely wide, effectively silencing her.

The door to the cell opened and the military Captain who was in charge of the town's garrison, looked down at her, a satisfied smile on his cruel face.

'They would have collected you also and taken you back to the capital. Apparently you are no bandit but just a poor defenceless girl who was abducted by Rueda's men. It is such a pity that I had to say, regretfully, that you fell overboard whilst being brought here and were eaten by Piranha fish.'

Tanya looked angrily at the man then overcome by her plight her eyes filled with tears. She would never escape this foul place she realised with dismay and bitterly regretted ever agreeing to work for Sturmberger. If she hadn't taken his job offer she never would have ended up in this mess now, she chastised herself.

'So my dear girl, you can now look forward to many hours of stimulating company,' the Captain laughed and nodded to his men. The one who had been fondling Tanya promptly tossed aside the rough wool blanket that had been covering her. Underneath it Tanya was quite naked, her legs marked with faint red lines from where they'd whipped her and her arms bruised from where she'd struggled as they had earlier held her down whilst they had taken turns to fuck her.

The Captain, whose hands hand been folded all the time he spoke behind his back now revealed what he had concealed behind him. At the sight of the electric prod Tanya tensed then twisted her arms ineffectually against the rough rope that was tight about her wrists.

'You enjoy my stimulating company, don't you my dear young girl?' the Captain moved closer. Tanya looked up wide-eyed with fear and shook her head, she tried to beg with him but the gag was utterly effective. The man crouched down beside her and smiled sadistically. Tanya felt his hand touch between her legs and she realised to her shame that she was slick with arousal. Even this cruel treatment in its way, she had to admit to herself, aroused her.

Closing her eyes, she wondered how she had become so slavishly devoted to such torment and even as she pondered this she felt a searing jolt of electricity delivered to her tethered body. With a gag muffled cry she arched her back, her young limbs straining against the ropes as she was subjected to another shock delivered to the tender inside of her thighs. She gazed up sorrowfully at the men standing over her, tears welling in her eyes as she knew that this was just the start and the session, like the one the day before, would last for hours. Once they had thoroughly exhausted her and her body was washed with pain they would then untie her, roll her onto the stone floor and her already throbbing sex would be subjected to a repeated shafting.

Tanya cried as she felt another jolt of electricity shock her already aching body and she bit down on the gag, shaking her head in urgent protest as this time the electric prod had been applied directly to her sex. Please, please, Tanya silently begged, somebody please make this stop. The torture did not stop though although in a distant office a phone could be heard to ring and a moment later Tanya was vaguely aware of the sound of approaching footsteps.

Dazed and breathless, she gazed up to see another man, a policeman this time, had entered the cell and was talking with the captain who from the expression on his face did not seem pleased with the news he had just received. After the policeman had left and the door was dragged closed, the Captain looked back down at Tanya as she lay panting, her body throbbing and limbs aching from her struggling.

'I find it hard to believe but someone is looking for you and he does not seem to be willing to be distracted from his object of finding you. I think we may have to discover that the Piranhas did not eat you after all but thankfully you are still alive and well.'

Tanya could hardly believe her ears but then the Captain had not finished speaking.

'Still, these people from England who have come to find you are still a day's journey from here. I am sure we can enjoy that time in each other's company can't we?'

BORN TO OBEY

by Lee Ash

The Gold Cup Challenge; the ultimate test of obedience. Every dominant wants the distinction of having trained the winning slave.

Jane and Liz are just two of the contestants, hand picked by their masters. Each girl has to overcome very different obstacles on her way to the Challenge. Jane has to contend with envy, hostility and sabotage, while Liz has to learn to accept her submissive nature and then learn total obedience.

As each girl fights her way towards the great day the stakes keep getting higher and the tests get even tougher. Only one slave can emerge triumphant for her owner – only one girl will be tough enough to endure the rigours of the Gold Cup Challenge. There are no guarantees for either Liz or Jane that they will survive even the first round. There is just their devotion to their respective masters.

BOUGHT AND SOLD

by TESSA VALMUR

As soon as Zoe Farquerson steps off the plane in the tiny kingdom of Al-Saram, she walks straight into trouble with the secret police. But she is not the innocent tourist she claims to be, she is a field agent for British Intelligence; and she has been betrayed.

Soon she is a helpless pawn in an international intrigue, caught between ruthless and dominant players in a game where allegiances shift as fast as the desert sands. But as a beautiful European girl, she is highly prized and there are plenty of people willing to pay any price to get her in their power.

BOUND TO PLEASE

by Giselle Lorimer

Charlotte is the classic 'rich bitch', a self-obsessed flirt who is concerned only with her own pleasure. But she indulges herself once too often and is seen masturbating. Suddenly finding herself in the hands of dominant and cruel men, Charlotte is catapulted into a series of trials and tribulations which have only one thing in common: each one involves more humiliation than the last. And each time she is convinced that she has reached rock bottom, her masters dream up something else, until she at last comes to realise that her destiny really does lie in being Bound to Please. And there is nothing she can do about it.

Giselle Lorimer's first book for Silver Moon: 'Enslaving Anna' marked a brilliant debut and signalled the arrival of a major new female talent in the erotic genre. 'Bound to Please' is an assured and highly erotic follow-up recounting the lovely heroine's step-by-step descent into complete subjugation.

PAIN AND PASSION

by Mark Stewart

Pain and Passion is the story of Angelique's journey into the dark world of submission.

Rejected and punished by her parents, condemned to the strict discipline of Nemesis House and the jealousy of the other girls held there, Angelique sets her sights on serving the man she worships.

However, the Baron is not a man who will let affection for any girl spoil his enjoyment of punishing her. Angelique has to learn that only by enduring whatever his fertile imagination can conjure up for her can she hope to be allowed to serve him.

SLAVE CORP

by Alex Geiger

"'Here we see President Carlson negotiating with the UN just before the Slave Laws were passed. She was, of course, a vocal opponent of such a measure."

Julie looked up and saw a conventional picture of the United Nations Security Council Chamber with all the delegates sat around their desks in a huge circle.

"And here we see one of her negotiating just after."

This time the shot was of an orgy. Valerie Carlson was on her knees, collared and chained, and servicing all the other male leaders.'

Slave Corp, the world's most powerful enterprise, in the wake of the passing of the Slave Laws, controls the female half of the world's population.

Julie, a beautiful nubile eighteen year-old, has just graduated from school as a fully trained submissive – but is she? The flame of something dangerously close to rebellion burns inside her as she sets off on a journey through a devilishly perverted London in pursuit of her true identity and nature, but first she must first pass through the most depraved instruments of pleasure and pain ever conceived. The da Vinci Chamber and Slave Corp's most monstrously perverted creation yet – The Diablo Device

INTO THE ARENA

by
Sean O'Kane
(The first of the 'Arena' novels)

Tara is a thrill seeker; a girl who pits herself against as many challenges as she can. But when she meets Conor Brien she finds herself facing greater tests than she could ever have imagined.

He is scouting for female gladiators to take part in the recreated Roman games he and his associates are planning to stage - and he wants Tara.

But before they are ready, these modern gladiators have to learn to please their owners and the crowds who will throng the stands and cheer them on as they battle against each other on the sands of the arenas.

On board a ship which transports them towards their new life, Tara and her companions are faced with stark choices. Will they submit to the harsh training regime which is imposed upon them? Will they march out to do battle for their owner?

Silver Moon have over a hundred titles of erotic domination and submission in their catalogue. If you would like to find out more and join our readers' club absolutely free, then write to;

Silver Moon Readers' Services
The Shadowline Building
Wembley Street
Gainsborough
Lincs DN21 2AJ

Tel: 01427 816710 (during office hours)

You will receive a free quarterly magazine with features, interviews, news, views and special offers plus the chance to order titles which are only available to club members.

Alternatively you can log onto:
www.adultbookshops.com

Free Book Offer

FREE BOOK OFFER

To claim your free book simply detach or photocopy this page and send it to:

Silver Moon Readers' Services
Shadowline Building
Wembley Street
Gainsborough
Lincs. DN21 2AJ

You will receive whichever one of the following books you choose absolutely free, delivered with discretion to your door:

Please send me (select one):

- ❏ Slave for Sale — by JT Pearce
- ❏ Tales from the Lodge — by O'Kane/Bridges
- ❏ Bush Slave II — by Lia Anderssen
- ❏ Beaucastel — by Caroline Swift
- ❏ Eve in Eden — by Stephen Rawlings

Name: ....
Address: ....
....
....
Post Code: ....